Into the Wise Dark

Other Books by Neesha Meminger

Shine, Coconut Moon

Jazz in Love

Into the Wise Dark

Neesha Meminger

Ignite

Ignite Books, New York

Ignite Books, NY

For information about this title, please contact info@ignite-books.com
Cover design by Eithne O'Hanlon
Author photograph © Craig Blankenhorn
The text for this book is set in Georgia
10 9 8 7 6 5 4 3 2 1
Meminger, Neesha
Into the Wise Dark / Neesha Dosanjh Meminger.--1st ed.
Summary: Time-traveling Parminder, a.k.a. Pammi, must stop a
power-hungry Able from the future from destroying the ancient
city she visits, where Ables like her live freely. If she is unable
to stop him, the city of Zanum vanishes forever, taking
Pammi and all other Ables with it.
Library of Congress Control Number 2011916535
ISBN 978-0-983-1583-2-5 (paperback)
ISBN 978-0-983-1583-3-2 (eBook)

To the feminine divine,
without which/whom none of this would exist.

Acknowledgments

I am deeply grateful to Olugbemisola Rhuday-Perkovich, Sarah McCarry, and Ibi Zoboi for reminding me to stay on the path, in their own unique and immensely valuable ways; Wiscon and everyone I've met there, especially Debbie Notkin, Lisa Cohen, and Jeanne Gomoll for stepping in and making sure I got there the year I needed it most; and the folks who make the CBS Con or Bust Fund happen each year. Because of you, I discovered a whole new world.

To Mathu Subramian, for her enthusiasm, fierce energy, and hopeful outlook. The Hidden History in Chapter 14 is for you.

I owe a heap of gratitude to readers who yearn for and demand a wider, deeper array of stories—tales that push and tear at the veneer of what we've been told is irrefutable truth.

A hundred thousand million thanks must go to Hollis, always, for being the fire and the fuel for all my endeavors.

To Satya and Laini, for teaching me, every day, to dig deeper. And deeper still.

And, of course, to the Great Wise Dark—the source of all thoughts, words, actions, and events.

I can see, and that is why I can be happy in what you call the dark, which to me is golden, because I can see a god-made world, not a man-made world.
—Helen Keller

The water in a vessel is sparkling; the water in the sea is dark. The small truth has words which are clear; the great truth has great silence.
—Rabindranath Tagore

Everybody thinks that this civilization has lasted a very long time, but it really does take very few grandfathers' granddaughters to take us back to the dark ages.
—Gertrude Stein

Part 1: Zanum

I have become the Dark. This wasn't something I set out to do. It wasn't even something I wanted. But that's what I am.

Pasea says we are all made from the stuff of the Dark—that we carry it within us and it is there for us to mold into whatever vision of reality we hold as truth. But most of us walk around not even knowing the Dark is there ...afraid of it, afraid to look into it, to even acknowledge it.

But me and the girls I met the summer after I graduated from high school—we had all seen it. We knew about the Dark. We touched it, merged with it, molded it into our version of reality. I didn't know how important my role was—rejected it, in fact—until much later.

This is the story of how I, a Traveler of the Dark, went back in time to give life to my ancestors. It is a story of how I consumed Dyal so that she became a part of me forever. And it is a story of how my ancestors ended up in the part of the world now known as the Indus Valley. We began in Zanum, far to the east of the Indus, where we had lived for many generations before the Conquest.

And that is where this story begins. In Zanum. But first you need to know who I was before, when I began Traveling. How everything started. And how I had to fight to hold on to my grip on the Dark.

Chapter 1

"How could hanging out with hardened criminals in a psychiatric facility be a lovely growth experience?"

My mom's mouth twitches—a nervous habit. "Darling, your history... what you went through is... it's over. You've moved beyond it and blossomed. You're now a normal, well-adjusted teenager and you might be able to help others who haven't gotten over their... issues."

"You'll love it, Pam," Dr. B. says, beaming. His cheeks get a rosy tinge when he's excited about something. "The founder of this facility, Ms. Schroff, contacted me to see if I knew of a bright young woman with an interest in the field of psychology, and you were the first who came to mind. We've set up an appointment for you to meet the staff this Saturday afternoon."

"You can take my car, darling," my mom says. She's doing that thing where she digs her thumbnail into the cuticle of one of her fingernails. "It's a beautiful drive—quite gorgeous I'd imagine, if you went along the bicycle path."

Right. This is exactly how I wanted to spend the summer after my senior year.

I shift my concentration to the TV in the background. Dr. B. is watching the news on Democratic Times. The narrator's voice is flat and emotionless. "The Casey administration has given the okay for Congress to pass a bill that would ban ethnic studies across the nation. The administration stated yesterday that programs like Anti-Oppression Studies in California are 'divisive and emotionally charged,' and have no place in a democratic and free society. Already, several groups have announced massive, city-wide protests..."

"Yes, there couldn't possibly be anything worse than teaching people to think for themselves, could there? To present another perspective and allow people to make up their own minds...?" Dr. B. says to the TV. "Definitely not in schools where young people are supposed to be taught to think!"

He sighs, looking away in disgust. "I should clarify," he says to me. "These girls are far from hardened criminals, Pams. They're high-functioning teenage girls who were traumatized early in life. They are receiving specialized training. Ms. Schroff sees something special in them—a capacity to do great things." He pauses for a moment to choose his next words. "The point is for these girls to use what they've learned from their early life experiences, including the traumatic ones, in some sort of leadership role that will benefit their communities."

Just my luck that Dr. B. is *the* Dr. Babaloo, the Indian-American Dr. Phil. He was pretty huge in Britain and he's managed to recreate some of his success here. Dr. B. doesn't technically live with us. He has a fancy-schmancy condo in the heart of town, but he's over pretty much every single night. Mom refuses to move in with him because she says she was just fine before him and she's just fine now.

Dr. B. has a lot of connections in his field, and when this Ms. Schroff asked about bright young women he might know... well, lucky me. Now, he and my mom are super excited for me to go as a Peer Support Counselor at the Margaret Schroff Leadership Academy and Residence for Girls.

"It's true, darling," Mom adds, taking her eyes off Dr. B. for only a second. "When I visited, they all seemed like lovely girls. I think you'd get so much out of sharing your life with them and hearing about theirs in turn."

There's that word again. *Lovely.* I try to stick with my negotiating voice, but the irritation leaks through anyway. "Why can't I just lifeguard, or work at the marina? Or paint houses for the summer like everyone else?"

Mom tightens her lips. "Because those jobs won't help you when you want to go to college, and Dr. Mace says working with girls who are where you used to be will help you reach full recovery."

My throat goes dry. "When did you talk to Dr. Mace? And *why?*"

Memories of sitting in his office rise to the surface. The feeling of somehow being paralyzed from the inside out immobilizes me once again.

I shake my head. It's over now. I've "recovered."

Mom watches me carefully, then examines her fingernails. "Dr. Mace and I touch base from time to time," she says. "Just to make sure everything is going well." She looks over at Dr. B. "Besides, Bubs thinks Dr. Mace runs a good clinic."

"They do seem to have a fairly progressive mandate, Pams. There are some well-recognized doctors on staff with your Dr. Mace." He glances at Mom. "I would probably have picked someone else for you, honestly, but your mother did a lot of research and this clinic has a stellar reputation. It's been lauded in all the journals."

"I don't want to go back there, Mom," I blurt out. "I thought we were all done."

"We are," she says quickly. "But since you're taking this year off, I want to make sure Dr. Mace is available in case—" She falters for a quick beat, then recovers. "In case we need him."

"We're not going to need him, Mom. I'm *fine.*"

"I know you are, darling. I'm just taking some precautions." She smoothes my hair back. "I want to make sure you're happy and well. You know we have a history of this sort of thing in my family."

Yes, I do know. Mom has told me over and over how her grandmother was delusional all her life, and that her own mother had tendencies to talk to people who weren't there. Clearly, it freaked my mom out. So much so that she kept a close watch on me from early on—making sure I didn't display any of the "symptoms" her mother and grandmother had.

"Well, you won't have to worry about me having a lot of time on my hands if I get this job at the center," I say, jumping on the only foothold I can see. Maybe if Mom thinks all my time will be taken up at this center, she won't make me go see Dr. Mace again.

She beams. "Oh, I do hope you get it! Imagine that—you could have your own show like Bubs!"

"It's only for the summer," Dr. B. says, with his back to us. His attention is back on the TV. "But who knows. They could extend it."

"That's fine," I say. "I'm doing the fellowship in the fall, remember?"

When I brought home a brochure from the guidance office at school, Mom and Dr. B. agreed to my attending a nine-month fellowship, starting in September, with an organization in Kenya called Sustainable Living. The brochure referred to it as "one of several overseas destinations that work with local rural populations in building stronger infrastructures."

Whatever. All I knew was it would take me far, far away from Mom. And Dr. Mace.

"Besides, didn't you say you wanted to major in psychology in college?" Mom asks.

I nod. *Yes, yes I did. I said that as I was listening to my iPod. I knew it was what you wanted to hear and would, therefore, guarantee that you'd get off my back.*

It had worked. She and Dr. B. had beamed like lighthouses. They immediately went about "helping" me.

"Well, there you go then," she says, with finality. "This is perfect. You'll go as—what was it, Bubs?"

"Peer support," he mutters.

"Yes—you'll be peer support for these girls."

Dr. B. turns to give me a big smile. "You'll do great, Pams. There will always be a counselor present. This is not your average treatment facility. It's one of the best there is. Have you ever heard of it—the Schroff-Davies Foundation?"

I shake my head.

"Margaret Schroff is a very wealthy, elderly woman whose father made great inroads into the field of psychiatry," he explains. "She created this foundation. One of her biggest projects, besides building new and specialized wings in hospitals, is setting up treatment centers for girls the foundation has identified as having significant leadership potential."

He swivels toward my mom. "All the girls were hand-picked from various group homes, hospitals, and psychiatric facilities when they were between the ages of seven and thirteen. They've faced tremendous challenges in their lives but they are, indeed, exceptional young women.

"Did I tell you about the article Ms. Schroff wrote in *Science Today*—the one about the connection between human emotions and energetic disturbances?"

I zone out as Mom gazes at him like he's a sunrise. When there's a break, I jump in. "Can I go now? I want to take a ride along the path before dinner."

"Okay, darling, but remember—tomorrow's the interview!"

I stare incredulously at both of them. "How did you know I would be okay with doing this?"

They speak at the same time: "It's such a fantastic opportunit—"

"We thought you'd be great—"

They look at each other and chuckle. Dr. B. speaks first. "We don't want to make decisions for you, Pams, but this is truly a once-in-a-lifetime opportunity. Everyone I know, including myself, would have jumped at something like this had we been offered such a chance when we were in school."

"And what else would you do all summer?" Mom asks. "Dr. Mace thought it would be good to keep you occupied."

I grit my teeth to stop the sentences in my mouth from spilling out. "Okay," I say. "Fine."

I grab my bike from the storage room downstairs and head to the bike path. On the way there, I pass by the steps under the highway bridge, which are normally occupied by a particular bunch of kids hanging out and smoking weed. Some of the girls are from my school—an all-girls' school with a focus on math and science. The girls that go there are from families that are among the wealthiest in the nation. That's what it says online, anyway, when you look up my school.

And then there's me. Mom and I are definitely not part of that "wealthiest in the nation." Everyone at school knows it, too. Me and three other girls are there because of special needs scholarships that the school provides to "extraordinary young women who display rare promise." Mom busted her ass to get me in there and worked nights to keep me there. She still busts her ass as a nurse, but she doesn't do nights any more.

I know I should be grateful.

I see some girls from school with a couple of guys. I grip the handlebars of my bike and nod as I walk by. One of the girls nods back and quickly returns her attention to the guy who's stroking the exposed part of her back between her tight T-shirt and the waistband of her jeans.

"Omifreakinggod!" she giggles, twirling a strand of hair around her fingers. "Seriously? Eww! I could *never*..."

I look up a heavy, rhythmic tune on my iPod and blast it as I walk up the hill to the paved area by the statue of William Cabot, the explorer after whom this park is named. But to everyone around here, it's the statue park.

I think about what Dr. B. said about the girls at the treatment facility: *They've faced tremendous challenges in their lives, but they are exceptional young women.*

I mount my bike and start pedaling as soon as I hit the bike path.

As much as the sight of those girls with dudes draped all over them annoys me, it triggers a familiar pang somewhere deep inside. How amazing would it be if my boyfriend was here with me? Live and in the flesh so I could put my arms around him, maybe hook my thumb through one of his belt loops, or sit on a bench at the statue park and talk about... whatever?

But Dhan's not here. Not even close. And if I ever share with anyone exactly where he is, they'll lock me up before I can take another breath.

I drop that line of thought quickly, and think about the five days a week that I'll be required to put in at the residence. With girls who were "traumatized in early childhood."

Translation: *crazies*. My stomach knots up. If anyone knew about half the things I kept secret, I'd be lumped into that same category.

In fact, I *was* lumped into that same category when I was seven. And guess who walked me straight into the psych ward, and into the office of Dr. Mace? My mom. The same mom who is now talking about what a lovely growth experience this will be.

The very thought of Dr. Mace and his lulling, hypnotic voice makes me dizzy. And here she is again, my own mother, throwing me into yet another pit of vipers.

I pedal faster and sail around a curve, past an old man with a bag of breadcrumbs perched on his lap. There are throngs of pigeons on his shoulders and at his feet, almost burying him in blue-gray feathers.

Peer Support Program, Dr. B. said. A new initiative they're trying out this year to give the residents a chance to talk to other girls their age who've had "more stable" upbringings. I suppose that would be me—with the more stable upbringing.

Hypothesis: *If girls traumatized at an early age interact successfully with peers not traumatized at an early age, they will integrate more effectively into society at large, thereby increasing leadership potential.*

Laughable, when you think about it. My mother has this funny selective amnesia. Part of me would love to remind her of *my* early childhood.

Mom and Dr. B. had been each other's first loves. When they were about my age, they were caught making out by my mom's parents, who immediately arranged her marriage to a more "suitable" boy.

The more suitable boy turned out to be my father, whom I refer to as Biodad. I don't remember much, but from the few bits of conversations I've overheard, Biodad used Mom as a punching bag. And the first time he hit me, my mom packed her bags and we took off to the U.S.

We lived with a family friend for a couple of years before Mom got us our own place. She worked nights so she could be around during the days if I needed her. And the family we stayed with was always around to help.

Then the seventeen-year-old daughter of the family we stayed with—Jazz—decided it would be "*so* romantic!" to get Dr. B. and Mom back together. She and her friends concocted a plan to make that happen. And it did. And here we are.

I ease around another curve in the road and sit up, taking my hands off the handlebar to blow on each one in turn. Despite the warmth of the sun, it's cool in the shade of the old, crooked trees lining the bike path.

I gave Dr. B. a hard time at first, but I actually like him now. He tries to stay out of mine and Mom's relationship and gives me plenty of space. He's okay for a guy with his own TV talk show.

I slow down over the small wooden bridge to see if I can catch sight of the swans that hang out in the stream sometimes. But the water is a clean, vibrant blue sheet and there is no sign of the swans, just the usual gaggle of geese and a few ducks.

Things could be worse than having to spend the summer with residents at a girls' treatment facility, I suppose. I could be spending the whole summer with girls like the ones from my school, which is exactly what I'd be doing if I worked at the marina.

I stop and lean the bike against the metal railing of the bridge. Two turtles are sunning themselves on a large, flat rock. I wonder what the girls at this facility are like.

I pick up a twig and snap it in half, dropping it into the flowing water below. It gets carried gently downstream, going to some unknown, predetermined destination. I sigh and turn back to my bike. If the girls at the center are anything like me, they could be in there for no reason at all.

Chapter 2

It started when I was seven. I saw a giant brown-and-gold cobra one night. It rose and fanned its hood, then stared calmly at me from the foot of my bed. I sat up and looked at it for several minutes before running out to tell my mom.

She gave me a hug, told me it was a nightmare and that I should go back to sleep.

I insisted it was not a nightmare. I wasn't scared, I told her, and that snake was real. She smiled and explained that we lived in upstate New York and there were no cobras there.

When I went back to bed, the snake was gone. I stayed up for a while, wondering if my mother was right and I had imagined everything. But I knew I'd been wide awake.

I looked for the cobra again, night after night, but it never reappeared. Then one night, during those same hours after I went to bed, but before I fell asleep, I closed my eyes and felt myself drifting. It was like going through a misty rain— reminded me of being in the cave behind the falling water at Niagara Falls.

In the darkness, I saw a golden, wispy thread and grabbed hold of it. When I opened my eyes, I was in a whole different place, and it was daytime.

I panicked, but there was a woman there. Pasea. She was kind and warm and soothing. She told me she'd found my body in the desert and something had called her to me. She said she was from Zanum, a land from the distant past—far, far away from where I lived, but it was okay, I would get home fine. She said everything would be all right and she would be there to help me.

"People like you have existed since the beginning of time," she explained, as she found a wrap for me to change into. "It is nothing to be afraid of. I am real, not imagined, and you are real. All of your experiences here will be very, very real."

Then she looked me dead in the eyes. "Never, never, let anyone convince you otherwise. You are descended from here, little one. Your power is greater than you can even imagine. There are people who will know this, and they will be afraid.

"But be unmoved, child," she continued, "the Wise Dark is the eternal womb—the life force. It is the darkness from which all events, people, and time itself emerge. Those who have the gift to navigate the Dark create the events of our collective destiny."

Each time I visited, I was farther along in their future. How quickly I jumped forward, or where I landed, depended on how I manipulated the Dark.

I trusted Pasea immediately. And I met Dhan, her grandson.

Dhan's mother died in childbirth and Pasea had raised him. He was very curious about the strange bahari, the "permanent visitor," among his people, but accepted my sudden appearances in his grandmother's home. He was easy about it all, perhaps because he was used to people having gifts, even if he and his family were not among the gifted.

In the early years, Dhan bombarded me with questions. "What is the name of your home? Do you like Zanum better? Is your home more beautiful? Is there more water? Do you have the same lizards?"

Slowly, my tongue and my ears grew accustomed to the thick, ancient language. A few minutes of my time could be hours in Zanum, and hours could be days, sometimes even weeks.

At first I had no control over how long I was gone, or how much time had passed since my last visit, but I looked forward to going every night.

When I first told my mother about the visits, she dismissed it all as a dream. When it didn't stop and I began to speak to my dolls in Zanum, using the same words each time for various objects, she scheduled the first available appointment with a child psychologist in a hospital where she used to work.

Dr. Mace.

I remember telling him, "Pasea says it is important for me to hold on to my memories of Zanum. She said people might try to take them away."

His gaze had sharpened. "Yes," he nodded. "Go on."

But the look on his face had stopped me cold. It was the way a prisoner might look at the key to his jail cell. My throat closed up and I said nothing more.

There were other things that happened in Dr. Mace's office that I couldn't explain. Chunks of my memory went missing. I'd be talking to my mother about someone from school or something, then—nothing. It was like falling off a cliff. Complete erasure.

"It's normal," he would tell my mother. "These things happen when the mind is struggling with a painful reality."

I complained daily about missing Dhan and Pasea, but my mother would only scrunch up her face, take deep breaths to fight the tears I could already see, and say that I needed to keep up with my appointments because I was "doing very well." Then she would pull me close. "I lost my mother and grandmother to these fits of delusions... I won't lose you, too."

After a while, through weekly sessions with Dr. Mace, Zanum began to slip from my grasp. I dreamed of calling into the darkness and hearing only my echoes in response. I clung to Zanum night after night, but it was like grabbing a handful of fog.

I stopped participating in school and was developing "behavioral issues," according to the guidance counselors. I was in danger of being kicked out of the private school my mother had worked so hard to get me into.

Soon, she got other family friends involved and called my grandparents in England for money. She took an extended break from work and monitored my every movement. She made sure I made it to every single one of my appointments with Dr. Mace and checked on me every night to make sure I wasn't having one of my "fits." And she kept Dr. Mace informed of everything.

It worked. I began to forget. The last visit I remember was when I was eleven. Dhan was eight then. Zanum was gone, no matter how desperately I searched for those beautiful, magical strands I'd found before.

Pasea said that time worked like a spiral staircase. Time slowed down or sped up depending on how you remembered it in your brain, how fast you moved through it to get to different points, and the decisions you made in the Dark.

When it was taken away from me, I felt empty, incomplete.

My mother was happy. Dr. Mace was happy. The counselors at school were happy. For three years I was normal. I was functioning well. I'd made "great progress."

Then, when I turned fourteen, I found a strand. And everything I'd been made to forget avalanched into my memory again.

When I saw that thread—so faint and wispy I wasn't sure it was real—I knew that I would never let Zanum slip from my grasp again.

Chapter 3

I stare into Nahut's liquid brown eyes, her ridiculously long eyelashes fluttering as she watches me. "I can't believe you still remember me, girl. Every time I come out here, you greet me like an old friend." I stroke her neck. I was just here last night in my time, but a full month has passed in Zanum since then.

"It's so weird. To me, it was just last night that we were doing the new moon rite," I say over my shoulder to Dhan. "I come back the next night and it's time to honor the next moon."

"I'm glad you've made it to both rites. Yonaweh and Miraly have a tendency to sneak off before nightfall and leave me alone." He comes up behind me and nuzzles the side of my neck. "Besides, offering rice balls and cakes—especially cakes—to the ancestors wouldn't be the same without you," he says, sliding his arms around my waist.

Dozens of moths flutter in a dance in my belly.

We started catching up around fifteen. It was the only time we'd been close in age since I'd begun visiting. He'd always been a kid to me. And then, suddenly, he was this hot guy.

For him, I'd be gone for weeks, or months at a time. For me, I'd just been there the night before. The way Dhan looked at me with his lopsided smile began to squeeze my stomach from the inside. By the time we both turned sixteen, I couldn't ignore, even if I wanted to, the current of electricity I felt whenever he was around.

"Those cakes are awesome." I turn around in his arms. He smells of musk and straw and hard work and muscle. My pulse kicks up a notch as I place a hand flat against the solid warmth of his chest.

He leans in to drop a light kiss on my lips. "If we're not back at Pasea's hut in minutes, she'll find someone else to watch you."

I shove him away. "I don't need to be 'watched,' thank you very much."

He grins, picking up a broom. "She'll find someone else to *accompany* you and explain Zanum rites and ceremonies."

Nahut nudges my head and I reach down for more grain, holding it up for her to nibble out of my hand. Already the day's beginning to cool. The sun is dipping to the west, away from where the rainbow was this morning.

I'm still blown away by how much work kids have to do here. From the age of ten, Dhan has been in charge of all the camels. He brought Nahut into the world on his own, while Pasea was away dealing with Council matters. I'd stood off to the side as the calf emerged, looking gray and slimy and not at all cute.

Dhan wiped some of the slime off the calf and let the mother smell it. "To help her bond with the baby," he'd said. "She's held the baby in her womb for thirteen moons and a few days—a long time."

But little Nahut—although camels are never really little—bonded quickly with her mother. Now she's the sweetest camel Dhan's got. He and Pasea have several. They raise them for the milk, meat, and hide, and sometimes they trade them with caravans that come in from deeper in the desert.

"Do you remember the time I mangled the words 'hot' and 'dung'?" I ask.

He laughs. "How could I not? You said 'I am dung,' instead of 'I am hot.'"

"Yonaweh never let me live that down."

Dhan furrows his brow. "'Live that down?'"

"He never let me forget it," I explain.

He nods. "He thought it was very funny."

"I was so embarrassed." My voice gets soft. "Lucky for me, you showed me the right syllable to emphasize."

He stops and smiles, leaning against the broom handle. "I also reminded Yonaweh of how he butchered the Lamian language in our last class—inserting innuendos that nearly sent the headmistress into seizures."

I smile and shrug. "He still calls me *N'ronga*."

Dhan snorts. "Yes—hot dung."

I throw a handful of grain at him. "I'll take it as a compliment."

He smiles into my eyes for a moment and a single flame licks the length of my spine. "If anyone dishonored you, Mika, including Yonaweh, I would break him in half."

I love the way he says Mika, the shortened version of my Zanum name, Mika'Arini. I stare at the grain in my hand, not trusting myself to look into his perfectly-etched face. Or the waves of his long, dark hair tapering into points, like paintbrushes dipped in shiny black paint.

"You totally took me under your wing when we were little." I dart a quick look up, forcing myself not to fall into his eyes.

He grins. "I had no choice. You kept getting yourself, and me, into trouble."

I toss him a mischievous smile and deliberately sprinkle a handful of grains on the ground. "You missed a spot."

He pokes me with the broom handle and I yelp.

Dhan's older than me now—I turned eighteen in the spring and he's almost nineteen. I'm desperately hoping I can figure out how to control the way I cross over so his time is more consistent with mine. The moments I spend here with Dhan make me want to walk away from everything I know back home, where I can't be myself with anyone, and stay in Zanum forever.

"It's good," he says, putting the broom away. He grabs a shovel and a bucket and efficiently begins to scoop up camel dung. "This... residence. It could be good for you."

I hold more feed up to Nahut, but one of the older camels nudges forward and grabs it before she can. "I'm worried it'll be like Dr. Mace's. If I ever, *ever* leak anything about this place, about you and Pasea, they're going to lock me away. I might never be able to come back." My heart stops for a moment at the thought.

Something dark flickers in his eyes for less than a heartbeat before he composes himself and goes back to shoveling. "It's very strange to me—the lack of acceptance in your time for differing perspectives on reality," he says, dumping the contents of the bucket into a wheelbarrow.

Zanumites use dung as fuel for their mud ovens and lamps. Pasea and Dhan collect it from their camels and distribute it to neighbors. You'd be surprised how happy people are to get a bucket of crap patties.

"We'll take the buckets around tomorrow," he says. "After the patties are dried." He rinses the bucket out and tosses it into the shed before closing the doors and sliding the metal bar in place.

The muscles of his back slide and flex under his skin, which is dark brown with a red-gold hue from hours in the sun.

"This is one of the first lessons we learn," he says. "*Truth enters in myriad guises; each an indisputable god.* It's a wonder your world fails to see the beauty of multiple truths."

"My world is the same as yours, dude," I mumble, "just some thousand years later."

He shakes his head. "No, your world is not the same as mine. There is nothing the same."

There's a hand inside my chest, squeezing my heart. I shove aside the clutching panic I feel whenever I'm reminded that I don't really belong here—or anywhere. That I'm neither here, nor there. Not now or then.

"Your elders believe this residence will be helpful for your education?"

I nod, pulling myself back. "My mom thinks I want to go into psychology."

"A spirit healer."

"No." A smile tugs at the corner of my mouth. "A head doctor."

He grins. "Your head, my spirit. It's no wonder the prophecies are of dark times ahead with much destruction and inequity... wars, death, hunger." He scans the sky, now ablaze with the colors of fire. "With thanks to Divine Mother, my people have never known hunger and strife."

"That's because Atesu uses her magic to command the water." Atesu is the Presiding High Priestess of Zanum, sometimes referred to as the priestess-queen. She has a seat on the Council, but she runs everything and makes all decisions about Zanum and its people. She is extremely skilled at controlling certain types of weather and creating protective invisible shields around events. Pasea says Atesu's magic protects all of Zanum.

"It's not 'magic,' Mika. You sound like the northerners with their great fears of what they do not understand." He takes my hand. "Yes, speaking to the element of water is Atesu's gift. She was born with it. But bringing the river's bounty to our city by applying the principles of energy and heat, by using incantations and manipulating the elements is a learned scientific process. It is revealed only to those who prove themselves worthy of mastering and wielding such power."

I feel the strength in his hand, the warmth of it. His fingers, rough and solid, interlace with my own. "How is a person judged to be worthy of doing something like that?"

He shrugs and leads me out of the fenced-in camel enclosure. "It's a process for those inducted into the path of priests and priestesses. For the rest of us it is one of the Mysteries."

He turns suddenly, looking serious and way older. "Did Mai-ma tell you there is talk that the Upper Kingdoms are looking to spread their reach—even as far down as Zanum."

Mai-ma is what Dhan calls Pasea. It means "mother of my mother."

I nod, recalling the conversation he and some of his friends were having a few nights ago. They were speaking very quickly, melding words together so I couldn't catch everything, but the anxiety in their voices was unmistakable.

"They say the invaders have taken prisoners as slaves—and the fate of a slave in the hands of a northern warrior is not a pretty one."

He sighs, and I can almost hear his thoughts. In addition to their usual tasks, most of the young people of his city have been training for years as warriors. "The prophets say," he continues, "that soon an invasion from the north will be upon us."

I trace his earlobe and a rolling sadness creeps up my arms like fog. "We'll fight," I say quietly, not quite believing my own words. "You're supposed to help lead your people from dark peril to an enlightened homeland far away, remember?"

He pulls me close and laughs without humor. "You don't truly believe those things Mai-ma says, do you?"

I wish I could do something to take away the worry that seems to have aged him decades in less than a minute. Instead, I look off at the red of the sky, deepening into wisps of purple and indigo behind him. "I do. And speaking of Pasea, she'll freak if I'm out after dark again."

"Yes," he murmurs against my neck. "She said you're under her care, and she worries you might end up in the hands of an unscrupulous warrior, if you're not careful."

"And I said that would never happen as long as I was in the hands of her unscrupulous grandson."

He throws his head back and laughs. This time it's a rich, warm sound. "She did not find that funny."

His laugh. It's a sound I would bottle up and use as a balm.

The last thing I want to do right now is let go of him, but I would hate it if Pasea decided I should be "accompanied" by someone else. I'd see much less of Dhan. I give the setting sun one last, long look before untangling myself from his arms. "Come on, let's go."

My stomach flips as he leans in for a kiss. And there's something in me, a kind of hunger that reaches out for him again. I don't want to go.

He pulls me so close against him that I feel his heart beating through my skin. He slides his hand down my side, along my ribcage and down to my waist.

I bury my hands in his hair. "Dhan."

"Mmm?" His touch is like a flame licking the entire length of my arm.

Every cell in my body wants him to keep going. But the part that's nervous about defying Pasea, and seeing less of Dhan as a result, wins out. "We really have to go," I whisper, dropping my forehead to his shoulder.

He tilts his head back with a sigh. "Yes, you're right."

We peel ourselves apart and I adjust my wrap.

Dhan takes a deep breath. "Let us return you to Mai-ma's hut," he says with a smile, "where you are safe from my wandering hands."

"I'm not afraid of your wandering hands."

He tightens his fingers around mine and we walk back through the lower part of the city, along the winding riverbank. The entire city is set up like a sun, with a cluster of five temples at the center. The largest, the Sun Temple, is surrounded by four smaller temples—one for each direction. The rest of the city extends like the sun's rays, petering off into the desert and cut short at the meandering river.

The river, where Dhan and I have spent hours learning about each other as the water flows by. I look at him out of the corner of my eye.

He's wearing a loose, sleeveless tunic over long, flowy pants, soft leather sandals, and his gold—a thin collar of hammered gold around his neck with a snake clasp at the back; a thick band of hammered gold encircling both biceps; and small, thin gold loops in his ears. Every inch of him is strength and confidence. He knows exactly who he is and walks in his skin with a kind of ease I haven't seen in most of the guys from my time.

The evening is warm and Zanumites are lighting oil lamps, placing them in their windows or on the steps leading into their homes. People are hanging out of their windows and chatting across the alley with one another. They smile and greet us as we pass. Flowering vines crawl down from rooftops, dusting the air with sweet scents that compete with the smells of burning incense and spices sizzling in mud ovens.

It should be a pleasant enough evening, but something is in the air. I can't put my finger on it. At first I wonder if I'm feeling the tug to go back home—a subtle, but perceptible yank, like an alarm clock, that means it's time to go back. But the more I focus on the feeling, the more certain I am that it's something else. I feel it more intensely as we go up the steps toward one of the temples. There's a sort of current in the air that has my hair standing on end.

"Dhan, something is..."

"Yes," he says quietly. He scans the narrow stone steps. "I feel it, too."

I stay alert to my surroundings, but allow myself to go back to the feelings of moments before, when Dhan was pressed against me. When everything inside me was wide open and *on*. I want to be like that always. Opening like a sunflower craning toward the sun.

As we near the center of the city, we pass several girls heading in the opposite direction. They're clutching bows and have quivers slung over their shoulders. One is carrying a breastplate made of leather and metal. They're all wearing the sandals of warriors—made with tougher leather than regular sandals, with straps set closer together to protect their feet.

The girls smile and nod to me. But they look at Dhan with unabashed interest and giggle softly as we pass. I can't help the fire that suddenly roars out of control in my chest. Even though I know they're not being rude—it's perfectly acceptable in Zanum for people to appreciate others openly, even when they're in committed partnerships—I want to yell, "Hello? I'm standing right here!"

I work to make my voice sound nonchalant. "You know them?"

He gives me a puzzled look. "They are warriors from my city. I don't need to know them to acknowledge them."

I stop and pull my hand away. The burning feeling in my chest blots out everything. Before I can stop myself, I blurt out, "They're flirting with you."

He frowns. "Flirting?"

"Yes," I say, exasperated. "Showing interest in you."

He laughs. "Yes." He pauses and looks at me. "Does this bother you?"

I glare at him. "*Yes.*"

He looks perplexed for a moment before understanding dawns in his eyes. I see that he's working hard to keep a straight face. This pisses me off all the more.

"We've had these conversations in the past, Mika. Things are strange where you come from. Here," he says, "lovers are not pets. We are adults—free agents of our own lives and destinies." He tilts my chin up with one finger. "We can have strong feelings for one another and still enjoy the company of others, no?"

Everything I can't control whips around me like a wind, magnifying the fact that "normal" is so far out of my reach. Normal love, a normal relationship, normal conversations with a normal boyfriend. Instead, Time thrashes me around in its jaws without regard for what I want, or where I want to be. All of that frustration boils over like a pot on the stove.

"What do you do when I'm not around?" I ask in a voice that sounds strained, even to my ears. I know I sound ridiculous, but I can't help myself. The need to stop time from flowing around me, to have things be manageable and under control, blots out everything else.

He leans against the wall and crosses his arms. "What do you do back in your time?" he asks, "when *I* am not around?"

I press my lips together. "I asked you first."

One corner of his mouth lifts into a lazy smile as he pulls out a phrase I used to use when we were kids. "I asked you second. That means I answer second."

"That's a pile of sheep turds and you know it."

He grins, but says nothing.

I look back in the direction we came from. The girls are gone. "I do *stuff*," I say. "It's mostly school, school, and more school. But when I have some down time, I hang out, go to movies once in while, read, ride my bike, skateboard, swim. But now that it's summer, I have to work." I shrug. "That'll probably take up most of my time."

I realize how silly that sounds. Kids here do way more work than any of the kids at home. They have less free time. Most have kids of their own, and are doing what they'll be doing for the rest of their lives by the time they're about my age. An image flashes through my mind, of some of the girls from my school and their boyfriends sitting on the bleachers in the middle of a fog of weed smoke. And I think about my plans for the summer—complaining to my mom about not being able to lifeguard.

But Dhan doesn't mention any of that. "I do the same," he says. "I study, I care for the animals. Whenever I have time, I play sports with Yonaweh and the others. I help Mai'ma Pasea in whatever she needs. If the Council calls for a task, I make myself useful. There is never any shortage of *stuff*."

I look at the ground, as if what I really want to say is down there somewhere, just waiting for me to unearth it. I can almost feel the currents of time swirling around us, his faster, mine slower, all of it out of my hands.

"But there are so many hot Zanum girls," I say softly, digging the toe of my sandal into the dirt. "And sometimes I'm gone for long stretches of your time."

"Hot?" he asks.

I sigh. "Beautiful, sexy, desirable…"

He nods. "And the boys in your time? Are they not hot?"

I stop digging and look up at him. "As if you would care what I did with other guys."

"Of course I'd care. I wouldn't stop you, but I would care." He looks at a point over my shoulder and I see him working hard to rein in his emotions. "Mika, you do not know what it is like for me. I never know when you will leave or when you will return. I never know how long we will be apart. And there is no way for me to contact you in between." He looks into my eyes. "I think of you every day. Sometimes it is like a physical pain not to have you here."

All the frustration cracks like a shell. The rage I felt seconds ago leaks out of me. I force myself to listen to his words, as hard as it is to hear them spoken. "My mother left me when I was very young, Mika. And you—you keep on leaving me."

I grab his shirt and pull him toward me. With my lips brushing against his, I whisper, "I don't *want* to. If I could stay here forever, I would."

He wraps his arms around my waist, tight. I know he feels as powerless and frustrated as I do. No matter how much I worry and turn it over in my thoughts, I can't seem to find the magic switch that lets me control *any* aspect of what I can do.

My heart is buzzing like a hummingbird's wings, a thousand million beats a minute.

He raises my hands to his lips and kisses my knuckles before gently tugging me back to the path.

When we arrive back at Pasea's, she's not there. Dhan stops just inside the doorway and turns to me, one arm around my waist. "I'm going to see what's going on. Something is off, but I can't quite figure out what."

I nod and kiss him, but something is pricking the edges of my awareness. The air has shifted and everything feels... different.

Just as he's about to let go and leave, Pasea rushes in. "Mika'Arini!" she says, as if she had forgotten all about me. She wrings her hands, looking unsure about what to do next.

"Is everything okay?" I ask.

"Yes, yes, all is well," she says quickly. "I must go to Center Square. There is a—" She stops. "No matter."

She buzzes around, grabbing an incense burner, a stone carving, several crystals, oils. "Please find something for evening meal on your own, Mika. Dhanmat, you may join her after your evening chores, but when she is ready to leave, go to your hut for the night and stay there."

Dhan furrows his brow. "What is it, Mai-ma? What's happening?"

She looks over her shoulder as she pauses at the door. Her lips are pressed together in a thin line. "Follow my instructions without question. And *you*," she says, zeroing in on me. "You stay here, understood?"

I nod.

When she's satisfied, she scurries out the door. I've never seen Pasea like this.

I look at Dhan. "What's going on?"

He shakes his head. "I don't know, but Mai-ma is worried."

I take his hand. "Come on. Maybe we can help."

He holds my hand in a firm grip. "Mika. If we deliberately disobey her, we—*I*—will be severely punished."

And right then, I feel the tug.

Dhan recognizes the look on my face. "Now?"

I nod. "Something must be up at home."

I swallow hard. Even if I don't cross back on my own, the pull will become strong enough to yank me back. That happened once and it's painful—physically excruciating. I woke up screaming and in a cold sweat, with my mother freaking out. I explained it away as a nightmare, but I can't have it happen again.

Pasea says the yanking back is probably a survival mechanism. She says some animals will halt labor in the middle of giving birth if they sense danger, then start again when they're in a safe place. Maybe some part of my consciousness knows I need to be back in my body because something urgent is going on, so it just snaps me back out of self-preservation.

Besides, Pasea says it's important for me to be fully present and aware when I'm crossing over. It's the only way I can learn to control my gift.

I glance at the door where she was a moment ago. I can feel the tug on the other end of the thread, wanting me to ascend that spiral through the Dark, back into my "real" body—a living, breathing shell waiting for me in my own time. But something big is going on here, something I feel I should know about. Something that feels like it absolutely involves me.

I wrench my hand free of Dhan's. "*You* obey," I say, and head out the door in the direction Pasea went.

"Mika..." I hear him grumbling behind me, but I know he's following.

After a few minutes of speed walking, I see Pasea's figure up ahead, in the shadows. It's now completely dark and the white fabric draped loosely about her body shimmers under the buttery glow of the moon. She looks ethereal, skimming along the path as if her feet aren't even touching earth, as she heads toward Center Square with her sack of incense and stones. Whatever's going on must be occupying every inch of her thoughts, because she doesn't even look around. She seems absolutely focused on where she's going and whatever's happening there.

There are very few Zanumites out. It's getting dark and most families are returning to their homes for the evening.

Dhan steals alongside me, grasping my hand, and we follow Pasea at a safe distance.

When Center Square comes into view, Dhan and I exchange surprised glances. A crowd is gathered there, in front of the sacred tree. I scan the faces from where we are.

Dhan points and I spot his grandmother elbowing her way to the front, just to the left of where we're hidden in the dimly-lit alley.

Normally, this is a bustling center of merchants and craftspeople selling their wares and calling out to potential customers. The woman who pops corn on a giant skillet near the alley that leads to Center Square has taken the skillet away and quieted the embers for the day. With the sun going down, people should be gathering their things to go home, satisfied with a day of socializing, trading, crafting, and selling. But now, the air is full of taut anticipation.

I pull Dhan in the opposite direction, so that we're skirting the edges of the square, until we get a view of what's going on at the front. We hang back in the shadowed entrance of someone's empty home, and keep out of sight.

I struggle to keep the urge to return home at bay, but the pull is getting stronger.

At the front of the crowd, on a raised platform constructed at the base of the sacred tree, elder members of the Council are seated on stools, facing the city people.

A chill runs through me. Pasea once told me that the sacred tree represents the people. So long as the sacred tree thrives, the people will thrive. Its roots go deep into the womb of Great Mother of All and its branches rise high into the light of knowledge and wisdom. But for a split second, I see the tree as a gnarled, ancient, frightening thing, doubling over in spasms. I shove the image aside and trying to scrub it out of my mind.

"It's the Council," Dhan whispers. "There was no ritual announced tonight."

He and I both know this has to be more than a regular ritual. I've been to naming ceremonies, including my own, rituals for calming the earthquake serpent, and rituals that helped ease the dead into the afterlife, along with the usual new moon ceremonies and rites to mark the beginning of seasons.

But I've never seen Pasea this worked up.

A few drummers squatting near the front of the crowd begin a slow and steady beat on convex wooden drums covered with animal skins. An old walnut-skinned man with deep creases on his face and about three teeth in his mouth, starts up a haunting melody on the vina, a wind instrument usually used by the snake handlers.

As they do at all ceremonies and rituals, the Council members begin a prayer, slow and rhythmic at first, then building until their chanting fills the night and ricochets off the walls around us. Some members of the crowd are caught up in the trance, swaying with the increasing rhythm of the words and music.

I'm rooted to the ground, feeling the energies above and around all of us. They are constructing something with the chants and music and drums and incense. I can feel it, something unseen, yet very real, around us. Some sort of invisible barrier.

Finally, one of the elders, a tall man with a long, white, woolly beard, stands. His face is raised to the sky and his blue tunic swings loosely about his thin body as he leaps and twirls to the beat. He leaps a few more times before holding up a hand.

Immediately, the drumming and music cease, and the chanting peters off. A transparent sort of barrier has formed around the area of the ritual. I can feel it all around me, except for the area right where I'm standing. Outside of the barrier, lightning flashes and the wind picks up. But inside, where the people of Zanum are gathered, the air is still.

The elder's eyes, which had been closed during his dance, flicker so that only the whites are visible at first. Then he opens them fully and seems to grow larger.

There's a gasp from the crowd as the elder's features shift, subtly and almost as if they haven't at all, and he becomes someone else.

Dhan confirms this with a whisper. "He's channeling an ancestor."

The voice coming from the elder's throat is not a regular man's voice; it reverberates like it's coming from far off in time. "Hear me, children of Zanum, descendants of Kumari Kandam, the land that lies beneath the sea! I am an ancestor-priest. We came across the waters and settled the land to our north, lands upon which you now tread." He looks around at the crowd. "We created for you great temples and left for you our wisdom and knowledge—knowledge that you were to build on." He casts a glance at the Council members, who all bow their heads low in reverence.

"There is one open Council seat," he rumbles. "Only those Zanumites bestowed with gifts from Divine Mother, and who have reached an elder's level of mastery, will have the opportunity to fill this Council seat."

A murmur ripples through the crowd. I hear some of the Zanumites within earshot.

An open Council seat!

...rare and highly coveted opportunity!

A seat on the Council means great power and initiation into the greatest of Mysteries...

I turn to Dhan in surprise. High priests and priestesses live very long lives, so open Council seats are extremely rare. "Ever since I've been visiting, there have been seven Council members. When did this seat open up?"

"It was Imbara," he says, leaning close to my ear. "She foresaw her own time to cross the Great Desert into the Dark."

"Is this always how Council members are chosen?"

He shakes his head. "Never. It is never public. It has always been a closed ceremony in the Serpent Temple. There must be a reason they want all of the gifted members of Zanum present."

His eyes scan the crowd. "It's almost as if they are searching for something... or someone."

I lick my top lip and taste the salt of perspiration, but I hang on. Something tells me I *need* to see this.

Dhan looks down at my face and puts his arm around my waist. "Come, Mika," he says, concern threaded through each word. "Let's go. You're looking pale."

I grit my teeth and hold on to him. "No."

The old, bearded elder booms into the crowd. "Who among you will prove their faith to Divine Mother, the Wise Dark, and That Which is Unknowable?"

Almost every Zanumite raises their voice in answer. "I will!" "Me!" "*I* am a faithful child of Our Lady!"

The man slowly walks the length of the thrones in front of the other seated elders. Then he turns again to the Zanumites and thunders, "This seat will remain empty!"

The Zanumites look at one another in confusion. One woman, with the ability to whip up earth and sand with only a few movements of her hands, conveys her astonishment. "But there have always been seven on the Council. How can we have an empty seat? The Law requires seven members for all rituals and ceremonies."

The elder sweeps an arm across the crowd. "Silence!"

The crowd obeys.

He pulls his sword out of its scabbard. "Your ancestors plunged into the depths of the sea at Her command! By Her grace, the Shining Ones were spared and led to this land to begin anew, but all were willing to offer their lives. Who among you will step forward now, in their footsteps—in noble sacrifice to Her?"

I gasp, clutching Dhan's arm even tighter. "What is he talking about?"

I feel him tense. "They're weeding out non-believers. Those who are not loyal—who would not give their lives for Zanum and the ancestors."

The crowd shifts nervously, looking around in stunned silence.

"Come now!" the elder booms. "We, your Council, have received guidance from Divine Mother! She who is known by many names and has hundreds of attributes—Our Lady, Holy Mother, the Divine Womb, That Which Is Unknowable, Her Holy Darkness—now demands the offering of three of our bravest souls in return for Her protection and grace, as we move into perilous times. Those who step forward in ultimate sacrifice will symbolically occupy this Council seat. Together, your energies and spirits will embody the seventh principle!"

I look for Pasea. I'm sure she will step forward and stop this madness. I remember hearing about some tribes in the desert who sacrificed a queen's waiting men and women when she died, burying them along with her. But this is different. This is asking people to sacrifice themselves for no good reason. At least none that seems good enough to me. Not that sacrificing yourself for a queen is a good reason, either.

But when I find Pasea, I see that she's seated stiffly on a stool, off to one side of the Council. Her expression is anxious, but she doesn't seem freaked out. Why isn't she freaked out???

Some of the Zanumites take a step back. Others avoid making eye contact with the seated Council members. I stare at Pasea. If anyone fits the description of "faithful," she does. But she doesn't have mastery over a particular gift, so she is what the Zanumites refer to as "latent."

Pasea is an expert of sorts when it comes to outsiders, or bahari, but she can't do some of the things that these people can. Neither can Dhan. His mother visits him and he can see her, but he doesn't call her up. That's probably why Pasea told Dhan to go home. If this ceremony is only for the gifted of Zanum, he shouldn't be here. Technically, she shouldn't be here, either, but because she's been studying bahari for many years, and knows more about us than others, she's allowed to some restricted rituals and ceremonies.

I've learned not to question much of what goes on in Zanum, even when I don't understand and it seems strange to me, like people marrying their cousins—which happens a lot.

I don't know if it's from the horror of what this man is asking of the people, or the tug to go home, but my legs feel shaky. I lean against Dhan for support.

He glances down at me and I know he wants to say something, but this time he doesn't. He puts an arm across my shoulders, and turns his gaze back to the scene unfolding before us.

The elder roars into the crowd as lightning tears through the sky on the other side of the barrier. "Are there none among you worthy of a seat on the Council?"

Finally, a young man speaks. His dark curls are swept back from his face and cascade to the middle of his back like a rippling waterfall. "I am Vinta. And I possess a rather controlled gift of Sight," he says, bowing his head. "But I cannot see this event nor its fallout in the Winding Steps of Time."

The elder inclines his head. "It is shielded, my child."

So that's what all the chanting and music constructed—a shield. But what, or who, are they shielding this event from?

Vinta walks to the front of the crowd and sinks to one knee before the bearded man. "My brother and I have traveled a great distance to be among you. We are not direct descendants of Kumari Kandam, but we both have the gift and were tormented when we lived among our own in the Upper Kingdoms. No one knew how to care for us or cultivate our gift. Our mother heard there were more of our kind here and sent us to join a caravan traveling east. Among you, we have found healing, support, sustenance, and love." He looks up at the elder. "I offer myself and my brother to Divine Mother, Great Honorable Council."

He looks over his shoulder to a man who is obviously his twin. "Haram, let us bow to the will of our leaders who are the embodiment of Our Lady."

Haram looks at Vinta with contempt. "Not I, brother." He says, chuckling without humor. "You have always been the one to seek adoration and praise from our elders. I have no need to prove anything. I do not agree to this."

Vinta scowls. "Haram! The Council has offered us what none other can. There is no other place for us. Do you not remember how it was when we were children? What do you fear? Death?"

His eyes crinkle in remembered pain. "You know as well as I that there are many things in life far worse than death." He holds out his hand. "Come, kneel with me—show your devotion."

Haram looks around at the faces of the crowd and sets his jaw. "I will not. And I advise you, dear brother, to come back among the good people of Zanum. These leaders have gone mad."

Several people shout in agreement.

I'm wondering about that, too. They want people to *sacrifice* themselves? This is so unlike the Council. So totally and completely, one-hundred-and-eighty-degrees opposite of everything I've known the Council to be.

I look again at Pasea, but she hasn't moved a muscle.

Vinta slits his eyes at Haram before turning back to the Council. Even from where I'm standing, I can see the anger on his face. "My apologies, Honorable Council. My brother knows not of what he speaks. I shall climb gladly into the lap of mortal death if it should bring Our Lady's favor upon my family, the Council, and all of Zanum." He turns to the Council members and they each nod in approval.

I take a deep breath to quell the rising nausea in my belly.

The ancestor takes Vinta's hand and leads him into a tent set up behind the sacred tree.

"Oh, my god," I breathe. I clutch Dhan's arm with my other hand. "Is he going to *kill* him?"

Dhan's eyes dart to Pasea as well. He shakes his head. "I can't believe he would."

I hear the same disbelief and shock echoed by the other Zanumites. The old man who once strung a beautiful necklace out of glass beads for me, shouts, "He is but a child!"

The sweet-maker, who I've seen turn salt into sugar, and sand into millet, using only a small fire and his chants, shakes his fist in the air. "Surely, this is a crime against Our Holy Mother and Child!"

There is a hummin tension in the square as the Zanumites and other Council members sit, waiting. The skies on the other side of the shield turn dark and menacing.

Dhan tightens his arm around me, but says nothing.

A long moment or two later, the elder returns. His sword is bloody and his face has a look of grim determination as he wipes it clean. "He was worthy," he says to the other Council members. "He went forth bravely and without so much as a whimper."

It's only when Dhan clamps his hand over my mouth that I realize I had opened it to shout something. *Anything.*

I bite down on his finger and he yanks his hand away. "Don't you *ever* do that again," I whisper.

He shakes his hand and rubs the teeth marks I've left behind. "We are *not* supposed to be here, Mika. I don't know what's going on, but I trust Mai-ma completely. If she is not worried, I am not worried."

He's lying. I can tell from the tension in his body that Dhan is totally worried. But he's right; I trust Pasea, too. She still has that anxious-but-not-freaked-out expression on her face and I try to relax, knowing that if she's not tearing through the crowd and screaming, there has to be a reason for all of this. I swallow and concentrate on staying upright.

"This is not a show of devotion," Haram says. He's shaking with rage and there are other city members physically restraining him from running up to the where the Council members are seated. "This is a farce put on by a superstitious group of elders masquerading as leaders!"

"What is superstition, my boy?" the elder asks, barely concealing the reproach in his voice. "Divine Mother? She is the very source of all you own and value! It is Her gift that flows through you. Without Her breath, all our great gifts lie dormant."

There are murmurs of agreement throughout the crowd.

Haram's eyes spark as a sob escapes before he shouts, "You have taken my only kin—my brother!"

The man levels him with a glare. "No one 'took' him. Vinta went willingly, of his own desire and devotion to the eternal Mother." Then, as if dismissing the whimper of a child, the ancestor looks out into the crowd again and raises his sword above his head. "One more! Who among you fears no mortal death? Who among you would cross gladly into the afterlife to serve She who is the source of all?"

"What outrage is this?!" shouts the sweet-maker, moving closer to Haram.

"You are not leaders," yells a woman I've seen heal the deepest of wounds with just the touch of her hands and a feather-soft breath. She moves to the side where Haram's supporters seem to be gathering. "The power to give and take life is not yours!"

"The Council has never failed us!" says a scolding voice. "You must have faith."

"The Council is drunk on power!" Haram flings out. "The Upper Kingdoms have no Council and no Divine Mother. They have one, sane, ruling king—one who, no doubt, would have put an end to this madness already!"

"If we do not have faith in our leaders, we have nothing!" another man says harshly.

"Who shall it be?" the elder roars again, ignoring the comments from the crowd. "Who among you is worthy enough to shed your blood for the great honor and responsibility of a seat on the Council?"

A man, Ghera, whom I've seen training in armed combat, steps forward. "Through Her breath, I command the flame," he says. "I humbly offer myself to my Council."

The elder takes the man into the same tent he took Vinta and returns moments later, with a newly bloodied sword. Right away, the crowd begins to split into two clear factions—those who support Haram, and those who agree with his self-sacrificing brother, Vinta.

The Council elder repeats the ritual a third time with an older woman, Maitreyi, who can communicate with the departed.

The edges of my vision begin to blur. Something important is going on in my time, calling me back. But I can't leave. Everything I've ever known about Zanum is up in the air. This place that always felt like a second home—like love and warmth and acceptance—has suddenly, in one evening, filled me with revulsion and shock. I can't go back until *something* makes sense.

When the ancestor returns this third time, he wipes the blade of his sword clean and faces the crowd. "The three souls who walked fearlessly into That Which Is Unknowable are the most faithful and brave among you. None other would be worthy of a seat on the Council. You, dear Zanumites, would accept no less."

I see some heads nodding in agreement.

Haram's voice cuts through the heightened emotions of the crowd. "The Council is a sham, bent on leading us all to certain death!"

"Haram speaks truth!" says a man whose son has competed in several camel races with Dhan. The man moves to stand next to Haram. "I have heard of the Upper Kingdoms—those kings are conquering many territories. Their people grow robust and have more of everything than we can ever imagine. Let us join with them!"

Haram seems emboldened by the small group of people who have moved closer to support him.

"The gods of the Upper Kingdoms would never require such a sacrifice!"

"No!" his supporters cry in agreement.

"They value this life, the beauty around us, love among mortal beings! They do not preach about the Dark and a divine mother and her holy child. They do not value all that is unseen over what is right in front of our very eyes!"

"Enough!" Everyone turns to Atesu, the priestess-queen. She nods to the bearded elder, who at once crumples to the ground.

Atesu waits a few heartbeats while the elder, the true owner of the body on the platform, comes back into his form. I'm amazed watching that larger-than-life person shrink back into an old, frail man in the minutest of shifts and changes.

Atesu motions for one of the waiting men. "Bring the elder priest some camel's milk and help him to his seat."

Then she turns to address the crowd. She raises her arms above her head and I can see the white serpent tattoos winding from her upper arms and ending as raised cobras on the inside of her wrists. Tattoos that mark her as the highest-ranking among priestesses—the priestess-queen of Zanum.

She's holding glass jars full of water, with what looks like stalks of grass floating in them. "Those of you who put unwavering faith in your Council, stand firm where you are. And *you*," she says, turning to Haram and his supporters. "At dawn, you will leave this city. Any blasphemer who agrees with you must accompany you."

He narrows his eyes. "We are to be banished?"

"Indeed," Atesu says. "You have questioned the very foundations upon which this city was built. You have spoken in favor of those in the Upper Kingdoms, whose goal it is to consume all that Our Lady has breathed into creation. Their kings have conquered our sister cities, leaving behind rivers of blood and slaughtered innocents, destroying shrines and fouling wells and water sources. They seek to destroy Zanum in the same manner."

Two tornadoes form behind Atesu, obediently spinning in place. She keeps her arms stretched over her head as she looks each of Haram's supporters over. "At dawn you will all be escorted into the wild and left to find your way. Do not return."

"You will live to regret this, old woman," Haram says in a low voice.

"I know I will not," Atesu says, matching his tone. Then, as if finished with him, she lowers her arms, handing the jars to a seated Council member. The tornado columns disappear at once.

She turns to the crowd. "And now, beloved Zanumites, I present to you your High Council."

Vinta, Ghera, and Maitreyi all walk out of the tent, each carrying a slain sheep.

I whip my head around to gape at Dhan. This time, I clamp my own hand over my mouth to keep from squealing or shouting.

He slumps his shoulders and lets out a long exhale.

I notice that Pasea's face is tear-streaked and wonder if she, too, was afraid those people were really being sacrificed. Was it nothing but raw, unwavering faith that kept her from jumping up and yanking them away from the man with the sword?

There is a collective gasp, and then cheers and cries of relief from the crowd.

Atesu smiles. "These three, Blessed by Divine Mother, were willing to offer their lives in order that yours may be protected by She who presides over all," she says, shooting a look toward Haram and his gathered supporters. "They showed who among you is loyal, and who among you would side with the enemies of Life."

Some of Haram's supporters voice their regret. The sweet-maker looks especially devastated. "We have been manipulated by our own Council!"

Someone I can't see shouts, "I will not leave Zanum—it is the home of my ancestors! I am a child of Kumari Kandam!"

A woman's voice overlaps that with, "Forgive us, Honorable Council! Allow us to remain among you!"

"You have been tested, not manipulated. Only your own foolishness keeps you from recognizing the difference," Atesu says. She gestures toward the three who had stepped forward to sacrifice themselves. "These three Blesseds were tested as well," she says, turning back to Haram and his supporters. "You have shamed and disappointed your ancestors and you have cut your connection with Zanum, Kumari Kandam, and your Council. Tonight, you will eat, pack your belongings, and rest. At dawn you will leave and never return."

She turns back to the crowd. "As Presiding Head Priestess of your Council, it is my duty to inform you that we have had a rare collective vision. We will require the energies and skills of nine members for what we are soon to face. The Seers among us predict a great storm of destruction moving steadily toward Zanum."

A gasp ripples through the crowd of faithful Zanumites.

"You, my beloveds, will be the seeds of a resistance that must live on for centuries to come. The armies of the Upper Kingdoms have joined forces, bringing with them their new gods and their new ways. We have seen that they do not abide by the Laws of Holy Mother, but seek to bleed and plunder Her stores until all are bereft. We must prepare."

Thunder rumbles as streaks of lightning shatter the sky outside the barrier. The crowd raises its hands in a battle cry. All except for the small, tense group of supporters surrounding Haram.

He stands with his fists clenched at his sides. "You have made a mockery of us all," he shouts. Even from where I'm standing, I can see the vein bulging in his neck as he turns to Vinta. "Since childhood, you have tried to better me, brother. At the bow, with a sword, and in skinning a lamb. You may now rest smug in the belief that you have bested me. You are the more faithful, a Council member, a *blessed* of Divine Mother." He spits that last phrase out.

"And you, as ever, have decided I am to blame for your shortcomings," Vinta throws back. He stands tall and stoic, even with a bloody sheep in front of him. "I have no desire to bring you pain. I acted according to my own inner Word, and I beseeched you to walk with me. You chose not to. You allowed fear to halt your step. You are fully grown, dear Haram, and the director of your own destiny."

Haram stares at Vinta, seething for a moment, before erupting again. "You dare to call me a coward, when you are complicit in staging my humiliation? I have had doubts about the Council in the past, and today they are all confirmed. Fear not, you who stand by my side! I will lead us to a home where we are not called to challenge our instincts; a home where we may live by our desires and answer to great kings!"

He turns to address Atesu. "We will not go quietly, old woman. Let all who stand here bear witness: I, and those who stand with me, will not leave a single one of you unscathed."

Something frozen and brittle clutches at me from the depths of my being as Haram's eyes scan the crowd and lock onto mine. It's like he knows I'm here. For just a split second, I see a disembodied shadow hovering behind him. But when I blink and look again it's gone.

"You are nothing but manipulative tyrants toying with your gifts—all in the name of a divine and holy mother who seeks to strike down the core of every man among us. This city, and all it stands for, shall be reduced to cinders before I am through." He flicks a glance in my direction. "My name will be known throughout the ages."

"Silence!" Atesu says, raising her arms. A blast of wind slams through the ritual area. Atesu narrows her eyes and speaks directly to Haram. "It is done. You are no longer welcome among true Zanumites."

She turns back to the crowd. "Tonight, we feast in celebration of your new Council. There is ample roasted meat, wine, and fruit—rejoice!"

My vision begins to darken amid the fading murmur of the crowd. I dig my fingers into Dhan's shoulder and feel my legs give out beneath me just as I hear him whisper, "No. Don't go, Mika..."

Chapter 4

"Pammi! Darling, are you okay? Oh, sweetheart, please talk to me!"

My eyes snap open. I'm peering into the panicked face of my mother. She's holding the phone in one hand.

"What's going on?" I ask, forcing each syllable out. Every bone in my body feels shattered.

"Oh, thank *god*," she says, snatching me to her chest.

Sheer survival instinct keeps me from screaming in pain.

"I've been shaking you for a good ten minutes!" She pulls away and searches my face. "You were having another one of your nightmares, sweetheart. Are you all right?"

I struggle to bring my heart rate back to normal, to quell the shrieks of agony that want to tear out of my throat. Every part of me feels absolutely battered. Like I've been yanked through several plate glass windows.

"I'm fine, Mom," I say through gritted teeth. "Just a bad dream."

"That was worse than a bad dream, Pams." Her eyes cloud with frantic worry—a worry I've seen before. "That was more like absolute terror."

It hurts to breathe. I work at keeping my face expressionless. "I had ice cream last night. You know I get really bad dreams after I eat ice cream." The look on her face tells me I have to do better than that. "Plus, you've got me going into some juvie home tomorrow, Mom—I'm nervous!"

Her face relaxes a bit, but the frantic worry lingers. "Oh, honey, it's nothing like that! Don't worry one bit. Bubs would never put you in a position that was unsafe. You trust him, don't you?"

I nod, resisting the urge to pass out. "Yeah, but I'm still nervous."

She kisses my forehead. "Of course. That's to be expected, sweetheart. Don't worry. Everything will work out just fine."

I sink back down, allowing the pillow to swallow my head. "I'm going to try to go back to sleep now. I'm exhausted."

I feel the bed creak after a moment, as she eases herself off. "Yes, darling. You need to get some rest. You really had me frightened for a moment there! I thought you were..."

She trails off, but everything she doesn't say is loud and clear. *I thought you were having one of your hallucinations, again, Pammi! Just like my mother and grandmother! I don't want to lose you, too, darling. Should I call Dr. Mace?*

I've heard it all a million times. I wish I could go back to Zanum, but I can't risk it now. There's no way I could relax and stay alert enough to cross over with my mom's radar on full alert.

I toss and turn with visions of bloody swords and storms of destruction crowding my thoughts, until I tumble into a restless sleep.

The next morning, Mom taps on my bedroom door. "Time to get up, darling," she says, poking her head in. "Don't want to be late for your appointment!"

I grumble and roll out of bed in grim determination. If working at this place keeps Mom off my back and lets me keep visiting Zanum, then it's worth it. Even if it means having to sit in offices that remind me of horrible things.

"I'm up," I mutter, rubbing the sleep out of my eyes.

"I'm going out for a bit with Bubs, but call if you need anything, all right?"

"Okay. I'll be fine."

"Don't be nervous, Pams. You're going to be great! And good luck, I want to hear all about it."

When the door shuts behind her, I climb out of bed. I would love to go back right now, and stay in Zanum. For some reason, though, right before I fall asleep is the only time I can go. Pasea said our body chemistry changes at night and that might have something to do with it. Or maybe that's the only time I allow myself to completely relax and still stay alert—kind of like being in a trance, asleep and awake at the same time.

But what happened last night was jarring. I feel a stronger sense of urgency about being able to go whenever I want, and to control the way time flows around me when I travel.

"If you can control the angle at which time bends," Pasea says, "You will go wherever you want to go. And you will decide how fast or how slow time flows, as long as it is still within the laws of the Dark. You cannot go to the same point twice and you cannot go backward," she says. "Wherever you land on a time point not your own is where you move forward from. Never backward."

I sit down and try to focus on what I need to do today. Pasea told me once, when I said I wanted to stay there forever, that I had to remember where I belonged. I wasn't a Zanumite and I never would be. "Divine Mother has breathed her gift into you, Mika'Arini. You may travel through Her Darkness, but you must always obey Her laws."

I haul myself up and dress in my one and only interview outfit—a pair of navy slacks and a cream-colored shirt. I try to eat a slice of toast, but not much is getting past my jittery stomach. Instead, I gulp down some orange juice and grab my mom's car keys, my skateboard—just in case—and a pair of sneakers.

I used to love skateboarding when I was younger and, every now and then, I like the feel of sailing along the pavement with my arms outstretched. The bike path between my house and the center is perfect for it.

I head off to meet the girls at the treatment center.

I find the Margaret Schroff Leadership Academy and Residence for Girls pretty easily. It's a huge brick house on a hill surrounded by old, sheltering trees. There are acres of land behind it and, off to one side, an orchard where a few men in hats are working under the sun.

I could swear that I've driven past here a million times and never noticed it before. How could anyone miss a huge estate like this?

I park in the lot and chirp the car doors locked. I walk up the wide stone steps and ring the buzzer as a camera clocks my every movement.

"Parminder Dhillon?" says the intercom.

"It's Pammi."

Mom and Dr. B. had said they would be expecting me, but I guess I figured the place would be more institutional-y and impersonal. Maybe more like the sleek glass and steel structure of Dr. Mace's office.

The door buzzes and I push on the handle. Inside, the place looks like a Victorian mansion. The floors are dark wood and the furniture is antique and solid. There are lush throw rugs everywhere and large framed pictures on the walls in the foyer. They have lights trained on them like hangings in a museum.

When I look closely at the little cards underneath each image, I see that they are all of different goddesses. Under one, an image of a large, rotund woman with full breasts and the entire world in her lap, there's this inscription: *Cybele, a.k.a. Magna Mater ("Great Mother" or "Mother of all Gods")*. Another, a photo of a small carved statue of a woman with rounded hips and big thighs, is labeled, *Astarte-Ishtar, ivory, ninth century BC.* I walk around to look at the third, a colossal image of a golden woman in profile. She holds a baby out in her hands and rays radiate from them both. The card underneath reads, *Saule, supreme goddess of the sun, a.k.a. the Great Sky Weaver. Baltic goddess governing life, death, and childbirth.*

Okay, this can't be a hospital. What kind of residential treatment center looks like a senator's mansion? And has huge pictures of goddesses all over the place?

The click-clack of heels snaps me back. A petite blonde smiles disarmingly as she holds her hand out from about ten feet down the hall.

"Hello, Pammi! I'm Celia Ramirez. It's so lovely to meet you." Her grip is warm and solid. "The girls are eager to meet you," she says, heading back down the hall. "Come, I'll introduce you, and we'll get started."

Down the long hallway, I see more framed images. I quickly scan the cards underneath each image as I follow Celia Ramirez. There's *Durga Maa*, sitting atop a lion; *Kali*, dancing on the skulls of men; *Mahadevi, the Great Goddess*; and *Lakshmi, the Goddess of Luck.*

I'm guessing that was the Indian goddess wing. My old complaint to Mom about there being no Sikh goddesses or female gurus flits through my mind. I hate that I know little to nothing about these stories and myths. They are so fundamentally Indian, yet most westerners know them better than I do.

Dr. B. had said today would be a "feeling out" session. That made me want to snicker—it sounded like something one of the girls from my school might do under the bleachers with dude-of-the-month. Childish? Maybe, but still funny.

Dr. B. said this "mutual interview" would give me a chance to meet everyone, and they would get a chance to meet me, and we could all see if we were a good "match." He makes everything sound so easy.

"Here we are," Celia says, leading me into a large, well-lit room.

On my right is a little area sectioned off as a kitchen, with a small round table in it. There's a teakettle on the counter and a fridge with charts that are neatly held in place with fruit magnets. The rest of the room is bright and colorful. This space has only one framed image. I squint my eyes and read. *Pallas Athene, Warrior Goddess in Arms.*

When I look to my left, I see The Girls.

There are three of them sitting in a circle of chairs and cushions. None of the girls look up or make any move to acknowledge me.

Actually, that's not true. One of them stares at me like she can see right through me.

I feel as if I've entered an entirely different dimension. Like Mom and Dr. B. don't even exist. Like nothing outside of this mansion exists.

Celia acts like she doesn't notice the fact that there's one girl who looks like she wants to pounce on me, and that the other two haven't batted an eyelash. "Well, here she is!" she says brightly.

She turns to me. "Pammi, this is Etienne Williams, Sharlene Levine, and Gayla Henderson. Girls, this is Parminder—er, Pammi—Dhillon."

Gayla looks up after a long minute. "Hey," she says with a limp wave.

Etienne continues to look at me with dark, impenetrable eyes. They're like magnifying glasses burning holes through the layers of my skin.

I can't see Sharlene's face because she's picking at something on the chair by her leg, and her hair is hanging down like a veil. But I can see her strategically ripped tights and her short jean skirt.

"Have a seat, Pammi," Celia says, motioning me into a chair next to hers. "We're at the end of one of our circle sessions and were just doing free share. We thought it would be good for you to sit in on the last bit of our session so you have an idea of the way we communicate around here."

I nod and take a deep breath. I don't know what I was expecting, but this is so not it.

Celia turns her attention to the girls. "Now, what was it about the orchard?"

Etienne finally takes her eyes off me. "Shar's got an issue."

"It's not *my* issue," says Sharlene. For the first time, I see her face. She's beautiful in a kind of plain way—like those girls on *Next Top Model* you'd walk right past on the street, but when you make them up and put them on a magazine cover, they're "supermodels."

"Joe's a nice guy," Gayla says, pushing her glasses up.

Sharlene leans forward. "Nice has nothing to do with it, Gay! Some 'nice' guys do all kinds of skeevy things when no one's looking."

Gayla digs the toe of her shoe into the rug. "Yeah, but I seriously don't think Joe's like that. I've been alone with him a million times and he's always respectful."

"It's true," Etienne says. "I don't think he would hurt a fly, Shar."

Sharlene jumps up. "Are you saying I'm *lying*?"

Etienne leaps out of her seat. "No one's calling you a liar— shit!"

Gayla bangs a fist on her chair and stands. "I didn't say that! It's just that..."

"What? It's just that what?" Sharlene says, almost shouting now. "All my life, since I was little, I've been told I was lying when I told!"

"You're not little anymore," Etienne says quietly.

"Everyone knows you hate those guys, Shar," Gayla says. "Even though we need them." She darts a glance at me. "They work here."

"I don't hate them," Sharlene hisses. "I just don't trust them."

The air around us is taut and alive. My heart is hammering and I realize I'm also on my feet.

Celia stands, too. She speaks in a calm, measured tone. "All right, girls—goodness. You nearly gave me a heart attack, Sharlene."

Sharlene's hands are balled up into fists as she glares at everyone. "I'm sick of you all implying I'm making shit up."

Etienne sucks her teeth. "You *do* make shit up."

Sharlene's jaw tightens. "They shouldn't even *be* here. I mean, why do we have guys working at an all-girls' school? We couldn't find any women to give those jobs to?"

"We have *these* male workers because Miss Maggie trusts them, Sharlene. You know that," Celia says, in a soothing voice. "We aren't a facility where no men ever enter the grounds, hon. Everyone is here because they have a unique and special task."

Sharlene whips her head around. "Picking fruit? That's a specialized task?"

"They're not just picking fruit, Shar," Gayla says. She seems to be telling Sharlene something with her eyes.

Sharlene focuses her fury on Gayla now. "Oh, yes—that's right. They're contributing their energy to the shield—"

Both Etienne and Gayla widen their eyes.

"*Shut up*, Shar," Etienne mutters through clenched teeth.

Celia sighs. "Girls," she begins, but the phone rings and cuts her off. She glances at it.

Sharlene withdraws into herself as the phone continues to ring.

"Oh, that dratted voice mail still isn't working!" Celia says. "I'll be right back, girls."

Both Gayla and Etienne are glaring at Sharlene.

"You almost blew it," Gayla says. Her voice is full of reproach.

"Gotta be more careful, Shar," Etienne says. "You could mess everything up for all of us."

Sharlene wraps her arms around her body and rocks back and forth. "Up yours, Tee. I could go on about all the shit *you* do."

Etienne relaxes into a grin. "But you won't."

Sharlene sinks back into her seat and, after a moment, Gayla sits down, too.

That leaves me and Etienne still standing. With Celia on the phone, I'm on my own and these girls have not rolled out a welcome mat.

Etienne makes a slow circle around me, looking me up and down. "So, newbie. What's wrong with you?"

My breathing is shallow, not quite making it past the knot in my chest. But I work to steady my voice. "What are you talking about?"

What's wrong with *me*? I'm not the one in a treatment facility. I bite back the words.

"Don't mess with her, Tee—she's an outsider," Sharlene says, giving Etienne a half smile. "You could mess everything up for all of us." Then she levels a suspicious gaze at me. "What *is* your deal?"

Etienne is about one-sixth of an inch from my right ear. I feel her breath, warm and moist, as she speaks. "There has to be something. They wouldn't let her in here if she didn't have *something*."

I stand rooted to the spot.

Etienne comes around to stare directly into my eyes, just inches away from my nose. She whispers, "What makes you different from everyone else you've ever known your whole life?"

A numbing kind of frozen spreads from my belly to my limbs. I can't breathe.

Etienne steps back slowly, with a knowing nod and the faintest hint of a smile.

Gayla, who has been watching the exchange closely, nods. "So, it's true. You're one of us."

Celia comes scurrying back from her phone call, takes one look at me and raises her voice. "Tee," she says sternly, "I *told* you to behave."

Etienne sucks her teeth again and puts on an innocent face. "What? What'd I do?" Then she saunters back to her seat, stretches her legs out in front of herself and never once takes her eyes off me.

"Honey," Celia says, taking me by my elbow and steering me toward the kitchen. "Pay no attention to Etienne. She gives everyone a hard time at first. She's really a kitty cat once you get to know her."

I can't picture Etienne as a kitty cat. A hyena, maybe.

Celia pours me a glass of water and I guzzle it down. My heart has not slowed its pace, and I can still feel the girls behind me, watching with more interest now than when I first walked in.

What makes you different from everyone else you've ever known your whole life?

"She's only trying to intimidate you," Celia says gently. "Ignore her. Let's go back into the circle. You'll be fine—I promise."

"Can I have some more water, please?" My voice comes out raspy.

I do not want to go back into that circle. In fact, I'm having serious doubts about this whole thing.

Celia refills my cup and hands it to me. I take my time sipping until she says, "Let's go back to the circle, Pammi."

I could be imagining it, but this time her voice does not sound as gentle. "I don't think—" I begin, but before I can finish, she steers me back to my seat.

"Behave, Tee," she says firmly. "Otherwise, you'll lose privileges again. Understand?"

Etienne presses her lips into a thin line and draws her fingers across her mouth, as if she's zipping it shut. Then she sits back and fixes her narrowed eyes on me.

"All right," Celia begins. "Where were we? Oh yes—Sharlene, what was it that Joe said in the apple orchard that upset you?"

Sharlene had her foot propped up on her chair, but now drops it in exasperation. "He thought I was some chick he could be a jerk around and that I would just, like, giggle or something." She looks down to inspect the remaining black fingernail polish on her pinky. Just like that: everything out, everything in.

"Is that what it really was, or is that what you believe it was?" Celia asks, leaning toward Sharlene. "How do you know what he was thinking?"

Sharlene keeps staring at her fingernail.

"That's not how I saw it," Gayla says.

Celia turns to her. "Tell me what you saw, Gayla."

Sharlene rolls her eyes without looking up from her fingernails.

My heart rate is slowing to a more regular pace and I'm breathing a bit more normally. Celia's probably right—Etienne is just trying to intimidate me. I can deal with girls trying to intimidate me and make me feel like I don't belong. I dealt with that plenty at my school.

"Shar said something about his IQ and how it was related to him working in an orchard for a living."

Etienne snorts.

"That was because he was staring at my ass," Sharlene says.

"He was *not*," Gayla says. "He was looking at the wormy apple you were picking off that low branch, you turd."

"Puh-leeze. I know when a guy is looking at my ass."

"Sheee-it," Etienne says, throwing up her hands. "Can we move on, already?" She slides down in her seat and folds her arms across her chest, a bored expression on her face. Her features are like one of my mom's perfectly chiseled Indian sculptures. Her lips are full, set into the dark velvety brown of her skin. But it's her eyes that unnerve me—half-hooded, with lashes that sweep up and down like fans.

I don't realize I'm staring until she gives me a wink. I look away quickly and feel my face getting hot.

The phone rings again. "Oh, that blasted thing!" Celia grumbles, getting up. She looks at Etienne. "Remember..."

"Yeah, yeah," Etienne says.

As soon as Celia's on the phone, all three of the girls lean in.

"Seriously," Gayla says. "What do you do?"

I lean back. "Do? Um, I just graduated from high school."

She waves her hand. "No. You know what I mean—what's your thing?"

I give them all a blank stare.

"She doesn't even know," Etienne says with a smirk. She looks at me with utter disdain.

Sharlene folds her hands between her knees and leans so far forward, she's almost off her chair. As if speaking to a four-year-old, she whispers, "All three of us," she points to each of them in turn, "and just about everyone here—we do things that no one out there can do. That's why we're here." She waits a beat before adding, "that's why *you're* here."

Okay, who *are* these people? Are they trying to ambush me? Is this some sort of weird test my mom set up with Dr. Mace? His voice reverberates in my head. *You cannot visit a place in another time while you sleep, Pammi. It's all in your head. It is something you are making up so that you can deal with the pain in your life.*

My voice is barely a whisper. "No, I'm not." I look at Gayla and her face is dead serious. "This is a residential treatment center," I say slowly. "You all were..." I trail off and start again. "This is a facility for girls who were traumatized in early life."

Etienne sucks her teeth for something like the seventeenth time, and Gayla just shakes her head. There's a long moment of silence while each of the girls looks hard into my eyes and everything gets sucked out of me. I no longer hear Celia chattering on the phone in the kitchen. All I see is three sets of knowing eyes, boring deep into my bones.

When Sharlene speaks again, her words ricochet throughout the walls of my brain. "I can go just about anywhere I want to, without leaving this place." Her eyes glint as she watches my face.

Slowly, I freeze. My mouth is clamped shut.

Gayla turns to Sharlene. "You're not supposed to—"

"Shut up," Sharlene says, keeping her eyes fixed on me.

My thoughts are a jumble. Where am I? What *is* this place?

Gayla darts a glance at Celia and bites down on her bottom lip. "We don't know for sure about her," she says quickly. "And Miss Maggie never told us about anyone new."

Things start moving in slow motion, like I'm underwater. My head swivels toward Etienne and I hear her say, "We know." She nods in my direction. "*She* doesn't."

Sharlene reaches out and, with a wicked half-smile playing on her lips, covers one of my hands with hers. "Think about it, *Mika*."

Somewhere in the distance, I hear my chair topple over. Then I'm standing up.

I hear Celia's surprised gasp as she spins around. I hear everything far away, drowned out by the sound of my own shallow breaths and the furious pounding in my ears.

Then there is Etienne's laughter, the door slamming behind me, and the pounding of my feet against the pavement.

Chapter 5

I run. I don't know where to—just away. I'm falling. The whole world has gone crazy. I see nothing. I hear nothing, except the words echoing inside my own head. *We do things that no one out there can do. That's why we're here. That's why* you're *here.*

Dry twigs crunch beneath my shoes. My interview shirt snags on a branch and still I run, as fast as I can. *She doesn't even know.*

I run and run and run.

And then I'm slipping. No sound. I'm falling through white mist and fog and there's a gentle, soft drizzle. I grab onto a golden strand to stop myself, but I keep twirling, like a dry leaf caught up in autumn winds.

I'm in the desert. The sun tears through the sky like a million bolts of lightning piercing through me all at once. I sit up and look around—nothing as far as the eye can see, except sand dunes. Red, rolling, beautiful dunes against a vivid, painfully blue sky.

I stand up and my two-inch heels sink into the sand. My mouth is parched. I shake the sand off my hands and begin to walk. But before I can take a step, a giant, brilliant white cobra slithers out from underneath the sand and rises before me.

I recognize it instantly as one of the Guardians of Zanum. I try to remember everything I've heard from Pasea about the four serpent-guardians, the white one in particular. I can't remember if this is the one that kills intruders slowly, sucking out her victim's entrails little by little while keeping them alive to prolong their agony.

I'm not an intruder, I want to say. I'm a bahari—I have a role here. But my voice is not cooperating. My throat is parched, as dry and scaly as the guardian's skin.

The giant serpent sways a little, gazing at me.

If they're hooded and swaying, they are content.

I hold my breath and stand stock-still. Sweat trickles down the hollow between my breasts, soaking the top of my bra strap.

After what feels like an eternity, the serpent lowers herself, turns, and makes a slow ascent up the sand dune.

Relief washes over me. But something calls to me and I follow the white cobra. I climb, using a thick branch with oak leaves stubbornly hanging onto it, as a walking stick. I realize I must have held onto that branch as I fell in the woods. I stumble and steady myself with the help of the branch until I get to the top. There I see, far off in the distance, shimmering patches of green dotting the horizon.

Zanum.

I look around for the serpent, but she's gone. Her wavy trail stops abruptly at the top of the dune and then—nothing. No trace.

I begin to run, but since I've had no breakfast this morning, the effects of the "mutual interview" catch up with me and I fall several times on weak, wobbly knees.

I heave myself up and keep walking. It looks like a long way to go, but as the city becomes clearer, I hear the familiar sound of a temple flute and the plinking of thumb pianos. I feel a renewed surge of energy and walk faster.

Slowly, first as a shimmering brown and white dot, then coming closer and into focus, is Pasea. As I come near, she holds her arms out. I collapse into them.

"Vinta sent me," she says. "The Gentle Guardian alerted him. How did you enter by that gate, Mika?"

I wipe my forehead with the back of my hand and peel away. "I didn't. I just sort of *landed* there."

She stares hard at what I'm holding. "That is from your time."

I look at my walking stick with the shock of vibrant oak leaves at the top. "I must have grabbed for it as I was falling."

"Organic matter—live, organic matter—came through with you..." There's a flare of alarm in her eyes. "That must be it!" she whispers.

"What?" I ask, knowing she is, once again, keeping something from me. "What must be it?"

"Come," she says. "Your elders will question your absence if you are here too long. I gather from your clothes that you were not near sleep when you crossed?"

I shake my head.

She turns, taking my hand and leading me through the paths, past city-dwellers who greet us and stare at my strange outfit.

I make a mental note to clean myself up before going home. My shirt is a mess and I have dirt smudges on my arms. I have no idea what the rest of me looks like.

"Pasea," I say, wondering how a woman over sixty can move so fast. "The treatment center—the girls there..."

She cuts me off. "We cannot speak of this now, Mika. We must have you return quickly. I do not know how the Dark works when a bahari slips through in times of stress, or when fleeing a perceived threat." Then she mumbles, almost to herself, "Besides, Atesu needs to know."

Atesu needs to know *what*? I want to ask, but I know I won't get any answers. Plus, she's right. I have no idea where I was when I slipped through, but wherever I was, my body is still there. If anyone finds me, it will look like I passed out in the middle of nowhere. I could get yanked back before I can cross over on my own.

Rather than taking me to her hut, Pasea takes me away from the city and straight to Atesu's hut. "Hut" is hardly the term I would use for the marbled floors and ornately gilded walls of Atesu's three-level abode, but it's the Zanum word for "home."

At the entrance, Pasea strikes a chime with a brass rod to signal our arrival, then walks straight in. Atesu is outside in the back courtyard. As we get closer, I see that she is rubbing her thumb against her fingers over a potted plant, sprinkling something into the dirt. Small beads of water form at the tips of her fingers and fall into the plant's dry soil.

"It has been a dry season," she says.

"Atesu," Pasea says, bowing her head. "Mika'Arini has slipped through a crack." I can hear the barely-concealed urgency in her voice as she adds, "and she has crossed the Dark with *live* matter."

"It's only a tree branch," I say, examining the splintered wood.

Atesu studies me and I want to squirm under her penetrating gaze. After a moment, she motions for us to follow her.

She moves quickly out of her home and through the stone pathways of Zanum, to the main temple in the center of the city. We get more than a few stares on our way there, but no one questions Atesu. They bow their heads as she passes.

We pass through the majestic arched gates of the inner mound, around which all of Zanum is built, and arrive at the Sun Temple in the heart of the city.

Atesu strikes the bell overhead and heads toward the stairs.

I've never been in the big temple before, let alone on one of the floors reserved for Council members and high priestesses. The arc of the temple rises up several stories high, and the structure tunnels into the ground as deep as it is tall.

Pasea once told me all temples represent rebirth. "Under the ground is conception—life lying in wait in the Wise Dark; on the ground is life in the sun, sensual pleasure, and physical reality;

and above the ground is transcendence, moving up among the stars through evolution."

There is no handrail, so I run my palm along the cool stone blocks that fit perfectly against one another to form the curving wall of the staircase. There are images etched into the wall—a story, or history of sorts, spiraling up the levels of the temple.

When we arrive on the third floor, Atesu reaches for my hand. "Vinta has summoned the other Blesseds," she says, leading the way to the High Council chamber. "You will join us."

"But I'm in the woods back home, and I—"

"Silence," she says. "Whatever you experience here, no matter how long, will be mere seconds upon your return."

I want to ask how she knows this. Nothing I've ever seen Atesu do has indicated that she can manipulate time. But again, it's one of the mysteries I've learned are a part of Zanum life.

As usual, I have a mouthful of questions, but Pasea's grip on my arm serves as warning for me to keep silent and respectful. She lets go of me long enough to fish a hammered copper cobra out of one of her pockets and slides it up my arm until it's encircling my left bicep. "Wear this," she says.

Every initiate into the Mysteries wears a talisman. Depending on the degree they've been initiated into, the talisman is either silver, brass, gold, or encrusted with precious and semi-precious gems. Though I haven't been initiated into the Mysteries of the high priestesses, I'm accepted at Council meetings because I already have knowledge of another great Mystery—the future.

The cobra talisman slides up my arm, cool and smooth. The cobra is my avatar because it was the first animal spirit to beckon me to the Dark, and to Zanum.

When we arrive at the High Council chamber, the Three Blesseds, the three people who "sacrificed" themselves at the ceremony by the sacred tree, are sitting in a small circle, in large, high-backed wooden chairs. Atesu sits in the spot reserved for her at the top of the circle and Pasea and I settle into the empty seats left open for us.

I wait. No one tells me anything until they feel like it—or, as Dhan says, "Until the time is appropriate"—no matter how much I plead.

Pasea has told me I'm not the first bahari to have entered Zanum's time, and the presence of people from other points along the timeline has been mentioned at some of the Council meetings I've been to. While everyone seems to know of our existence, no two baharis simultaneously visit a point other than their own on the Winding Steps.

I've been coming here for most of my life. And still, no matter how connected I am to Zanum, I will always be a bahari – a permanent visitor.

Atesu begins by invoking blessings from That Which Is Unknowable and then blessing the space we're in. Her wavy white hair frames her head like the hood of a serpent as she holds her arms out, then up, while uttering a string of sacred words.

"Atesu," Vinta begins, once Atesu lowers her arms, "the bahari has been spotted." He looks at me. "She was at the Council appointment ceremony."

Atesu glances at him before zeroing in on Pasea. "You were to instruct the bahari *not* to attend the ceremony."

Pasea's face is ashen and she looks the way I feel. "I did," she whispers.

Atesu's eyes flash. "Then why was she there?"

I flinch from the force of her words.

"My apologies," Pasea stammers. "I was rushing—"

"Nothing to be done now," Atesu says, cutting her off and turning to me. "Bahari Mika, we have stressed this before and I shall stress it again now—you must do as you are told while in Zanum. *Do you understand*? What you have done may result in dire consequences for my people."

"It already has," Vinta says.

Atesu turns to him. "Speak."

"It seemed there is someone on the bahari's trail. They have been for some time. They may have followed Mika'Arini to the Council appointment ceremony."

Atesu frowns and, for the first time since I've been visiting Zanum, she looks worried. "A bahari present at a sacred ceremony that has been carefully shielded, and is forbidden to all but the most powerful among us, leaves all Zanumites vulnerable. It is the equivalent of leaving a gate wide open to intruders."

Ghera, one of the other Three Blesseds, says grimly, "Then we don't know how much of the ceremony was witnessed by those who seek to destroy us."

Atesu nods. "So it has begun," she says under her breath.

Something horrible has begun because of something I did. "*What* has begun? All of this involves me—can someone *please* tell me what's going on? If I've done something terrible, maybe I can change it!"

Maitreyi, the third of the Three Beloveds, runs a hand through her graying hair and sighs. "This cannot be changed, child. You may only move forward from your first point of entry into another time. Now, your—*our*—only way out of this is to move forward from it." She turns to Atesu. "She has every right to know what her destiny involves, Atesu."

Atesu looks at me and I shrink under the fire of her gaze. "My child," she says, her voice taut. "I'm afraid there is someone from the future—a future even beyond yours—who is bent on the destruction of Zanum and all of our descendants. It seems he means to use you to achieve his goal."

I stare at her. "But why? How could I possibly help destroy anyone?"

"That," Atesu says with a sigh, "is not to be spoken of. To speak it gives it power."

"Mika, you must learn to master your gift," Pasea says, her voice ringing with urgency. "Otherwise, everything we are doing, all our efforts and struggle, shall be in vain. Our descendants will..."

"Enough," Atesu says.

Pasea stops speaking and casts her eyes down. "Forgive me." She looks up at Atesu again. "I vow to do everything in my power to make amends for my error, Atesu. I shall prepare Mika to the best of my ability."

"Mika'Arini," Ghera says, leaning forward. "It has been prophesied that the invasion from the Upper Kingdoms signifies the beginning of the end of our way of life. The invasion is led by the kings of the North, with Haram and his supporters at the helm. As a bahari with the gift of traversing the Dark and navigating the Winding Steps of Time, you have a very important role."

I swallow hard, digesting his words.

"Remnants of our time, our people, are embedded in you," Vinta says. "This knowledge is important in your task."

The urgent tone of the Blesseds and the palpable tension in the room make my mouth go dry. Why *me*?

"You must, however, begin with reducing your visits to our world, young bahari," Atesu says.

I begin to protest, but she holds up a hand. "It is far too dangerous for you to continue visiting. You have been spotted. Now your hunter knows precisely what he is looking for, when before he did not. You are a living portal into Zanum." She looks at a point on the floor. "We are all called upon now to do what is required."

Vinta stands and walks over to me. He takes one of my hands in both of his. "Mika'Arini, you may be required to go against everything you've been taught, everything you've been told is true, but you will have to trust your instincts. When you Traveled through this time, I had a vision. There were young children crawling over the remains of their loved ones, and snatching food out of the hands of corpses…" I feel a shudder pass through him. He takes a deep breath before continuing. "Such brutal devastation. If I had to, I would be willing to kill my own brother to make sure the future I've seen never comes to pass." He searches my face. "What are you willing to sacrifice?"

I stare back at him, at a complete loss for words. What *am* I willing to sacrifice?

Atesu's mouth is a thin line as she turns to everyone in the circle. "We have little time. Zanum is the cradle of the resistance— the greatest resistance of all time—one that will play out, over and over throughout the centuries, in cycles, until we either self-destruct as a species, or evolve into the higher beings of our collective destiny.

"Our accumulated knowledge must be preserved. The Ancients foresaw this day and developed a plan. It is carved into the Sacred Tablets, to be read only by initiates—we must have faith in the wisdom of our ancestors."

"Dhan," I say, remembering his words from the other night. "He's the one who's supposed to save the Sacred Tablets."

Atesu shakes her head. "No," she says. "Dhan is to be sent to the field with the rest of our young men."

The discussion fades away.

Dhan is to be sent to the field.

Why didn't he tell me?

The thought of not seeing Dhan again blots out everything else. Not lying by the river in his arms. Not listening to his heart beating against my ear.

I want everything to stop so I can catch up. The possibility of leaving Zanum—and Dhan—forever never, *ever* entered my mind.

"The other Council members will be here soon to prepare for the Birth of Life festival," Atesu says. "Stay for that before returning, Mika'Arini."

"Dhanmat will meet you outside," Pasea says, turning me toward the arched exit. "I will see you before your return home."

Dhan isn't there when I come out. I sit on the backs of my heels and wait. My heart is like a stone in my chest. How could it be possible that I might never see him again? How could it be possible that the only thing that makes sense in my life might no longer exist?

Soon, I hear a soft shuffling behind me. I stand up, reaching for Dhan. For a moment we just stand there, tangled in each other's arms. Then I bring his head down and kiss him fiercely before shoving him away.

"Why didn't you tell me you were going out on the field?" I want to crush him in a hug and smack the crap out of him at the same time.

"I just found out." He runs his fingers through his hair and stares at a point on the wall. "Things are moving too quickly."

"Atesu said you're going—"

"Into combat," he finishes. "This came upon us faster than expected, so there is much to learn."

My throat goes dry. "But you weren't supposed to be a warrior. You're supposed to tend to the freaking camels!"

"Come," he says. "The festival has already begun." He sets his jaw, takes my hand, and begins to lead me toward Center Square with long strides. "Some things are much bigger than us, Mika.

Sometimes we have no choice but to move through what comes at us."

It's an effort to keep up with him. My mind is racing, trying to make sense out of everything. But my only thought is: *No.*

"Mai'ma warned me this might be a possibility since I first saw you. I never believed it would truly happen."

I grit my teeth. "Why didn't anyone warn *me*?" I watch a large white bird with black wingtips and long thin legs take to the air, sending a raucous flapping all around it as others of its flock follow suit.

He shrugs. "Stars shift, planets realign. We are not in control. No one can know for certain what is to come."

We walk in silence for another few minutes. My skin feels like there are a million ants crawling over it. I want to run and pound the pavement—release the adrenaline shooting through my veins.

"But now, this night, let us forget what is coming and celebrate birth and life."

There's no way to forget, I want to say.

We spot Yonaweh and Miraly as we near Center Square and they come toward us. Dhan grasps Yonaweh's hand in both of his, in the Zanum greeting, and Miraly squeezes me in a hug.

"This full cycle's festival is bittersweet," Miraly whispers to me. Her eyes are shining with unshed tears.

Yonaweh's face is set in hard, grim lines, but he nods to me. "N'ronga, it is nice to see you."

I swallow the lump in my throat and can only offer a nod. I realize that, for the first time ever, I am in the same boat as many of the Zanumite girls my age—girls who have boyfriends going to the battlefield, elders they love who might be lost, a home in danger, an uncertain future.

But for now, the people of Zanum are gathering in the streets and the atmosphere is thick with a mixture of apprehension and the desire to forget, to escape for just a little while and celebrate good things, like the never-ending cycle of life-death-life.

Yonaweh and Dhan duck into a nearby hut to change into all-white tunics, while Miraly and I go into another hut to change into all-white wraps. When we emerge from the huts, the guys are waiting for us.

Yonaweh grabs a bunch of large, gold-painted syringes and hands one to me and one to Dhan. Then he squirts vivid blue liquid from the syringe all over Miraly.

She squeals and runs for cover, snatching another syringe in the process and aiming it at straight at Yonaweh.

Before I know it, Dhan has his syringe pointed at me and a surge of saffron-colored water splashes all over my wrap.

I gasp, shocked for a moment by the cold water, but quickly give chase as Dhan takes off, weaving in and out of the crowd. I lose him in the process. I'm hit by streams of electrifying color at every turn.

I run, duck, and dodge, getting caught up in the joy of the moment and forgetting the meeting with Atesu. Forgetting what is to come.

I feel giddy. Like a kid—playing and getting dirty and knowing it's okay. I run to the nearest urn filled with colored water to recharge my weapon, and scan the crowds for Dhan. But everyone is camouflaged by a mess of colors all over their skin and clothes.

I see a quick flash of a familiar shadow, but when I look more carefully, it's gone.

I'm squirted from the side by a little boy and playfully squirt him back, then duck for cover in a narrow alley.

Arms grab me and pin me against the wall.

I've always felt safe in Zanum, even during the darkest time of night, but panic surges through me. I swallow a gulp of air, ready to scream.

"It's me, Mika."

Dhan.

I let the air out in a sigh and pull his head down for a sloppy and breathless kiss.

He leans back and smiles, leaning his forehead against mine. He slides his hands under my wrap.

My grin melts into a kind of yearning I've never felt before. Molten lava streams through my limbs. I dig my fingers into his shoulders.

He kisses me deeper, pressing me back into the wall until I can't breathe.

But it's still not enough. Not close enough.

Suddenly, I thank whoever and *whatever* that I had enough foresight to make an appointment with the local clinic back home for birth control pills a few months ago. When I asked Dhan what Zanumite girls did for birth control and STIs, he'd looked at me with some confusion and said, "Herbs."

Right. I decided to stick with what I knew worked in my time.

As if reading my thoughts, he looks deep into my eyes. His breath mists my lips in shallow puffs. "Shall we go somewhere more private, Mika?"

I falter for half a second. Am I ready? I *want* to, more than ever, but is this the right time?

He registers the doubt on my face and releases me.

We break apart, leaving me feeling cold and damp.

"I'm sorry," I whisper. I press my fingers against my temples while he leans his forehead against the wall next to me.

He shakes his head. "No, don't apologize." Then he leans over to scoop a handful of green water from a nearby urn and fires it at me. He grins before taking off around the corner.

"Urgh, you—!" I take off after him again, just like when we were kids.

When all the colored water has been used up and people have washed themselves and finished feasting, the night ritual begins.

I feel bloated from over-indulging in wine and grain-cakes, roasted meat, and fruit, but I'm more content and satisfied than I've ever been.

The Council meeting from earlier today seems far away, almost like it never happened at all. I brush thoughts of it aside, not wanting to ruin the glow.

Dhan and I are sitting under a tree with Yonaweh, Miraly, and several others when Pasea approaches. "Come," she says, motioning for us to follow. "It is time for the procession."

Everyone stands obediently and follows her to the middle of Center Square. There, under the sacred tree, is a large, wooden wagon with a stone statue of Divine Mother. Each hair is exquisitely carved in perfect detail. She is bare-breasted, with a large round belly and wide hips. The wagon is covered with blossom garlands and glitter, and at her feet are offerings of food, gold coins, finely woven wraps, and other small and cherished items.

Atesu stands at the head of the procession with a torch, and the rest of the eight Council members flank the sides of the wagon with equally bright torches. A small band of musicians is assembled in front of Atesu.

She motions to a man behind her and he lifts a conch shell to his lips three times, blowing a call into the night. The trumpeting sound spirals into the very center of me. It is the signal to begin. The musicians start a slow drumbeat as the procession begins its journey through the city.

Atesu and the other Council members take up a chant that the crowd repeats in unison.

The rest of Zanum, minus the children—who are at home being watched by some of the oldest of elders—follows behind the wagon, repeating the words of their Presiding High Priestess. We are pressed together, arm in arm, or hand in hand.

I am sandwiched between Dhan and Miraly and I can feel the vibration of their bodies as the drumbeat pounds through us all. The chanting and drumbeat, the tight grip of Dhan and Miraly's hands, the sway and creak of the wagon... all coalesce into a floaty, dreamlike atmosphere. I'm not part of this world, or any world, really. My feet feel like they're not touching anything solid, like I'm moving through the Dark.

We wind our way to the banks of the river where the wagon rolls to a stop. Atesu and the High Council members gather around a ceremonial bonfire, its arms already reaching into the inky sky.

The drums beat faster, and the chanting becomes more lyrical. A song—or is it instructions? I am compelled to move my body. I dance in a trance-like state with the rest of Zanum and I lose myself. I merge with the earth, the people, the sky, the night, the stars.

The moon shines bright and full, lighting the statue of Divine Mother, watching over us. The night is still and beautiful. I wonder if Atesu has anything to do with how perfect the weather is.

I whirl and dance. I move my body like the winding river, like the serpent that represents my spirit. Out of the corner of my eye, I see Dhan watching me. The look on his face sends pulses of electricity zinging through my body. I move toward him, weaving slowly through the bodies between us, and sink into his arms. The music peters off.

I hear the rumble in his chest as he murmurs my Zanum name and, in that moment, Mika'Arini is exactly who I am. Pammi seems somewhere far away, in another distant world.

The fire is half the size it was earlier, but it's still burning bright. Almost everyone has coupled off, swaying together to a beat that is no longer audible. The couples are of varying gender mixes and, in some instances, I spot tiny circles of three or more, arms linked, everyone swaying in perfect synchronicity.

"What now?" I ask.

Dhan looks around. "Now we do what we wish. Spend all night talking, or celebrating the life force and honoring the gifts of Divine Mother."

"How exactly do we do that?" I ask, tracing his jawline with the tip of my finger.

He smiles. "Everyone does it differently. It's up to the people celebrating."

"I see."

"There is no coercion. No one does anything they don't want to."

A thought occurs to me. "You've done this many times without me."

"Yes."

I'm silent for a moment. I feel the beat of his heart through his tunic. I want to squeeze him tightly. Stamp my imprint on him somehow. Hold him close and never let go. "Who did you celebrate the life force with last year?"

Now it's his turn to be silent. "Mika, you know we do not have the same—"

"I know. I'm just asking," I say.

He sighs. "I danced with Yonaweh and Miraly and some of the others, then I was overcome with exhaustion and went home."

I can't help the relief that washes over me. I feel him shake his head above me, but he says nothing more.

We spend the rest of the night kissing under the moon and swaying together as if the music had never stopped.

When it's time to return, Dhan walks me to Pasea's hut.

"Dhan," I begin. But I let his name hang there between us, not knowing what else to say.

We gaze at each other silently for a moment. His face looks the way I feel—a dark cloud, full of thoughts and emotions needing expression. But neither of us knows how to harness all that thunder, lightning, and pelting rain into words that make sense.

"What's going to happen now?" I ask.

He doesn't answer immediately. He leans his forehead against mine like he had earlier, during another moment of uncertainty. For the first time since I've known him, he seems at a total loss.

"We battle," he says finally. "In our own ways, we battle to end a war. One that will spark many wars that will rage on, well into your time and beyond."

By the time I climb into my cot, on the second floor of Pasea's home, the sky is beginning to lighten. Dhan lies down next to me and I cling to him for as long as I can.

My breathing is ragged. I'm going to crumble apart. He kisses my face, my shoulders, my neck. I don't stop him or pull away. Right now, I couldn't care less who found me and where. The possibility of losing Dhan and Zanum a second time leaves me feeling shredded and raw.

He holds me as I try to relax enough to cross back, but I don't want to go. I want to delay it as long as possible—to hold back time so that it doesn't rush forward like a giant tidal wave and take away everything that means anything to me.

I don't want to think any more. Not about winding steps of time, battles, or wars. I plunge fully into my skin where every sensation is heightened by the night's ceremony.

Dhan's hands move down my ribcage to the dip in my waist. His fingers find the knots and fastenings in my wrap and I fumble with his.

I feel tears trickling out of the corners of my eyes and into my hairline, wriggling through the strands at my temples. Heat and fire waft against the cold pit of dread in my belly. I strain and arch to crack that hard stone, to let it bleed and open and bloom.

We swirl together in the pain, the bliss, both of us terrified and euphoric in this one moment. A moment I wish I could stop and freeze and cradle in the palm of my hand. If ever I could stop and manipulate time, this would be the moment I would harness. Before things tore apart and were flung in opposite directions.

And then I shatter and melt in an infinity of explosions.

I would drift away, a hundred thousand petals on the breeze, if Dhan's arms weren't holding me.

Soon, I feel him shudder with a force that could only be called Life.

He brushes the hair away from my face and kisses my skin, his eyes shiny and his lashes damp. He talks me softly through the breathing exercises that Pasea has been teaching me since I was a little girl.

Before long, there is a humming in my arms and legs. I can't feel where my hand ends and where his begins.

I don't want to leave.

I close my eyes and grope in the darkness for the delicate strand that connects my time with his. Me to him.

I don't want to go!

I pause as the darkness engulfs Zanum behind me, and force myself keep moving.

I have to. Zanum is not my home and not the time I was born into. I quell the rising panic inside and go back to breathing.

I sense the thin, web-like strand off to one side and reach for it. Once I have it in my grip, I hold on and begin the journey back. It feels like forever this time. Grief mingles with a strange elation.

My first time. At the festival of the Birth of Life. Nothing could be more fitting. It's exactly how I feel—like I'm awakening. Like I've crossed through a gate of no return. It's good and scary and I want to laugh and cry and dance and collapse and sing and scream.

Who do I share this with? Not my mother. Not Dr. B. I have no grandparents. And I have no close friends.

The loneliness of the journey back threatens to split me in two.

The white mist appears, far away at first, then closer until it folds me in. And then a gentle drizzle as the heat of the sun subsides, and the smell of freshly chopped grass recedes into the distance.

Chapter 6

I open my eyes. The feel of Dhan's touch lingers, still fresh on my skin. But under my fingers there is another texture.

Leather.

I sit up too quickly and a shooting pain slices through my head, temple to temple.

"Easy does it," says a voice behind me.

I turn. Behind a huge wooden desk, an old woman sits at a computer. She clicks on something with her mouse, then stands and comes to my side.

"I am Margaret Schroff," she says. "But everyone around here calls me Miss Maggie."

I stare at her. I get the same feeling of awe I get when I'm in Atesu's presence.

She looks into my eyes as if she's peeling away layers. "And you are Pammi."

I nod, but even that takes effort. I want to dissolve. I lie back down and rub the throbbing area between my temple and ear.

The old woman walks to an overstuffed armchair at the foot of the couch I'm on, reaches down and hands me my pocketbook. "You left this behind when you ran off earlier."

I clutch the pocketbook to my chest as she lowers herself into the armchair.

She laces her fingers together on her lap. "You'll be fine in a few minutes." She looks at me, weighing and measuring what she sees. "You look like you've had to say a difficult good-bye."

I feel myself beginning to unravel. My chest is tight. The feeling of Dhan's fingers on my skin dissipates, like wisps of smoke.

She never once takes her eyes off me. "I knew a girl once," she says in a soft voice.

I fight the urge to bolt—to scream and shout at whatever forces are squeezing me in their grip. But I set my jaw and turn back to the old woman. I have no idea where she found me and what she is planning to tell my mother about it.

"This girl was a very special girl. She had ideas and dreams and plans. *Grand* plans." She crinkles her eyes and looks over my shoulder, out the window. "She was what we call an Able—she was able to do things others could not. Things that made people very afraid when they found out what she was capable of."

I sit up, listening now.

"This lovely little girl claimed she could fly back and forth in time." She pauses to look into my eyes. "Can you imagine?"

I avert my gaze as blood pounds in my ears. Who is this woman? This facility, the girls... parts of it remind me of Dr. Mace. I don't move a single muscle for fear of giving away something—anything.

She smiles. "She would wake up every morning and tell everyone around her of her adventures during the night. At first, they humored her. How charming for a girl so young to have such a vivid imagination!"

She looks back out the window. "But soon, the girl began to describe actual events, as if from the perspective of someone who had lived through them. Events she had not yet been taught about in history classes and, sometimes, events that contradicted what was taught in those classes.

"As is so often true in our world, people became afraid of what they could not understand. Her parents took her to doctors who gave her medications. They left her for months at a time in treatment centers and facilities where she could be watched and monitored, hooked up to wires and screens that showed the patterns and waves of her brain. As if they could find some key to the universe."

I'm gripping the arms of the couch, every muscle tense.

Miss Maggie draws a long, steadying breath. "As a teenager, this girl spoke of using her gift, a gift that allowed her to see long-term consequences of certain seemingly small actions, to make significant changes in the lives of the people she loved—significant changes in the fate of the very world we live in."

A zinging vibration jolts through me and I leap out of my seat.

Miss Maggie snaps out of her memory and nods. "That is most likely your parents wanting to know you're all right. I called to let them know you had a brief spell—most likely dehydrated. Go ahead, answer it."

My cell phone. I take it out of my pocketbook and call my mom.

"Pammi! Are you okay?"

I take a breath and sit back on the couch. "Hi, Mom. Yes, I'm fine. I should've eaten more this morning, but I—I just wasn't that hungry."

"My god, Pammi, you gave us such a fright! Having Ms. Schroff call to say you'd passed out—"

"I'm okay, Mom," I say, cutting her off. "Just resting up and having some water. I'll be back soon."

"Are you sure? Shall Bubs and I come up to get you?"

"No! I mean, yes I'm sure. I'll see you soon."

"Okay," she says. "But call if you need to, okay?"

"I will. Bye, Mom." I slide the phone back into the zippered front compartment.

"She's a loving mother," Miss Maggie says.

"Yeah. What happened to the girl?" I whisper. Could there possibly have been someone else exactly like me?

I'd heard Pasea and Atesu talk about other bahari, but I'd always assumed these were people I'd never run across. People in other places, other times, and nothing like me. But someone in my own time, nearby even, who knows what it's like to feel alien? To have your heart ripped apart because you love someone you can never be with?

Her gaze drops to the backs of her hands. "It dulled—the ability to go where she went at night. It went in bits and pieces, until it was completely gone. Until she was only a shadow of her former self."

She leans back in her chair and looks up at the ceiling. "The doctors and her parents congratulated themselves on their success."

I nod. "I know what that's like. You're dying inside, but not allowed to show it. You have to keep smiling and pretending everything is fine."

"Yes," she says, shaking her head. "She is the reason I started this treatment center, Pammi. Girls like her, Ables with extraordinary gifts and talents, exist all around us. Most lose their gift or suppress it through effort, or their gift is taken from them.

"But some of us," she says, "hang on more tightly to what we *know*. Even in the face of some of the most brutal consequences. That's what all of the residents here have in common. They have all hung on and nurtured what they have been taught is impossible."

I reach for the pitcher of iced lemon water and pour myself a glass. The pitcher clinks against the glass as I struggle to steady my hands.

Somewhere in the back of my mind, I'm still wondering if this is a trick—if she's trying to get me to admit to something, to give myself away so she can say, "Ah-ha! Off you go to Dr. Mace!"

"But why am I here?" I ask. "It's clearly not to be a peer support counselor. I've gathered that much."

She laughs, but her eyes darken with intensity. "Time travelers are like living portals when they visit other times. You were at an event you weren't supposed to attend, Pammi. And by doing that, you allowed Mantel access to a shielded event. You've disrupted everything."

I stare at her. "Who's Mantel? And how could you possibly know all that?"

"Some of the girls in this center get glimpses of events from other times. Especially if those events affect this center and its residents. We call them Seers, these girls. They are not always accurate..."

"Wait—" I shake my head. "There are girls at this center who know what I can do?" I pause. I'm about to add, "Not that I can do anything," but realize it's too late. This old woman can see right through me.

"Vaguely. Most of the knowledge about what you do comes from me, but don't worry. I understand how important it is to safeguard that information."

I take a moment to digest that. Someone who knows my secret, but won't tell anyone?

"This center is relatively new. I wanted to set it up many years ago, but only managed to gather the resources I needed within the last decade or so. The center has only been open for a few years and girls graduate when they are eighteen. But most of them have stayed on to work as counselors or staff." She pauses for a moment. "Pammi, it is a matter of urgency that you understand something. There are elements, in the distant future, working very hard to find ways to eliminate Zanum. All Ables can trace their ancestry back to Zanum in some way. And *you*—you can be the enemy's greatest hope or its most powerful rival."

That gets my attention. "How? How can I be anyone's rival when I haven't even met them? And how could I be someone's greatest hope in destroying people like *me*?"

She leans forward. "I have been watching you since your first visit to one of my hospitals. You are powerful. Mantel's people—doctors like your Dr. Mace—worked diligently to erase your knowledge of self." Her eyes flash. "But you resisted, my dear, and have come out virtually unscathed. This is what frightens them and what they want to harness for themselves. They have been trying to reproduce your ability, your *gift*, for many years with the most advanced technology. They've hired the most highly trained inventors and engineers, spent billions of dollars in research. They want what you have, but they want it in its most potent form—*you*.

"When I received the report that a call had been made to your former doctor, a renewed hope surged through me, Pammi. I had every one of my watchers on alert. Mantel's people thought you were simply another low-level Able they'd managed to neutralize, but you came back, stronger than ever."

Watchers? Watching *me*? *Received the report*? *Low-level Able*? This is all a bit much. "Who is Mantel?" I ask again, my voice slightly louder.

She sits up, stiffening her spine. "He is Haram's future incarnation. His pride was wounded at the Blesseds ceremony and now he wants to destroy Zanum and control the power of all Ables. He's been trying to neutralize people like you and the girls at this center for hundreds of years—people who might not cooperate with his plans."

She spreads her arms and looks around. "My first order of business when I set up this center was to develop the girls' powers enough to hold up a shield." She raises her chin in pride. "The girls are doing a stellar job, but I did call in some of the men from our sibling center—the boys' residence—to help reinforce our efforts. So far, it has been strong and impenetrable."

She drops her arms and turns to me. "Mantel wants you because you keep thwarting his plans. Your connection to Zanum is strong, as if you are a living extension of the city here, in this time." She smiles in wonder. "Amazing, really. As if Zanum hurled a chunk of itself thousands of years into the future to ensure its survival."

"It feels like home to me," I whisper. "I would do anything to keep from losing it."

She nods. "Yes. I imagine you would. Mantel has been trying to find you for that very reason."

My head is spinning. I stand up so suddenly that the contents of my pocketbook spill onto the floor. I need to get out of here. None of this makes any sense. If I were in Zanum, I might believe some of this talk of Ables and an evil, destructive guy from the future. But this is *here and now*. And there's no one else in the world like me, right? I'm a freak and I have to hide my freakishness—that's how it's always been. Only in Zanum can I truly be myself. That's the truth... isn't it? I sink to my knees, blindly shoving everything back into my pocketbook, wondering, more than ever, if this is a trick.

"No," I say, shaking my head. "I'm not like the girl in your story...I'm not an Able. I can't—"

She holds up a hand. "I have a lot of resources, my dear. You'd be surprised what people will do if you give them enough money." She pauses for a moment to let that sink in before continuing. "I know you have a psychological history. At the age of seven, you were taken to a hospital because you were having recurring nightmares and hallucinations."

The room begins to tilt a little. I take another long sip of the water.

"I have many people who work for me in psychological treatment facilities and hospitals throughout the country. They don't all know what it is I do, or why, but they are paid very well to notify me when a girl is brought in for evaluation exhibiting certain symptoms or behaviors flagged by me.

"All of the girls here were brought to me from traditional facilities and hospitals."

She stands up, takes the two steps between her chair and the couch I'm on, and kneels next to me. She cups my face in her firm, cool hands. "Like the other girls here, you have a gift, Pammi. I have been waiting for you, but needed to make certain you had fully regained your ability before inducting you into our program." She searches my face. "And now I am certain. Your vitals were excellent, but your consciousness was elsewhere when we found your body." She pauses for a moment as if collecting the right words. "You, Pammi, could give us a fighting chance against Mantel."

She stands, walks to the door and places a gnarled, veiny hand on the brass handle. "Go now," she says, turning to face me. "Celia will help you clean up before you head home. Rest tonight. Tomorrow, you begin training."

Chapter 7

I have no idea how wrecked I look, but Celia asks no questions. She hands me a washcloth and a bag with a clean shirt in it. "This should fit you," she says, leading me to a large bathroom.

I wash the sand and dirt off my face, finger-comb my hair, and pull the shirt out. It's just a shade darker than the one I'm wearing. I change into it and take a damp paper towel to my shoes. I wipe off as much of the dirt and scuff marks as I can.

"Much better!" Celia remarks when I come out. "Here's a sandwich," she says, handing me a paper bag. "You need to eat something. Here's a sandwich for the ride home."

"I feel a bit better." Not entirely true, but at least not looking like a total wreck will help keep my mom off my back. And I am hungry.

Celia walks me out to the car, rattling off the hours and days I'm expected to work. Monday to Friday, nine-thirty to four-thirty. She mentions something about a weekly stipend, and then opens the car door for me.

"You're okay to drive?"

"I'm okay." Another lie. I am miles from okay. I pat the paper bag. "Thank you for the sandwich."

She nods. "You're welcome. I've set some time aside for you on Monday before you're scheduled to start. It's important for you and the girls to have another chance to connect and establish trust. I'll have someone pick you up if you'd like. Let me know by Monday, okay?"

I nod. "Mom said I could use the car if I got this job."

She smiles. "Excellent! We'll see you on Monday, then."

I put the car in reverse and back out of the driveway. I call my mom to let her know I'm on my way and drive slower than the speed limit as I eat the sandwich in about three bites.

I need to think. For the second time in one day, I want to stop time from moving forward—to shout, "HOLD everything, folks," until I can make sense out of it all.

I spot a parking area where a section of the bike trail starts, and pull over. I've been along this part of the trail before on my board. It runs along the river by my house and all the way up to Maine. I had no idea it ran past Miss Maggie's mansion. Was that because of the shielding she was referring to? Was that why I've driven past here a thousand times before and never noticed the center?

I sit for several long moments in the car. My insides feel heavy and full, like every emotion, *ever*, is in there waiting to come tearing out. I look around. There are no other cars. I take a deep breath and let out a scream. It's weird screaming in the car alone. I feel self-conscious. But the scream doesn't want to stop. Soon, I don't even notice that I'm sitting in a parking lot alone, screaming at no one, in my car.

I pound on the steering wheel like a maniac, yelling at Pasea, Atesu, Dhan, my mom, god, whoever. I know it doesn't change anything, but it helps me feel just a little bit better.

After I'm done, I slump in the seat, tired out. A few minutes of ringing silence later, I pull my skateboard out of the trunk, slip off my heels, slide my phone into the small pocket in my pants, and grab my iPod. I turn to a heavy, tribal fusion song and take off.

I know I must look strange as I sail along the path. This brown girl in bare feet, too old to be on a skateboard, with burgundy streaks growing out of her long-ass hair, and wearing an interview outfit.

But I feel better. Emptied. I'm sailing through the wind with no one around me but the trees. For this one moment, I am in control. I snake the board along the path, keeping time with the music.

Images of Pasea, Dhan, and Atesu run through my mind, followed closely by the unbearable thought of never being able to see them again. I can't even venture into the part of my brain that knows why, and what's supposed to happen to them in their future—my past.

My past.

What *is* my past, exactly? I remember so little of it. England. My mom with her arms stretched out in the swimming pool. Rain. I remember lots and lots of rain. Green moss crawling up trees, the gray of the sky and buildings and roads.

I see a small opening in the trees up ahead and turn into it. I jump off my board and walk, taking care not to step on anything sharp, down a narrow footpath leading into the woods. I love being barefoot. If it weren't for all the bottle caps and broken glass, I'd do it more often at home. I stop at a clearing by a stream. In the periphery of my vision, a deer bounds away.

My past. England. Biodad. Mom and I "escaping" to America. The all-girls' school. Mom working nights. Zanum.

Dr. Mace.

My pulse goes into overdrive. Some of our sessions were a complete blank. I would forget about them as soon as I walked out of his office. But others I remembered in stark relief.

In one, I'd just turned ten. "I don't remember anything we do here."

He smiled that non-smile, his vacant eyes sparking for just a moment as he reached for the file with my name on it. "Here," he said, sliding it across the table between us.

I flipped through his notes, surprised to see detailed accounts where I told him everything. Every single moment I spent in Zanum, every discussion, a description of everyone I'd ever met there.

All the blood had drained from my face as I closed the file and put it back on the table with trembling fingers. "I—I don't remember ever telling you any of this."

A pitying look. His voice dripping with fake compassion. "It's one of the ways our mind protects us, Parminder. It blocks out painful memories." Then he'd looked over his shoulder, as if for approval from someone I couldn't see.

I sit down on a log and focus on the sounds around me, but keep getting pulled back into the scenes running through my brain.

When Zanum came back it was the beginning of a complete and utter separation of my worlds. The biggest secret I've ever kept.

A secret that a stranger now knows.

Miss Maggie's world has collided head-on with my carefully maintained secret. She has been "following my progress" since I was *seven*.

A chill races up my spine. How do I know I can trust this rich lady who takes girls out of hospitals and puts them in her own facility?

I don't know, exactly, what Miss Maggie wants from the girls at the treatment center, and from *me*, but I know about keeping secrets.

And the girls. Could I ever work with girls like that? They seem so... I don't know, *hard*. Etienne is verging on cruel, though in a different way than the girls I went to school with. The girls at school hit on my shame spots—not having the right clothes, the right shoes, the right whatever. And that I'm not giggly and acting like a moron at the sight of every male. But Etienne... she's cruel because she has known cruel.

Gayla is the only one who seems semi-normal. She's kind of like me, only white and with glasses. She seemed a bit jittery at the meeting, but hey—so was I.

And Sharlene. From looks alone, she resembles the girly-girls in my school. Sharlene would fit right in with the popular girls, with her attitude and amount of bared skin. But she's not like those girls. *I can go just about anywhere I want to, without leaving this place.*

"How do I go home and act like everything's fine? Or like I was before Miss-Maggie-the-human-asteroid hit my planet?" I whisper into the trees. "What am I supposed to say to Dr. B. and Mom when they ask how it went?"

I turn down my music and listen to the woods. Jays fly overhead. A woodpecker in the distance somewhere. The stream meandering its way back to the ocean.

A clear, solid thought begins to form somewhere deep down, and I realize there is one thing I know for sure. Keeping Zanum a secret since I found it again has been like trying to hide my own skin.

I am going back to that center.

It's the one place I might find others like me. Others who have had to keep a giant secret stuffed up inside. Others who look at the options around them and don't see themselves fitting anywhere.

I don't know if I fully trust Miss Maggie and her stalking, spying ways, but those girls are like me... Ables. They see the whole iceberg—what's under the water *and* above it—while the rest of the world sees only the tip jutting out above the surface.

I've spent almost all of my life feeling like a freak. And with those girls at that center... well, at least I'm not the *only* freak.

I stand up, dust myself off, and walk back to the bike trail. My phone buzzes as I set my skateboard on the ground.

"Hi, Mom."

"Pammi, where on earth *are* you? Are you feeling better? Did you eat something?"

"I'm fine, Mom. I was just a little woozy. Celia at the treatment center made a sandwich for me. I stopped to skate along the bike trail for a bit and think about this new job and stuff."

"Okay, well, thank goodness you're all right."

I mumble that I'll be home soon and then fight the urge to get in the car and drive all the way to Canada. I hate that I have to act like this was a regular job interview and I'm a regular gal deciding whether or not to take a regular job.

At dinner, Mom and Dr. B. are all over me about the interview.

"Tell us all about it, Pams!" Dr. B. says.

"Well," I begin, choosing my words carefully. "I really think I'll learn some valuable skills working with those girls."

"Splendid!" he says, grinning. "I knew it would be a fantastic fit."

"Have they told you which days of the week you'll be working?" Mom asks, reaching for another paratha.

"Monday through Friday," I say. "And I get a stipend." I work hard to play the part of an excited graduate with a new job for the summer.

"Good," she says, sounding satisfied. "That should keep you busy."

Mom's face is aglow and Dr. B.'s smile could charge up a city block. Nothing out of the ordinary here, folks.

I'm relieved when Dr. B. changes the topic. "Kinder, do you remember that clinic I told you about—the new one down the street from the studio?"

Mom nods. "The women's clinic that your friend started?"

"That's the one. It was raided the other day. The National Medical Association is charging Pat with running an illegal practice."

Mom shakes her head. "That's awful! She seemed to be helping a lot of women."

"Yes, that's the problem. She was using herbs and food to help women who couldn't otherwise afford medical care." Dr. B.'s nostrils flare in anger. "Much more profit in keeping people sick, isn't it?"

"Oh, come on, Bubs," Mom says. "There you go with that conspiracy line again."

He spoons more raita onto his plate. "I grew up brown and Indian in Britain, Kinder. If I didn't believe in some sort of conspiracy, I'd be a complete fool."

Mom leans across to kiss him on the cheek. "And that you are not."

I let them carry the rest of the conversation, smiling and nodding in all the right places, until I'm done. Then I excuse myself, saying I'm tired and want to chill out before bed.

I watch a romantic comedy online, check people's updates on PictureMe.com, then brush my teeth and say goodnight to Mom and Dr. B. "I'm beat. I'll probably be comatose tonight."

Mom gives me a look, but squeezes me in a hug. "Sweet dreams, darling."

Dr. B. gives me peck on the cheek. "Good work today, Pams. We're really proud of you."

When I'm finally in bed, I slow my breathing to a steady, consistent rhythm. Calming my mind is almost impossible and it's much harder to concentrate knowing that someone is out there following me now. I cast about in the darkness for some indication of this other person and sense nothing. This relaxes me somewhat. Whether it's a false sense of security or not, it helps me move into the Dark.

Soon, the silky, shimmering strand comes into focus through the darkness. I feel the familiar calm as I move through the veils of time. I hear the sounds of Zanum in the distance, coming closer, until I'm in the cot in my room inside Pasea's hut.

"Mika, you've been asked to reduce your visits here!"

I sit up, throwing my legs over the side of the cot. "I know," I say. "But I didn't feel anyone else in the Dark with me."

"You will not feel him," she says, her eyes sparking. "They know how to shield their presence!"

Icy talons creep along my insides. What if he was there? What if I've led him straight here—again?

"I'm sorry," I whisper, closing my eyes. "I keep screwing up."

She stares at me for a moment before her eyes soften at the edges. "Come," she says, grabbing my wrap and draping it around my waist. "Since you are already here, you can help. Villages to the north of us have been conquered. The invaders, guided by Haram and the others, move ever closer."

My heart does a free-fall into my stomach and I allow her steady gait to carry me along. "Where are we going?" I ask, after a few minutes.

"We are helping to fortify the wall around the city. We must move quickly."

"But aren't there other things we should be doing?" My voice comes out raspy.

"Do not question the wisdom of an elder, Mika'Arini," Pasea tosses back, not breaking her stride.

"I'm not questioning, just wondering. Wouldn't I be more useful in other ways? Especially now that there's more important—"

Pasea stops short and turns. "I said do *not* question the wisdom of an elder," she says again. "Don't you think you've done enough with your disobedience?"

She couldn't have stunned me more if she'd slapped me across the face. Pasea has always been warm and gentle, never harsh. But I see the tension in her stooped shoulders as she hurries ahead of me. And I look around at the faces we pass. Every one of them is the same. Etched with fierce determination, but tinged with worry.

This is big. Bigger than anything I've ever known.

I stumble behind as she continues to lead me to the edge of the city. The warmth of her hand, holding firmly onto mine, is comforting.

Once we reach the outskirts of the city, I see that Zanumites of every age are helping to move large, smooth stones onto rolling boards and pushing and pulling the boards to the wall. A system is set up with a pulley and levers to hoist the stones up, creating a high wall barricading invaders out.

Or Zanumites in. In the distance, before the endless rolling dunes begin, I see one of the serpent guardians—the black cobra—up and hooded, watching everything.

The hairs on the back of my neck rise and I'm suddenly very afraid for all these people. And even though things are getting done, I wonder if cranes and bulldozers might be faster than the energy work used by elders and high priestesses to move things through space without touching them. But everyone is toiling together like a single machine. Women and men smooth stones and carry water; groups of men and women wheel large, perfectly-formed stones to the wall; the elderly and very young are closer to the center of the city, preparing food and tending to infants.

I see woven baskets full of offerings—grains, fruit, wine, dyed cloth, jewelry. These will be sent down the river at night to honor the ancestors and Divine Mother, and to ask for their protection and guidance. A tree has been chopped down from near the river and stripped of its branches. It's decorated with bright adornments and strings of berries, like a Christmas tree. Another appeal to powerful, unseen forces.

A shriek pierces the air. Pasea grabs my hand, half-dragging me into a large, dome-shaped building.

There are gold accents and fish shapes etched into the deepest shade of blue on the walls. The door is thick and made of stone, but moves easily when Pasea pushes against it.

A woman's moans fill the halls, one running into the next, and we follow the sound into one of the center chambers. Several women are there, scurrying around getting things, cleaning things, hurrying.

The woman who screamed is leaning forward and rocking from side to side with her arms around the shoulders of another woman. Still another woman is behind her, massaging her back, and a young girl of about thirteen stands by a large tub of steaming water, holding a pitcher.

"It is Armenra's time," Pasea says, as she goes to stand next to the woman massaging the screaming woman's back.

The woman says something in a voice too low for me to hear above the moans.

Pasea grabs a rag and wipes Armenra's forehead, murmuring something in her ear.

Another scream. The women quickly move the screaming woman to a sort of squatting stool where her knees rest against two padded planks and the area beneath her bottom is open. Someone is on each side, holding her up, while another woman squats in front of her, alternately offering encouragement and shouting commands.

The intensity of the moment presses against all my anxiety—about the future of the city, about the hunter following me through the Dark, about Dhan. My insides are at a complete standstill.

More screams, deep and primal, until I see what looks like the wet black head of a baby.

I grip Pasea's hand. We watch, transfixed, as the screams usher in this new life.

Armenra's final scream is the loudest and longest and deepest, by far. A baby spills out of her body, into the hands of the waiting midwife.

"Bring in the father," the midwife commands, and the youngest of the women runs out.

A few minutes later, a slight, dark-skinned man with a shaved head hurries in. He's carrying a potted plant in one hand and a small pitcher of water in the other. He carefully places the potted plant at the new mother's feet, touching them with trembling fingers, and whispering softly. A prayer, or blessing, maybe. Then he stands and places the pitcher of water on a table near his wife's head.

He dips his fingers into the pitcher and sprinkles water on her belly. "In this moment, you are Divine Mother incarnate. May your blessings shower upon us, this great city, and the new life you have allowed through the greatest of Gates, and preside over us in wisdom, longevity, good health and prosperity."

One of the women hands him a spoon with some sort of golden concoction in it. The father takes this spoon, bends over the baby and chants something.

"Now," Pasea whispers into my ear, "after offering the honey and butter oil to the child, the father will whisper the baby's secret name into her ear. This is a name he and Armenra have chosen beforehand, but it is revealed to the child only at her first initiation."

"No one else knows what it is until then?" I ask.

She shakes her head. "It is kept secret to protect the child from malevolent spirits."

Then the father cuts the cord and the baby is bathed and massaged by the midwife. After handing the child back to Armenra, the midwife ties a talisman around the baby's neck and the father takes the umbilical cord outside.

"To bury it," Pasea says. "It is a death of sorts."

All at once, the stillness inside me gives way and I have to sit down. Life, death, and rebirth are all around me. This new life seems so vulnerable and fragile in the midst of preparations for battle outside.

Chapter 8

When Armenra is asleep with her new baby at her breast, Pasea and I go back out to help with the wall. But the world seems changed to me. Seeing the birth of that baby has filled me with a new mix of wonder, urgency, and hope.

Arms encircle my waist as soon as we emerge. "Mika."

"Dhan!" I turn in his embrace so that I'm facing him and snake my arms around his neck. "You're here!"

He smiles. "Briefly. Soon, we ride to join the others."

He smells like straw and sweat and a little wine. I hold on to him as tight as I can.

He glances around until he spots Pasea, busy at a task. "Let's go to the river," he says, taking my hand.

We head away from the bustle of activity and slip out toward the sound of flowing water. Dhan keeps his eyes on the path in front of us, not speaking for a while.

"Things are not good," he says when we're far enough away. "The invading army has far more men than we first imagined, and they carry advanced weaponry."

"When—when do you have to go?" I try to keep my voice even.

"Tomorrow."

I stumble over a fallen branch as the terrain becomes greener and the river comes into view.

Tomorrow. The wonder and joy I felt just moments ago drains away.

We find a smooth, dry boulder by the edge of the water and climb onto it. We sit next to one another for a long few minutes, staring out at the water.

Water that has been flowing since the beginning of time.

How many battles has this river witnessed? How many lovers have splashed through those waves?

I turn to look at his profile. There are deep lines of worry etched into his face. I move so that I'm in front of him on the flat surface of the rock. I take his face in my hands and kiss him, trying to convey everything I'm feeling through that one small bit of contact.

When I pull away, he caresses my cheek with the back of one finger. "Are you well, Mika?"

I nod, not trusting myself to speak.

He buries a hand in my hair and leans his forehead against mine. "I don't know how long I will be gone, but I cannot imagine not seeing you again."

His words tear at me. I pull out of his embrace and sit up, hugging the fabric of my wrap around me, as if it can protect me.

I look away into the distance. The river flows past like always, oblivious to the pending invasion, to Dhan's *tomorrow*, to an unknown, faceless follower in the Dark. I climb down from the rock and walk to the edge of the water. I dip my hand in and watch the water part around my fingers to continue on its way, heading swiftly and surely toward its predetermined destination. For a moment, I'm transported back to the night after a sports match, when Yonaweh decided to get *real* honest with me.

I was watching from the side of the field where spectators gathered. Yonaweh and Dhan were playing on opposite teams. Each team had a distinct headdress. The players used what looked like hockey sticks that had little nets at the bottom. At one point, Dhan managed to finagle the ball out of Yonaweh's net and ran with it to the other end, missing the goal marker by mere inches. Yonaweh's team ended up winning.

The players from both teams threw playful jabs at Dhan for missing the final goal, and he gave back as good as he got by picking up on their fumbles. Some of the players' girlfriends brought food and pitchers of wine, so everyone decided to go to the river to celebrate afterward.

I really wanted to be alone with Dhan, but knew that he would want to spend time with his friends, so I tagged along. Everyone spread out sheets and blankets, and food was passed around.

Dhan relaxed and enjoyed the banter with his friends. I followed much of the conversation, but at one point I zoned out. They were using too much slang and speaking too fast for me to keep up. I got up and walked to the river.

I crouched down to watch the moon dance across the ripples. When I heard someone come up behind me, I turned, expecting to see Dhan.

"Greetings, N'ronga," Yonaweh said in his deep voice.

"Hey," I said, going back to the river-moon exchange.

He crouched down next to me. "Everyone is over there," he said, jerking his thumb toward the sounds of his friends. "Why are you here, alone?"

I breathed in and looked out over the river. "I like being by the river at night."

He looked across the water. "Dhan is enjoying himself."

I nodded, smiling. "He is."

"He would enjoy himself more if he had a mate who could join him with his friends."

I looked at him for a moment before shrugging. "I guess."

He found a stone nearby and tossed it into the water. We both watched as it made tiny *ploop* and sunk beneath the ripples.

"It must be lonely for my friend," he said. "And it must be lonely for you here."

I waited a beat. "What are you trying to say, Yonaweh?"

He shrugged. "You are bahari, Mika'Arini. You will never be Zanum. This is where Dhan belongs. Don't you think he deserves to be with someone he can build a life with?"

"Build a life with—?" I took a deep breath. "Why don't you let Dhan make that decision?"

He smiled. "Dhan is blinded by love. When a man is blinded by love, his friends must help him make decisions."

"Friends help their friends celebrate what they're happy about," I said through clenched teeth.

"Yes. If the friend is, indeed, happy."

"Yonaweh." The voice behind me was steely with anger and unmistakably Dhan's.

I tried to say *something*. "It's... it's—"

Dhan ignored me. "How do you dare to speak to Mika'Arini in that tone?"

"Dhanmat. Brother. You are my closest friend—"

Dhan's voice was soft, but the anger that coursed through his words sent chills through me. "Tonight you have not acted as a close friend, let alone a brother."

Yonaweh stood up taller. "Dhan, I do not want you to be unhappy. I want you to have what every Zanum brother deserves."

"Which is?"

"A good Zanumite woman who can share laughter with his friends. Someone who is *here*."

Dhan clenched and unclenched his fists. "Yonaweh, speak with care. You are not an elder. Mika'Arini is a bahari—she is respected among us. She is an initiate and she is not to be disrespected. The Council will put you to labor for many weeks if they hear what you have said to her."

The muscle at Yonaweh's jaw jumped. "No, you take care. I am not the only one who has these views. Look around. Listen to what your friends say. When the bahari is no longer in our world, then you will remember my words."

Dhan's eyes flashed. When he spoke next, it was with measured precision. He turned to address the rest of their friends, all of whom had stopped what they were doing to listen.

"Mika and I are together. We shall be together until one of *us* decides otherwise. None of our elders have any issue with this. If anyone else does, let them speak now, to my face."

Silence.

Miraly finally broke the chilled vacuum that separated the three of us from the celebration. "Mika is always welcome among us, Dhan."

"Then let this be our last exchange on the matter," Dhan said with finality.

Yonaweh muttered something under his breath and brushed past us to join Miraly and the others.

Everyone returned to what they'd been doing, but they were more subdued now.

Dhan took my hand and led me away from the gathering.

When we were a safe distance from the others, I stopped. "Dhan…"

He stopped a few feet ahead of me, but didn't turn to look back.

"Is he right?" I chewed on my bottom lip. "Maybe this… maybe *we* aren't… Maybe you should be with a—"

He took one long stride toward me and cupped my face in his hands. "I should be with *you*," he said, looking into my eyes. "No one can tell me who to love. No one can tell me you are not every bit as much a part of Zanum as I am. You may not live in my time, Mika, but a part of your soul is here, or you wouldn't have found us."

Then he pressed his lips against mine in a kiss that shattered every ounce of doubt I might have had.

I turn now, back to the same timeless river. I feel Dhan behind me, before I see him, and force myself back to the present. "Everything's changing so fast, Dhan. I feel like I'm just standing here, in the vortex of this giant storm." I cup some of the cool water in my hands and splash it on my face before turning to him. "Did you know that there's a name for people like me—in my own time? We're called Ables."

He smiles. "Yes. Finding your name is like coming home, isn't it?" He grazes a knuckle gently against my cheek. "Come," he says. "There is something I want to show you."

He leads me on what seems to be an aimless walk along the water's edge. After several minutes, we arrive at a clearing.

Colossal stone slabs have been set in a giant circle. The boulders are sanded down into crude square shapes and are all exactly the same distance from one another. They have inscriptions etched into all four sides, like huge stone tablets.

"I feel like I'm on hallowed ground," I say, running my hand over a couple of lines. "Are these the Sacred Tablets?"

"No—excerpts. But they are coded so that none but the initiated can read them. They are part of a map."

We begin to walk the outer periphery of the circle. There are flecks of what looks like gold embedded throughout every stone, and when the sun hits them, I have to turn away from the glare.

"A map leading to where?"

He shakes his head, running a hand reverently along one of the slabs as we walk by. "That I cannot reveal. Zanumites have been working on these for generations, since the moment the invasion was predicted. The hope is that these stones and others like them, scattered from point to point, remain standing throughout the ages, able to communicate with future generations—building the layers of knowledge, one upon another, until all of humankind ascends to the stars. When I was very young, I came often to sand and polish these with Mai-ma."

I stare at them, trying to make out the meaning of some of the symbols. "Why haven't you brought me here before?"

"It is for Zanumites," he says.

He walks to one of the three larger slabs placed in the center of the circle and begins to read, right to left in the Zanum way. "Overcoming our inner animal nature is humankind's greatest battle. If we do not succeed, we fail as an entire race. Great courage is required of all of humankind. In courage, we find strength we did not know we possessed."

He puts an arm around my waist and traces the intricate outline of a lion engraved between two paragraphs. "Mika..."

I look up and see that his eyes are dark, round—full of unsaid things. I reach up to stroke his cheek.

His voice is hoarse. "This may be the last time I see you."

I close my eyes. "Don't say that."

He pulls me into an embrace and kisses me hard. This kiss is not like earlier. This one cuts like ice. In it is pain and confusion and fear and uncertainty.

I absorb it all, filter it, and kiss him back with all the love and tenderness I feel for him.

Slowly, reluctantly, I untangle myself. "I will see you again."

He pulls me back into his arms, this time burying his face into my neck.

I feel myself threatening to fall apart. Pieces of me come loose and fly away, clinging to a Zanum that hasn't changed yet. To a Dhan that isn't lost to me yet. I cling and cling.

Until the wailing of an alarm jolts us both back to reality.

We race back. When we slip through the opening in the wall, everyone is rushing around, shouting.

"What's going on?" I ask, my fingers tightening around Dhan's.

"You have to leave *now*." He takes my hand and pulls me through the chaos until we reach Pasea.

She doesn't conceal the surprise—and rage—in her eyes. "Where have you two been?"

"It is entirely my fault, Mai-ma. Apologies." His voice is strong. Something has changed in Dhan and I hold tighter to his hand.

After several tense moments, the anger in Pasea's eyes flickers, then diminishes. She sighs. "I suppose you are entitled to a farewell."

Despite the confidence in his tone, I see Dhan swallow before he leans down to give me a quick kiss on the cheek, and one last, long look full of unspoken words.

And then he is gone.

I want to run after him, to hold on to him and hide him. To take him away with me. But Pasea has a vice grip on my wrist.

"Mika'Arini, this must be your final visit. Do not return. Atesu and the High Council members have ordered the portal where you enter to be sealed."

My heart freezes. "They can do that?"

She avoids my eyes. "It has never been done before, but we have never faced the threat we now do. The Council thought it best for your safety and ours to close that portal. You will no longer have access to Zanum."

"No!"

"Yes." The creases around her eyes deepen. "Your presence here could be catastrophic for both of us. Go now. Leave at once."

"Pasea!"

Pasea, who has been like a second parent to me, spins on her heel and walks away.

Part 2:

Miss Maggie & the Girls

I couldn't stay away. Night after night I went back, following the thread that had always been there, to the mist that always cooled my skin. I listened for the familiar sounds of a place I'd come to know like my own bedroom.

But there was no mist. There were no sounds. When I arrived at the end of the thread, there was a giant wall.

The first night, I banged on it, shouting to Pasea to let me in. I slammed against it with my shoulder. I walked and walked in either direction, for what felt like an eternity, to find a way— some way—of getting through.

I gave up only when I knew for certain that it was useless. Zanum had been torn from me once again. Only this time, it wasn't by Dr. Mace, as I'd feared all along. This time, it was by those I loved most.

Chapter 9

I collapse on the bed and drift again, into thoughts of Dhan's hands on my skin, his hair slipping through my fingers like water, the feel of his laughter as it rumbles through his chest when he's holding me. One part of me is thinking, "You have to accept it, Pams." But the other part—the bigger part—is thinking, "No *way*. There has to be something I can do."

I go online and search for "time travel" and a whole bunch of links to sci-fi novels and fantasy authors pop up.

"What are you looking for?"

I snap my laptop shut and wonder how the hell I didn't hear my mom come into the room.

But there's no one behind me. I look at the door. Closed. I stick my head out into the hall. Nothing but the sound of Mom's deep, rhythmic breathing.

Okay, *WTF.*

I know I heard something. I look around my room again. Nothing. Not a single thing out of place. No sign of anyone.

I shake my head and go back to my computer. Giving the door a quick glance to make sure it's closed, I open my laptop and go back online.

But my skin is crawling. I *know* I heard a voice. It was soft, but clear. As someone who's been told all her life that she's imagining things, I know when something's for real. I might've bought it when I was a kid, but now I know things happen in this world that no one can explain.

"You heard me, didn't you?"

I leap out of my chair and look wildly around my room. "Okay, who are you?"

There's a soft giggle. "I *knew* you'd be able to hear me! You know who I am."

I put my hands out in front of me to see if I can feel any shifts in the air as I walk around the room. "Where are you?"

Another giggle. "You can hear me, you can hear me! Can you see me, too? I'm everywhere! I'm in the air!"

I stop in the middle of the room. It feels different. The air here is still—that kind of dead air that sits heavy over the earth right before thunder rocks the skies. That's what it feels like in this one spot, but a bit warmer.

"You found me."

The words are like ripples of warm air against my earlobe.

"Sharlene."

"See? I *told* you you know who I am."

"Why are you here?" I ask. And then a chill runs up my spine. "Have you been here before?"

She laughs. "How do you think I know about your other name—which is really pretty, by the way." She says it again, rolling the 'r.' "*Mika'Arrriniiiii.*"

I knit my brows. "How *do* you know?"

She doesn't mask the annoyance in her voice. "For someone in a school for smart girls, you say the dumbest things."

I resist the urge to snap back. Right now I need information. "How do you know?" I repeat, praying my mom doesn't hear. The last thing I need is for her to come in here and find me talking to my bed.

An exasperated sigh. When Sharlene speaks again, she uses the same tone she used at the center—as if she's talking to a three-year-old. "When Miss Maggie told us there'd be a new Able, someone *important* joining us, I did some investigating."

"Miss Maggie said I was important?"

"Not in so many words. But that's what she meant." Then she adds, "don't get all big-headed. She says the same thing about all of us."

I sit on the edge of my bed. "So what kind of 'investigating' did you do?"

She starts moving around the room. When she speaks again, her voice is by the computer. "I watched what you searched for. I listened for names of doctors—we're all familiar with Mantel's people. When I heard your doctor's name, I knew you had to be one of us. I went to his office to see what I could find."

"But you seemed so unsure of me when I came to the center."

I feel the energy move, like a shrug, in response.

"People are flagged all the time. Not all of them turn out to be Ables."

I swallow the dryness in my throat. "What did you find out?"

Now her voice comes from near my bookcase. "Your mom called there recently. The doctor's assistant had your file out on her desk. Open for the entire world to see. There was a whole section in there about your visits to Zanum. How you started going when you were seven, until they 'made progress' and your 'hallucinations' stopped."

"It's been three years! They've kept my records, even after all this time?"

"Are you kidding?" She gets that same tone in her voice—the one that lets me know, with no uncertainty, that she thinks I'm a complete moron. "Once they get a file on you, it *never* goes away. You're in the system, baby."

Those last few words hit me like cement blocks. It's like having a stain that you can never get rid of. Like a barcode tattooed into your skin.

"Is that the only place you can go?" she asks.

I nod. "It's the only place I've ever been. I never thought of going anywhere else—didn't want to. When I was little it just pulled me to it one night, like a voice calling from around the corner. Not scary, but familiar. I trusted it immediately."

"Yeah," she says. "All of us were pretty blindsided by our abilities. But when I realized I could go anywhere and they couldn't keep me locked up, I took *off*, baby! I was almost never in my body. At first, they thought I was in a coma, and then they thought I had some form of autism. They kept trying to find a diagnosis..." She trails off, then gasps. "Someone's coming. I have to go."

"No, wait!" I want to know so much more. She knows some of what I've been through.

But I feel the shift in the air and I know she's gone.

My skin feels like a tuning fork, buzzing and vibrating. On one hand, I feel as if I've been permanently stamped as some sort of deviant. Like no matter where I go, or who I become, I can't outrun this mark of "weirdo" etched into my permanent record. But on the other hand, I've found someone who might understand me.

I think of Sharlene's words. *We're all familiar with therapists and psychiatrists.* Clearly, I'm not the only one with a permanent record.

Sharlene can be in two places at once—her body in one place, and *she* in another. When I go to Zanum, my body, or at least a version of it, comes with me. An outer shell stays here, breathing and alive. I just look like I'm asleep.

But Sharlene's body is there, too, looking like she's asleep. The only difference is that she's only wherever she goes *in spirit*. She doesn't take on a physical form.

But does she go back and forth in time?

Time traveler. I volley the words around in my head. Pasea and Atesu call it "traveling the Winding Steps of Time through the Dark." Does Sharlene travel through the Dark, or through time? What's the difference?

From what I can tell, Sharlene is unseen when she goes different places. But I *felt* her. I could hear her. She seemed surprised about that.

She knows my Zanum name from reading my record. I remember how detailed some of those accounts were when Dr. Mace showed them to me. I had revealed so much! Too much.

Sharlene must know a lot about my earlier visits, then. Does she know about Dhan? Has she been here before? Can she teach me to do what she does, travel *undetected*?

I sit down on my bed as ideas whip around in my head like birds taking flight. If I could figure out how to go different places whenever I want, I could visit Dhan whenever I feel like it. I could have a real boyfriend like every other normal girl on the planet. Or at least more real than what I have now. *But more importantly, I could go and find him on the battlefield.* The thought of him being injured out there, or worse, cuts through me.

No. I can do something. I know I can. It's my fault he's out there.

If I could travel like Sharlene, I could find out what the invaders have planned, help Atesu come up with a strategy to save Zanum, or *something*. Pasea always told me I was one of the most powerful bahari she and the elders had seen in many years. I'd always thought they said that because I overcame whatever Dr. Mace was trying to do to mess with my memories.

But now Miss Maggie, the founder of the center, tells me I am a direct link to Zanum. Why haven't Pasea or Atesu ever mentioned that to me? Was it like everything else they kept from me—for my own good? What if they were wrong?

What if I'm not attempting to alter the natural course of events? What if this *is* the natural course of events? What if I am *supposed* to change things?

I think back to when I "slipped" through to Zanum after that first visit to the center. I found my way there somehow, on my own and intuitively, when I desperately needed to. And I ended up somewhere close to the city, in the desert.

And then a realization thunders through me: *There must be another portal into Zanum.*

Mom leaves for work before I wake up on Monday morning. There's a note on the dining table, in her neat, loopy handwriting. "Good luck today! I've left my car keys on the hook for you. Love, Mom."

I have no idea what time I finally fell asleep, but when I last looked, the clock read 4:09 a.m. I'm supposed to be at the center at eleven and it is now ten o'clock. I yank a brush through my hair a couple of times and slip into a pair of jeans and a loose cotton blouse. I grab Mom's keys and head to Bean-Me-Up Cafe for an egg-and-cheese sandwich.

It's hard to eat because I'm so jumpy, but I force the sandwich down on the drive up. I can't wait to talk to Sharlene. I'm nervous because of the way I shot out of there last time, and the prospect of facing Etienne again does nothing to calm my nerves. But I might discover another portal into Zanum.

I have little conversations with myself all the way to the center as thoughts from last night crowd through my brain. How do I find this portal? And how am I supposed to stop a major, historical battle, exactly? *You'll have help.* From whom? *It doesn't matter—what's important here?* The answer to that one is simple. Dhan. Pasea. Zanum. *Dhan.*

I park the car, check myself in the rearview mirror, and walk to the huge front door.

The camera makes a whizzing sound as it follows my movements. As soon as I raise my finger to the bell, the door buzzes open. "Come on in, Parminder—er, Pammi."

"Sorry I'm late," I say, as Celia approaches.

She glances at her watch. "No worries. Come, I wanted to have a bit of time with you before we go in to see the girls."

I follow her into a small room. A large desk takes up most of the space, but the walls are lined with rows and rows of old-looking books. I scan the titles as I sit across from Celia, who settles into a wooden swivel chair behind the desk. Almost all of the book titles are in languages I can't make out.

"Given the direction your last visit took, I want to chat a bit about our mutual expectations. Would that be all right with you?" she says, looking at me over the top of her glasses.

I nod. "I might've overreacted a little." Something is making me uneasy. I don't know if it's the room, or being back at the center, but the little hairs on the back of my neck are standing on end.

She gives me a sympathetic look. "Yes, well, I'm sure you'd agree that it's important we all go into this with our eyes open, Pammi. We have a wonderful group of girls here, and Miss Maggie has picked these particular girls for you to spend time with."

I try to ignore the weird feeling and focus on Celia. "Why *these* girls?"

"Miss Maggie sees great potential in an interaction between you and these three. She picked these girls, and you, after much careful consideration."

I wonder what, if anything, Celia knows. In situations like this, where saying something could easily be incriminating, I've learned it's best to keep my mouth shut.

"I'm told your purpose here is to train with Miss Maggie and the girls, and share bits of your day, your goals, and your life experiences with them. This will give the girls an idea of what life is like outside of the center, so they are better able to acclimate once they leave. Each girl has individual therapy as well as groups and circles but, other than supervised outings, very few of these girls actually interact with peers from the outside world. This environment is the safest place for our residents. But they need someone from the outside who understands them, someone like you, Pammi, to give them a sense of what's going on out there."

"I don't know if I'm the right person to do this."

"You are the perfect person to do this. You've been through what they've been through. These are girls who've been traumatized in early years and you've lived through that as well.

"You'll notice that none of our girls have cell phones. We don't have televisions and the girls have limited access to computers and the Internet."

She pauses for a moment, like she's not sure whether she should say what she's planning to say next. "Some of the girls find their own way of connecting with the outside world, however. That's to be expected—they're curious, they're teenagers. They want to rebel." Her voice becomes softer, weighed down with sadness. "But they always come back. It's a harsh world out there. Particularly for our exceptional and brilliant young ladies."

Her eyes flash. "There are many out there who do not value the beauty of our girls' gifts. But here, they learn to strengthen themselves, and their leadership skills, until they are ready to interact with the larger world. And you are one of the steps to helping them do that."

"I am so not the right person to show anyone how to be normal," I say.

"And yet you've managed to do it! Despite all the challenges you've faced."

But I'm a freak, I want to say.

From somewhere just off to the side, I hear a whisper. *You are not a freak.*

I look around to see if someone came into the room without my noticing.

Celia frowns. "Is something wrong?"

"Um... Is there someone else here?"

She gives me a strange look. "Pammi, there are only the two of us."

I shake my head and sit back down. "I'm sorry. Never mind."

The whisper gets clearer. Closer. *RELAX.*

I stand up. "I think this might be a big mistake."

No! I'm not going to hurt you. Sit down, Pammi.

Is it in my ear or in my head? Dr. Mace's voice used to sound like this—coming from *inside* my ears, instead of outside of them.

But this voice is not Dr. Mace's.

"What's a mistake?" Celia asks.

"Erm, sitting in this chair." I grab a wooden chair from the corner and sit down on it, instead.

Celia knows some things, but not everything. We all think she was an Able once, but her ability was lost or removed or stunted somehow. She works here at the center and asks no questions. She's super loyal to Miss Maggie, and she totally loves us.

I nod as Celia continues talking.

The counselors and teachers here all know this place is different. Some know exactly what's going on, but others don't. They sign confidentiality agreements when they get hired and again when they leave. But there are rumors that everyone who works here has their memory wiped clean before they leave.

Celia's mouth has stopped moving and I realize she's asked me a question.

"I'm sorry, what was that?"

"Are you sure you're all right, Pammi?"

"I'm fine, I just—it's a lot to take in, you know?"

She nods sympathetically. "When we bring girls in from the outside, it's always a bit of a shock in the first few weeks. Then they find that our girls are not all that different." She grins and adds, "Perhaps a bit more colorful."

I fidget in my chair. "Pammi," she says, "as I mentioned before, if you have any questions, now is the time to ask."

Oh, right. Questions. How about, *Who's that talking in my head?!?!*

You'll find out soon, comes the answer.

I resist the urge to gasp in surprise. I may not be able to ask questions of this voice out loud, but whoever it is can hear my thoughts.

"I don't have any right now, thanks. But I'm sure I'll have some later."

She smiles and stands up. "Of course," she says, walking past me to the door. "Let's go say hello to the girls, shall we?"

We go back to the room I was in last time I was here. Celia pats my arm and directs me to the rug where the girls are sitting amongst piles of colorful cushions.

Something's different this time and I feel it right away. All eyes are on me as I approach.

I sit down next to Celia on a big cushion. "We're so glad to have Pammi back, aren't we, girls?"

"Glad you came back," Gayla says, smiling. Her glasses frames are an electric blue today.

Sharlene hugs her knees and picks at a frayed cushion cover. She's wearing army pants with a zillion pockets and zippers, a black, lacy shirt that looks like something out of a lingerie catalogue, and pink flip-flops. "Did you sleep well, Pammi?" she asks sweetly. "You look a bit tired." She widens her eyes in feigned innocence.

"I had a very annoying visitor last night," I say.

She cocks her head to one side. "Really."

"Really."

Celia watches our exchange.

Etienne smiles and leans back against a long, stuffed, roll cushion.

Sharlene shrugs, a smile tugging at the corners of her mouth. "That's a shame."

Celia, seemingly satisfied that no blood will be shed, heaves herself up. "Well, I'll let you girls get better acquainted. I'll be in the kitchen doing a bit of catching up on my notes. Just give a holler if anyone needs me."

I watch her walk away with some of the same trepidation I felt last time when she left me on my own in here.

Welcome to the crew.

I turn to Gayla. "Thanks."

Only when Sharlene smirks do I realize that Gayla hasn't said anything out loud.

"That was you!" I gasp.

"Yes," she whispers. "Keep your voice down. We don't know what Celia knows, so it's better to play it safe and not say anything."

"Can you do that whenever you want?" I ask, amazed that I can hear her now, loud and clear in my mind. "Can you hear my thoughts, too?"

"No and yes. I'm working on having more control over when I can do it. But I can hear your thoughts when I tune into them. Otherwise, no."

"And you can talk to people in their heads?"

"I can insert my thoughts into their heads and read theirs. I can see their memories and what they see as it's recorded in their brain."

Holy crap. "Wait—you can see through other people's eyes?"

"No. What we see is not exactly what's there. I see how people interpret what they see. So, if I'm reading a kid's brain, I read their terror of the dark, instead of just seeing a dark room."

"Wow," I breathe. "That must've been tough when you were little."

She shrugs, but I see a shadow of remembered pain cross her face. "It was hell. But it's like that for most of us, right?"

She looks at Sharlene, whose face softens as she reaches out to rub Etienne's arm.

"Gayla and I had similar experiences when we were kids," Sharlene says, turning to me. Her face is still hard, but she seems curious, like she's testing the water. "We both knew things we shouldn't have known because we could go places no one else could."

"It scared people," Etienne says.

"I went into people's heads," Gayla says. "And Shar went actual places and heard conversations that were happening right then—people making plans, cheating on partners, doing awful things behind closed doors."

I went into people's heads. I remember the feeling of uneasiness when I entered Celia's office. It was the same feeling I would get in Dr. Mace's office. And it was followed by Gayla's voice inside my head, just like Dr. Mace's.

That must've been his ability, too. "I think I had a doctor who did that."

Gayla nods. "Mantel uses people like us to control others."

"When you're a kid, you can't control your ability," Etienne says, "and people see you as a monster."

"Or nuts," Sharlene adds softly, looking at the rug. "And you get sent to places with rows of steel rooms, and you get hooked up to wires, or drugged until you don't remember your own name. And the tests—over and over again. So many tests."

Gayla stares at a point on the wall. "Yeah, the tests. To see how different things alter or heighten your ability. Deprivation, extreme temperatures, isolation."

My mouth is dry. "Did all of you go through that?" I whisper.

"All of us," Etienne says, looking at me, "except you."

I feel my back go rigid. "How do you know what I went through?"

"You're not here," she says. "You didn't get rescued from a hellhole where no one gave a crap about you. You didn't get drugs shoved down your throat when you wouldn't take them. You went to a nice, private, plush school and your mommy took good enough care of you so you didn't end up in one of the places we did. And now," she nods toward Celia without taking her eyes off me, "she says you're here to show us what it's like to be normal."

I clench my jaw. "You know nothing about me," I say, matching her tone.

"Oh, but *I* do," Sharlene says. She has a glint in her eye. "Tee's right. You've got a pretty cushy setup there, Mika."

Etienne grins, but it's a grin that doesn't show up in her eyes. "You'd be surprised by what I know, newbie."

I realize that's true. I have no idea what Etienne's gift is.

"You guys, cut it out," Gayla says. "You know you like it here. We've got a nice setup now, too."

I ignore Sharlene and Etienne. "I keep hearing about this Mantel guy. What do you know about him?"

They all look at one another.

Sharlene is the first to speak. "None of us have ever seen him."

"But we all know of him," Gayla says. "Some of the Seers get glimpses into the past and the future."

"Most of the time they're wrong," Etienne says, rolling her eyes. "And sometimes we're not even sure if what they're seeing is a vision or a bad dream. Everything at this place is hit or miss."

"They're not always wrong," Gayla snaps. "It's still fairly new. It takes years to get everything running smoothly, especially since it took years to screw everything up."

Etienne gives her a bored look. "Yeah, whatever."

Sharlene shrugs with one shoulder as if responding to a question only she has heard. "What we do know is that Mantel wants to control our abilities for his own use." She begins picking at an unraveling thread on her army pants. "Only Miss Maggie and some of her most trusted teachers know what's really going on. And even then, no two people know the same things. That way, if the shield is ever breeched, there's still some protection."

I feel like I'm being inducted into one of the Mysteries of Zanum. I wonder how Miss Maggie keeps others from knowing what she doesn't want them to know, especially others who can do what Gayla and Sharlene can.

"She can't keep everything a secret," Gayla says, as if reading my mind.

Did she read my mind?

"She tries," Gayla continues, "but some of us can access her thoughts. So what she does, instead, is teach us to respect boundaries."

"But some of the younger girls' abilities are too chaotic to control," Etienne says, popping a piece of gum into her mouth.

"She uses the older Ables, who have more control, to help out," Gayla says.

I focus on Gayla and Sharlene. "Help with what?"

"Help teach the younger ones," Sharlene explains. "And to help keep things from people who don't need to know them."

I look around. I knew there were teachers and other girls here, but I haven't seen anyone else.

"There's another building set off a bit in the woods," Gayla says. "That's where the school is. And a bit further in are the dorms. The shielding there is much stronger."

I'm about to ask if she is, in fact, reading my mind, when her face shifts into a sheepish expression.

"Sorry," she says, blushing. "I didn't mean to eavesdrop. Sometimes I forget to pull myself back out."

I feel a kind of lifting sensation. Like one of my mom's chunnis or a light scarf has been covering my head and someone slipped it off.

I stare at her.

Sharlene laughs. "You should see your face right now."

Again, I feel heat rise in my face. "It's a lot to take in."

She shrugs and starts chewing on a fingernail. And right then, I see her as she might've been as a seven-year-old. I look at Etienne and Gayla and picture them as kids, too. Surrounded by people like Dr. Mace.

Etienne's right. I, at least, had my mom. And I had Pasea and Dhan and Atesu and a whole other home, a place I could go where I was loved and safe. None of the residents at this center found that until they came here. This place saved their lives.

All at once, I feel a rush of emotion. I want to sag with the relief of having found somewhere I can fully be who I am, of having a name for people like me. A place in the present, a place I don't have to hide from my mom and Dr. B., or anyone else. I know I still have to hide what this center is all about, but there are people like *me* here!

A surge of protectiveness fills me. The same protectiveness I feel about Zanum. I would never put this center, or its residents, at risk. I decide right then and there that I want these girls as friends. Even Etienne. And I'll do whatever I have to to make that happen.

I ask Etienne the same thing she asked me that first day I walked in here. "And you? What's your thing?"

One corner of her mouth lifts into a half-smile, but again, it doesn't reach her eyes. "I bring back the dead."

My stomach twists.

Sharlene rolls her eyes. "Gawd, Tee. Do you have to be so dramatic?"

"Tee can channel people from the past," Gayla says.

"How did you figure out you could do that?" I ask. I'm a little afraid of the answer, but still want to know. I can't imagine being a kid and suddenly channeling someone through your body, never mind looking to the grownups around you to explain what the hell was going on.

Etienne's face hardens. "Watch it, newbie," she says. "Don't ask questions you don't really want to know the answers to."

I'm about to tell her, again, that she knows nothing about me. That she has no idea what I can handle. But something stops me.

Sharlene reaches out and laces her fingers through Etienne's. "Take it easy, Tee," she says gently. "She's one of us—not completely an outsider, you know?"

I watch the two of them for a moment and recognize their interaction. It's the way Dhan talks me off a ledge.

Gayla is watching me intently and I know, instinctively, that she's the one who stopped me from telling Etienne off. "Get out of my head," I say through clenched teeth.

"I'm sorry," she whispers, letting go. "But I don't want Celia hearing you guys fight. That's the last thing we need. Right, Tee? Haven't you had enough privileges revoked?"

Etienne and I both look at Celia.

I feel like an idiot for almost putting us in jeopardy. Putting *them* in jeopardy. I remind myself that I can just walk out of this place.

"Exactly," Gayla says.

I look at her and realize the scarf feeling is still on my head, right before it lifts away.

Chapter 10

Now that I can't visit Zanum, I'm having a lot of trouble falling asleep. I toss and turn every night, thinking about Dhan, wanting to be with him, desperate to know if he's okay.

Each night, I flip through my memories. Savoring them usually helps lull me to sleep. Sometimes Dhan comes to me in my dreams and I wake up not being able to tell if I'm there, or here. Then or now.

I know it's not real when he's the young Dhan, the nine-year-old boy I first met, but when he's the grown-up Dhan, I can smell the hints of cinnamon on his skin and feel his sun-warmed arms...

Like the other night. I had one of those naked-limbs-entwined dreams and woke up sweating and breathing heavy. My body was alive with a chorus of crashing currents. I stayed up for a while, trying to remember when it was, the very moment, that I knew I was in love. Trying to pinpoint the exact point of transition from childhood friend to a love that invades my every thought and emotion is like trying to nail down a wisp of smoke.

When lessons are of a "less sensitive nature," we train in the large open room with the kitchen where I first met the girls. But when we're working on something that Miss Maggie wants to keep away from others, we train in her office.

For the next few weeks, in Miss Maggie's office, I get to see what everyone's ability is. Etienne, as Gayla said, channels past lives. People kind of enter her body and take it over, like they're putting on an outfit. The first time I saw that in one of our lessons, it freaked me out.

Miss Maggie had been in the middle of explaining the different densities of the four elements to us when Etienne got this weird look on her face and said, "Someone's knocking."

Miss Maggie stood absolutely still and looked intently at Etienne. "Who is it?"

Etienne's face was taut for a split second before she relaxed. "It's Harold," she said with a little smile.

Miss Maggie relaxed as well. "Harold, I have only a few minutes, but it's lovely to see you again, dear."

Etienne became a ten-year-old boy, complete with runny nose and shy, darting glances about the room. I had to work real hard at remembering that was *Etienne*. Harold took over her body so completely that I forgot Etienne was in there. Until she came back, of course.

When it was over, Miss Maggie took a few minutes to explain it to me while Etienne recovered. "Etienne channels past lives, Pammi—something you ought to be familiar with from your visits." She held the back of one hand against Etienne's forehead for a moment before continuing. "These souls speak through her and tell us things we need to know."

"Sometimes they're polite," Etienne said looking out the window. "Like our guy, Harold." She looked smaller somehow, after her experience. Her face looked thinner, pale, and drawn.

Sharlene reached over to stroke Etienne's arm. "And sometimes they come ripping through, without any warning at all."

"That must feel like such a violation," I said. "I can't imagine having your body taken over like that."

"No, of course not," Etienne spat. "We know there's lots you couldn't imagine happening."

I bit back the words I was about throw at her and Miss Maggie jumped in to continue from where she left off before Harold interrupted us.

Gayla's ability unnerves me the most. Over the course of several lessons with Miss Maggie, I learned a lot more about what Gayla is capable of. When she's in my head, either going through stuff, or inserting her voice into my own thoughts, it's beyond scary. I can't tell if *I'm* thinking the thoughts, or if they're hers. The real discomfort comes afterward, when you know she knows things about you. Maybe even things *you* don't know and maybe don't want to know.

Gayla can pull up a file of memories your brain might've locked away under DO NOT EVER BRING TO CONSCIOUSNESS as easily as clicking on a link on a website.

"I'd like to have a family one day," Gayla said to me after one of our sessions, "but I can't do it if I don't know how to control this thing. Every time I get close to someone, I start listening in on their thoughts without realizing it. And sometimes I catch things I shouldn't, and feel betrayed by things they haven't even done—things they've only *thought* about doing."

And I thought *I* had a hard time hiding what I did. It's easy to see how someone like Gayla could be trained to become a female version of Dr. Mace.

What Sharlene does is the closest to what I do. Like she said that first day I met her, she goes anywhere she wants. She's been to almost everywhere on the planet.

"Antarctica?"

"Yep. Lots. I go there when I really want quiet. You go there and you feel like it's just you and god in all that whiteness. All that quiet."

I picked another place from the index of the atlas I was holding. "The Galapagos Islands."

She made a face. "Once. Pretty, but will not go there again. Mostly animals. Prehistoric-looking ones. Dinosaur-ish. Kinda smelly, too."

"I thought you can't sense anything when you travel. How did you smell?"

She shrugged. "Whatever. I could just tell."

Most of the sessions are as exhausting as physical workouts. But I go to each one more determined than ever to find another way into Zanum. To somehow retrace my steps on that day I slipped through.

"You seem so tired these days, Pams," Mom says at dinner after one Saturday. "Are you enjoying the work at the center?"

I finish chewing the piece of broccoli in my mouth before answering. "I am, Mom," I say truthfully. "I'm learning so much."

"Still, maybe you should take a day off and do something fun with your friends."

What friends? I want to ask. But I shrug and push some rice around on my plate. "I will. I guess I'm just excited." I look up with what I hope is a sincere expression. "I'm actually working in the field I want to go in. Not many high school grads are in this position."

"Absolutely right," Dr. B. says, nodding his head emphatically. "This could position Pammi beautifully to soar into the profession, Kinder. Stop worrying so much."

Mom allows a small smile. "You're right. But I just wish you went out and had more fun. You're too young to look so tired. Plenty of time for that when you get to be my age."

"You look stunning," Dr. B. says, leaning over to plant a big greasy kiss on her cheek.

She laughs and wipes the grease off. "Perhaps you'll one day have a show like Bubs, here," she says, giving me a wink.

"If you ever decide to go that route, Pammi, let me know. I know some sharp agents," Dr. B. says.

I nod, relieved to be out of the hot seat.

"Did you hear about the protests going on in New York City?" Dr. B. says.

"What protests?"

"You need to pay attention to the news a little more, Pams," he says, pointing a fork at me. "And not that rubbish on Wolf TV. There's a whole lot going on in the world right now and it affects all of us. People are rising up all over the globe, demanding change. Demanding equal distribution of wealth and resources. Resisting the efforts of the elite to control everything."

"What are the protests about, exactly?"

"They're in the heart of the financial center. But they're also in Los Angeles and London and Paris and Barcelona. People want change. They are tired of a small few holding the bulk of the world's wealth."

"A lot of those people are young and comfortably middle-class, Bubs," Mom said.

"That may be how they started," Dr. B. agreed. "But more and more non-middle-class and non-young folks have joined in, Kinder."

"It's dangerous," Mom says to me. "Don't you even think of getting involved in all this protesting business. I won't have you arrested. You stay focused on school and this new internship and you'll be just fine."

"Don't worry, Mom," I say. "I couldn't agree more."

~ * ~

Today, we're all sitting in our usual circle-on-the-floor formation in the kitchen room and waiting for Miss Maggie. Once a week, we meet with one of the senior teachers who are also Ables. They've all gone through Miss Maggie's personal training. These senior teachers know how to use what they do like a muscle. They can make their ability strong and powerful and fast, or light and soft and gentle at their command. It's amazing to see that kind of control, and to think that someday I might be able to have the same control over what I do.

But I quickly see what Miss Maggie has been saying all along. None of the other Ables, including the teachers, are even close to the kind of stuff me, Etienne, Gayla, and Sharlene can do. The senior teachers' abilities are noticeable enough to make regular people freak out, but they're only a fraction of what the four of us can do.

I feel Gayla reach out. *What do you know about Miss Maggie?*

I look at her and shrug.

She puts a finger to her lips and nods toward Celia.

I give her a mental rundown of what I know about Miss Maggie—the story she told me that first day I slipped through to Zanum by accident. That she would stand between us and anyone who tried to take our ability away.

Yep. We all got a version of that story.

There's a pause and I can tell she's reading someone else—either Sharlene or Etienne.

She can sort of broadcast her thoughts to a small group of select people—people like us who are sensitive enough to pick her up. For us, the broadcastees, it's like watching people talking to one another from far away. You can hear the faint, distant rhythm of conversation, but can't quite make out what they're saying.

Gayla comes through loud and clear again. *What did she tell you about the girl—the one who could time-travel?*

At first I try to recount it for her, but then I realize it's just easier to show her. *See for yourself.* I go back to the memory.

I feel her pull away.

Hmm. Nothing.

Another pause.

We've all been wondering who the girl is. The most obvious connection is that she's Miss Maggie herself.

I assumed it was. I can't help thinking that Gayla could just look into Miss Maggie's memories and read it there for herself.

I don't do that!

It's a loud, sharp thought, like getting pinged by a rubber band, but in your *brain* and multiplied, like, a thousand times. I reach up immediately to rub my temples.

"You all right?"

I look up into Celia's concerned face.

"These girls do have their quiet spells. I'll admit it unnerves me a little, too." She looks around. "What are you all doing in those sharp little minds of yours?"

I continue rubbing my temples, still feeling the sting. "I might be getting a headache."

"Do you want an ice pack? Tylenol?"

Gayla's face is contrite. *Sorry.*

I shake my head. "I'll be fine, thanks."

WTF? I form the thought nice and loud for her.

I told you I can read you when you're thinking regular! If we were in a room talking, you would've asked me out loud why I didn't just read Miss Maggie's thoughts.

We're not speaking out loud.

No, but we're all engaged in a discussion and I can't just turn off. Normally I try not to snap like that. I'm sorry. It's a tender nerve, I guess.

I reach across and touch her arm. Hearing her in my head gives me a little of what she's feeling in a way that words could never do, like her emotions are woven into every thought.

Celia comes back with an ice pack for me. "Here, put this against your temples, Pammi. It'll take the edge off a little and maybe bring down any swelling there might be in the blood vessels if you're about to get a migraine." She shakes her head. "Those are very common around here."

I want to get back to talking about Miss Maggie. I shoot a quick look at Sharlene and Etienne. Sharlene is staring at the rug, intent on picking threads from it. Etienne has her hands shoved deep into the front pockets of her hoodie and she's pulled the neckline up almost to her ears like a turtle. Her eyes are closed and her head is dropped back on the seat of the armchair behind her. Gayla has had a book in her lap, opened to the same page for the last fifteen minutes. And me, sitting here rubbing my temples talking about a headache.

I almost laugh. Celia thinks the *quiet* is giving me a headache!

She stands up and puts her hands on her hips. "What's in the works, ladies?"

And just like that, the connection disintegrates.

"Crap," Etienne says. "Is it a crime to want to be alone with your thoughts now?"

Sharlene huffs. "Nothing's in the *works*, okay?"

"We're just waiting for Miss Maggie," Gayla adds.

Celia gives each of them a long, hard look before heading back to the kitchen. Without turning around, she says, "No funny business, girls. I can smell it when you're up to something."

Right then, Miss Maggie walks into the room.

"I'll take it from here," she says, nodding to Celia. "Go on and take your break. It looks like you're about ready for one."

Celia gathers up her files. "Gladly," she says. "Later, girls!"

"What were we talking about, ladies?" Miss Maggie asks, looking pointedly at Gayla.

Gayla gives her a sheepish smile. "We were comparing notes about the story you told us. The one about the girl."

"Hmm. I thought that might come up." Miss Maggie looks at each of us thoughtfully. When she gets to me, she asks, "How are you finding it here, Pammi? I spoke with your Uncle Babaloo and he seemed pleased with everything."

"He's not my uncle. He's my mom's, um..." I hesitate before spitting it out. "Boyfriend." Even after all these years of them being together, and no matter how much I like him, I still feel weird about calling Dr. B. my mom's boyfriend. Especially since Mom really impressed upon me that I was not, under any circumstances, allowed to say that in the presence of other Indian people.

"We just call him Dr. B.," I add.

"Very well," she says. "Dr. B., then."

"It's going well," I say truthfully. "I almost feel like a resident."

"Yeah, except you get to walk out of here every night, without the stigma of a long record attached to your name." Etienne's voice is like the jagged edge of a broken bottle.

"Not that it's any of your business, but I do have a record attached to my name," I snap.

Sharlene darts a look at me, then mumbles, "As if you *want* to walk out of here every night, Tee. And besides, she's telling the truth. I've seen her record."

I want to fling my ice pack at Etienne. "What the hell's your problem?"

Gayla looks from me to Etienne. "Come on, you guys."

Miss Maggie sits quietly, watching our exchange.

"You're wrong, Shar," Etienne says. "I would love to be able to walk out of here each night and go to a nice, cozy family with my own cushy bed and friends, then put this 'experience' on my college application."

I'm coiling up like a snake, ready to strike. For some reason, Miss Maggie's presence has shifted the vibe. There's huge static in the room. And I want to throttle Etienne. I don't know how she gets this reaction out of me, but it drives me insane. She's basically challenging my right to be here. As if I asked to be here in the first place!

Miss Maggie is still watching us. So are Gayla and Sharlene. But I only notice them out of the corner of my eyes. This is between me and Etienne. We stare at one another, each of us hovering on that edge, ready to fire.

"Why don't you go, newb? You don't fit in here," she says.

"Why should *I* go?" I say, matching her tone. "I'm an Able, just like everyone else here. *You're* the only one with a problem."

"So you think," she says with a humorless smile.

I'm taken aback. I look at Sharlene, but she doesn't meet my eyes. Gayla wrings her hands and I feel her try to reach out, but that feeling gets yanked back almost immediately.

I look at Miss Maggie. "Say what's on your mind, Pammi," she says.

I draw in a deep breath. "Look," I begin, not sure how to proceed. "It's true I haven't had the kinds of experiences you all have had, but I *have* had some. I know what it's like to keep a huge part of yourself locked away and secret, hoping—praying no one finds out and discovers what a freak you are. I had sessions with doctors who tried to convince me that what I knew was *true* was just a figment of my imagination.

"Up until I learned there might be others like me, I thought I'd be living half a life 'til I died. I'm not going to give up Zanum, and I can't leave the time zone I was born in. Giving up either would be like amputating all my limbs. I'd only be half alive if I acted like either of my worlds didn't exist."

I pause and look around. They are all looking at me, but I can't read anyone's expression. I square my shoulders and look directly at Etienne. "I'm not going anywhere. I belong here just as much as you do, maybe even more."

Etienne's mouth drops open and she leans forward, ready to blast me.

I continue quickly, before she can speak. "No one dragged me here kicking and screaming. I came here not knowing exactly what this place was. And now I'm staying, knowing full well what it is and who lives here. I'm not going to let you or anyone else drive me out."

I wait for her to say something, but she sits there, tense and leaning forward.

There's nothing but silence for a long moment. Nothing but silence and the steady pounding of blood in my ears.

"I'm happy to have you here," Gayla says.

"Did you say that out loud?" I ask.

She giggles. "Yes. Everyone heard me."

Sharlene nods. "I heard her. What Pammi says makes sense, Tee."

Etienne opens her mouth to speak, then snaps it shut.

Miss Maggie's eyes crinkle almost imperceptibly. "Let's move on now, girls."

Gayla just sends me a feeling of warmth, kind of like a brain hug.

Etienne glares at each of us in turn, then slumps back against the armchair.

Chapter 11

I park my mom's car in our lot and chirp it locked. I wonder for the thirty-nine-thousandth time if Mom will ever agree to move into Dr. B.'s swanky condo so we can have someone else park our car.

When I get to the apartment, I am alone. I walk to my room and shut the door. I sit there, staring off into nowhere for what feels like a long time. I want to be back at the center. Back with Miss Maggie and other people I don't have to hide myself from. I want to keep learning how to control this thing that I can do. I want to be there every minute of every day until I figure out how to get back to Zanum.

The front door lock clicks and my mom's voice carries through the apartment. "Pammi?"

"In my room!"

"Well, come on out of there, love," Dr. B. calls. "We've brought Thai take-out!"

Mom sticks her head into my room. "Are you okay?"

"Yep. All good, Mom."

She smiles before ducking back out. "All right, then come on out and join us."

"You are in control, love," Dr. B. says later, as I pick at my dinner. "Whatever you want to do with your future is entirely up to you."

Mom nods, holding a fried piece of tofu deftly between chopsticks. "You have so many more opportunities than I had at your age."

I push the Pad Thai noodles around on my plate. This is what Ms. Zauberman, my English teacher from first year, would refer to as irony—Dr. B. telling me how much control I have over my future and my mom talking about all my options.

"Not hungry, Pams?" Dr. B. says, eyeing my plate.

"My stomach feels a bit unsettled," I say. "May I be excused, please?"

Mom gives me a concerned look. "I really do think you need a break, darling."

"I will. Soon," I mumble, getting up from the table.

That night, I go back to my memories—reliving, in as vivid detail as I can, the moments I've already spent with Dhan.

Dhan and Yonaweh had worked it out after that little scene by the river. Yonaweh even apologized to me.

"N'ronga," he'd said sheepishly. "I was out of line. I had too much wine and was not thinking clearly. You are the chosen mate of my brother-friend and I honor you."

"But everyone else..." I let the sentence dangle between us.

"That was not fair of me. Whatever others think is none of my business and should not be a concern to you or Dhan."

I didn't know if I'd ever be able to trust him completely, but he'd been Dhan's best friend since they were toddlers. Dhan loved him like a brother, so I had to make an effort. Because that was exactly what it would be—an effort.

But word about that night must have spread among Dhan's friends. Whatever thoughts anyone had about Dhan being with a bahari girl they now kept to themselves. The girlfriends made more of an effort to be nice to me, especially Miraly, and whenever we were in a group, everyone seemed to take great pains to include me in the conversation.

One afternoon, we were on a picnic with Yonaweh and Miraly. She brought a bunch of food, and Dhan and I took some of the cooled herb brew that Pasea had made the night before.

We spread a couple of sheets on the grass and the guys stripped out of their tunics, taking off and splashing into the river.

Miraly looked after them and shook her head. "Only their bodies are growing," she said. She pointed to her head. "In here, they are still ten-year-olds."

I smiled. "I don't know. It looks fun."

She laughed. "Perhaps we should join them after eating."

We watched the guys for a few minutes. "I hope there are no hippos in that water," I said, remembering what I'd heard about hippos mauling swimmers who swam too close. It was easy to do—they looked just like big rocks if you weren't paying close enough attention.

"Those two could tackle the heaviest of hippos into submission," she said with a grin.

I took a handful of grapes and popped one in my mouth. "Miraly, do you think you and Yonaweh will get married?"

"Married? Oh, you mean commit as soul partners for life—as you do in your time." She looked out at Yonaweh splashing water on Dhan and considered the question. "It's possible."

"Do you love him?"

"Absolutely," she answered. "As you love Dhan and he loves you."

"But... I don't understand having more than one person in your life," I said.

She picked up a smooth pebble and rubbed the dirt off. "Yes, Yonaweh has mentioned this. He and Dhan have spoken about it at length."

I was surprised, but I guess I shouldn't have been. Dhan should be able to confide in whoever he wanted to. And Yonaweh was his closest friend.

"Don't you feel jealous, or betrayed, when Yonaweh is with someone else?"

She had a bunch of pebbles now. She shook them in her hand as she weighed my words. "No... I have other lovers, too. But I do feel sad, or lonely, if the company I truly want is Yonaweh's and he's not available."

"Do you ever worry that he might love someone else more than you?"

"That is certainly possible," she said, sifting through the stones she'd collected. She kept the smooth, flawless ones, and tossed the others back. "But I love him. I want him to have the best life he can create. And I believe he wants the same for me."

She turned her sharp features toward me. Her skin was a honey-golden amber, and unblemished, like the stones in the basket of her slim fingers. "I trust Yonaweh will be kind to me if his feelings change—that he will not be cruel, or harsh, with someone he has been so close to. Do you trust that Dhan will treat you with kindness and respect, regardless of what happens?"

"I hope so," I said quietly. I watched Dhan swim with lithe strokes toward a floating log, and prayed the log wouldn't move and reveal itself to be something else. Something alive and angry.

I flipped Miraly's words over and over in my mind until the guys came back to the sheets and shook their hair, raining water droplets all over our hot, sun-soaked skin.

Miraly shrieked and took off after Yonaweh.

Dhan plopped down next to me and grabbed a hunk of bread, which he slathered with tomato-walnut spread and shoved into his mouth.

"Thanks for the shower, dude," I said, shoving him playfully.

"You're lucky I didn't do what I was going to do."

"And what would that be?"

"I can't tell you," he said, guzzling down some more herb brew. "I may yet decide to do it."

"Oh yeah?" I flicked a grape at him. "Well, I can come up with things to do, too."

He caught the grape and popped it into his mouth. "I have no doubt."

"Dhan," I said, choosing my words carefully. "If you found someone else you liked a lot, would you tell me?"

"Of course," he said, without hesitation.

"Would you break up with me?"

He scrunched up his face in confusion. "Break up?"

"Not want to see me any more."

He grabbed a towel, bunched it up, and put it behind his head as a pillow. "I would never break you up," he said softly. "I can't imagine life without my Mika."

In moments like these, I gave him a pass on messing up phrases. "But what if you liked this person more than you liked me?"

He laughed, then caught himself and sighed. He pulled me closer with one hand cupping the back of my head. "I would never throw away all the years we've spent together. And I pray that you would never walk away from me... but there are no guarantees. What I know now is that I want you with me, Mika, in this life and the next. In whatever form you take—friend, lover, or family, or... livestock."

"*Livestock?*" I threw another grape at him. It left a splatter mark on his forehead like a squashed green bug. I giggled and reached for another one.

He caught my wrist before I could throw the next grape and pinned me down on my back, holding my arms above my head. His hair hung wet and cold, brushing against my bare arms as he straddled my waist.

"That's not fair! You're bigger than me."

"Exactly. You must know your limitations."

My eyes bulged. "*Limitations*?"

He chuckled. "That's what I said."

I remembered a move we learned in a self-defense workshop at school and pulled my heels up toward my thighs, bending my knees as deep as they'd go. Then, in a quick and sharp move, I thrust my pelvis up while bringing my arms down.

I caught him by surprise. He wasn't expecting the move and toppled forward. He let go of my arms to stop his head from hitting the ground and I used the opportunity to shove him off me. I scooted out from underneath him and stood up triumphantly, grabbing a huge bunch of grapes.

As he pulled himself up, I started pelting him with the grapes. "Take *that*! I'll show you limitations! I know of no such thing!"

"Wait until I catch you," he said, mock warning lacing his words.

"*Never*!" I yelled and ran, turning every now and then to shoot a grape behind me.

He ducked and weaved to avoid the onslaught of fruit, but he was on me before I could get very far. He tackled me, taking care to make sure my head didn't hit the ground.

This time, he pinned me down flat and lay his whole body against mine, holding my arms above my head.

"Ha-ha! Victory is mine," he declared smugly, placing a quick, soft kiss on my lips.

"I let you win," I said, my chest heaving against his. "And I got you good! You look like a windshield splattered with bug guts."

"Windshield? Bug guts?"

"It's, um, when you drive in a car. Sometimes bugs splatter against the windshield because you're going so fast."

He rolled off me. "Yes, a self-powered chariot."

I nodded.

We lay quietly for a few minutes as he traced my eyebrows with one fingertip.

"I wish I could visit your world, Mika, even if for just one day," he said softly.

A thousand little balloons imploded in my chest. "I wish you could, too," I said. "But none of us can live in a time we weren't born into, right? It's against the Law?"

He nodded. "I don't worry about you taking other lovers... but sometimes I wonder if I'll lose you, as well, Mika. If you'll walk away and then come back to me in my dreams, the way my mother does."

All the words I could think of went up in smoke. I had never thought about it like that before.

"But I'm not a dream," I whispered. "I'm real. I'm *here*, Dhan. I'm going to keep coming back until we're both old and wrinkled." I swallowed the lump in my throat, and with it the knowledge that I was offering false promises.

But I wanted to hope. I wanted to cling to the possibility that those words could hold us. Could somehow become true if spoken aloud.

When I go to sleep, it's with the sadness in Dhan's eyes sitting like a brick in my chest.

Miss Maggie said that today I work on going to Zanum at will. I conveniently haven't disclosed the fact that I've been forbidden to return. Because, really—how am I supposed to learn to control my ability without using it? And though they've sealed off one portal, there's nothing forbidding me from "accidentally" finding another one. I am a teensy bit worried about Pasea and Atesu's wrath. But not enough to stop me from trying.

When I get to the center, the other girls haven't arrived yet. I help Miss Maggie set the cushions up and move some chairs around so that we can sit on the floor in a circle.

I feel Gayla coming before she walks in. "Knew you were here." She gives me a sheepish look. "I did a sweep of the room before I came in."

I smile. "I could tell."

Etienne swaggers in and avoids me like a disease. "Hey, Gay," she says, icing me as she passes.

I glance at Gayla, shrug, and sit down in a small rectangle of sunlight.

Sharlene glides in after Etienne, just as Miss Maggie claps her hands together and asks us all to take our seats.

"Ladies, let's get to work. While Pammi is here, we will concentrate our efforts. During your regular classes, you will continue doing the exercises assigned and honing your skills."

I see the muscle at Etienne's jaw jump.

Miss Maggie turns to me. "Pammi, let's start with getting you seated in the correct posture. Please cross your legs in front of you and look straight ahead."

I do as she asks.

She raises my chin a bit with one finger, then stands to look at my profile. "Shoulders back. Yes, like that. Now keep your head level and close your eyes. Breathe in to the count of four—"

"Someone's knocking!" Etienne's voice cuts through Miss Maggie's even, rhythmic instructions.

My eyes snap open. At first, I think this is another of Etienne's tricks to get on my nerves. But then I see Miss Maggie tense up.

"Who's there?" she says. "Announce yourself."

Etienne is sitting straight up with her eyes wide open. She begins to tremble.

Miss Maggie goes right to Etienne's side. "Who are you?" she demands. "Make your presence known at once."

Etienne's eyelids flutter. "Have I arrived?" her voice booms. "It was a very long journey."

"Identify yourself," Miss Maggie orders again.

"I am Dharam," says a voice that I know is Etienne's but does not sound the least bit like her. Whoever this is, they are clearly someone who's used to giving orders, not taking them.

Miss Maggie kneels in front of the stranger looking out from behind Etienne's eyes. Her voice is sharp. "State your business."

"I have descendants here." Dharam surveys the room. "I have been summoned to convey a message."

"Summoned by whom?" Miss Maggie asks.

"An ancestor," Dharam says dismissively.

Miss Maggie hesitates for a second, then sits back. "Speak freely," she says. Her voice is still tense.

"I am from a land before your recorded time. A land called Kumari Kandam that now sits at the bottom of the sea. It was the will of That Which Is Unknowable that our beloved home should perish in flames, a great phoenix swallowed by the waves. One hundred and forty-four of us survived—priests, priestesses, and initiates alike. We made our way to the mainland and grieved. We mourned the loss of one of the brightest civilizations ever to inhabit this earth."

His eyes rest on a small, wooden goddess figure on Miss Maggie's bookshelf. "After our grief subsided, we continued. We shared our arts, our music, and our knowledge with the people we met in our new home. We taught them the wisdom of the goddess, Words of Magic, and the poetry of alchemy. We taught them to build temples that would withstand the mightiest of storms." His voice drops a notch and I lean forward to hear him. "At some point in your history, we came to be known to some as Dervids, and to others as Dravidians. But whatever name we were known by, our wisdom and knowledge spread in all four directions."

He pauses to clear his throat and ask for water. Miss Maggie pours him a glass.

"Many centuries after my birth," he says, setting the glass down, "twenty-seven hundred of our descendants, the descendants of Kumari Kandam, were saved from a mass genocide that swept through our part of the world. The destroyers knew what they were doing. They were wiping the earth clean of the goddess. They destroyed all images of Her, erased our scriptures, our wisdom and knowledge, and in their place offered the people lies. They began this process before arriving at Zanum, and continue it until this day you sit in. They shall continue for many centuries in the future."

"Please continue," Miss Maggie says.

"Haram was my son. He has revisited this plane in many incarnations and now lives far in the future from this time, known to you by the name of Mantel."

I gasp and he zeroes in on me.

"He and Vinta did not know they were rightful descendants of Kumari Kandam. But their abilities were strong among their own people, and a direct reflection of their origins." He stops to shake his head. "I am deeply disappointed in the direction he has taken."

Then he looks around at each of us again. "In my time, the goddess lives in harmony with her consort. In the time of Zanum, she sows her seeds of resistance as her face is removed from the stories of creation, a balance so vital to a world that will soon go terribly astray. But Her seeds are nurtured and carefully guarded by those of us who support the old ways.

"Still, Haram's rage is powerful. His agony is an endless hole into which all of creation shall perish, if he is not stopped."

This time Miss Maggie's voice is a whisper. "What guidance do you have for us?"

"Haram, in his incarnation as Mantel, knows that among you is a Traveler who works to restore the old ways. You must take great care. Haram is more powerful as Mantel than he ever was in his own day. With the assistance of the Traveler, Haram wants to turn the power of the Law against Life itself."

"I would never help anyone—" I blurt.

Miss Maggie slices a hand in the air to shush me. "How?" she asks.

He scowls. "He intends to return to the day of a sacred ceremony, during which Three Blesseds were divinely chosen, and kill Vinta."

"Why doesn't he just Travel there himself?" Miss Maggie asks. I have a feeling she already knows the answer, though.

"He is not a Traveler. He must harness and use the ability of another to assist him, a sibling. Together, through horrific means, they have managed to live beyond their natural lifetimes." He looks back at me with a raging fury in his eyes. "You are our hope. May you rise tall and shelter the seeds of our goddess before they are—" He raises a hand and opens his mouth to say more, but Etienne slumps back.

"He's gone," she says, her voice thin and raspy.

Miss Maggie stares off at nothing, as if she's dazed.

Sharlene jumps up. "Tee!" She looks at Miss Maggie. "She doesn't look good!"

Miss Maggie blinks, then snaps back to attention. She scurries to grab a blanket from the couch and drapes it around Etienne. "Sharlene, please bring her some water."

Sharlene moves quickly as Gayla hovers over Etienne and Miss Maggie.

I hang back, not knowing what to do.

Etienne takes the water from Sharlene and guzzles it down. "Wow. That took a lot out of me."

Miss Maggie rubs Etienne's shoulders and back. "Yes, the more powerful they were when they were alive, the more power they demand from you when they're dead."

"What was he talking about?" Sharlene asks.

Miss Maggie stands up. "He was letting us know that we cannot afford to fail." She walks briskly to her desk and jots down a few lines before continuing. "Pammi, back into your posture. Girls, close your eyes and concentrate like your very lives depend on getting this right." She presses her lips together. "Because they very well could."

Everyone does as she says, including Etienne, who no longer has any hint of attitude.

"Pammi," Miss Maggie says, crouching down next to me, "you must use every ounce of focus you can muster and put everything you've got into this. Do you understand?"

I nod. That guy who came through Etienne was no joke and everyone in the room knows it.

"Close your eyes and breathe," she says.

Miss Maggie's hand covers mine as she matches me, breath for breath.

After a few minutes, we are breathing collectively, as if all five of us are one body.

Everything begins to drift and fall away. The world around me ceases to exist and all I can hear is the in and out breath. Everything is white—white light everywhere. And there is only the rhythmic breathing, like the sound of waves far away.

I wait for the drizzle, the soft mist, but it doesn't come. A thrill runs through me as I hear the sounds of Zanum far off in the distance, but something is in the way, and it's not the wall I've been running into. It's something I've never felt before. I try to move closer, to move through it, but I'm pulled back like there's a giant rubber band around my ankle.

I wait until I'm calm and try again. I move toward the invisible barrier with my hand out, hearing familiar Zanum voices on the other side. Everything in me wants to run toward them.

I inch closer when I feel no barrier. Hope tingles through me, waking every muscle. Just as I'm about to take step closer, I'm yanked back and plunged into darkness.

I'm falling. The breaths are gone and there is no light. I claw at the air to grasp something, *anything*, but there is nothing solid. I scream, trying to bring myself back to the center, but it is an endless drop.

The last thing I hear before the crash is Gayla.

It's okay, Pam. I'm here with you.

Chapter 12

The crash is like a giant chandelier exploding in my brain. It feels like tiny shards of glass are embedded in the soft tissues of my skull, piercing deeper into my flesh every time I move. I pry my eyes open, bringing my hand up immediately to block the harsh glare of light.

"Get away from here!"

I turn to the voice. I still can't see clearly, but I can make out the figure of a girl, about my age, crouching to my left. I try to sit up, but have to hang my head to bear the throbbing.

"Are you real?" she whispers, peering at me now.

"Water..."

She eyes me for a moment, then holds her hands out in front of her. A glass pitcher materializes in them, half-full of water. She pours the water into a cup that appears in her hand.

The water revives me a bit. As the throbbing subsides, I sense something. *Gayla?*

Oh, thank god you're okay!

I squeeze my eyes shut. *If you could call it that.*

We were all so worried! We didn't know what happened to you—where are you?

I look around. *I have no idea.*

I check out the girl. She has straight, jet-black hair and her face is like a pale, buttery moon. Her eyes are this weird see-through gray. She's wearing a kind of mesh metal outfit that restricts her movements. I'm relieved to feel the thin scarf feeling over my head as Gayla reads the image.

Pammi, I'll leave your thoughts alone, but can I share what you see and say?

I give Gayla a mental nod and try to sit up again. This time I almost manage to sit, but I'm still slumped over and weak. I wonder if this is what Etienne goes through each time she channels someone.

"Are you one of *them*?" the girl asks. Her voice is full of suspicion.

"One of who?"

She doesn't answer, but searches my face instead. Something about her looks unnervingly familiar. "You're not, are you? You're just a simple Able..."

I take in my surroundings. There are millions of points of light around us and we are suspended in space in what looks like a clear bubble. There is not a single sound—just silence pressing in from everywhere.

I struggle to breathe. "Where are we? It looks like we're just hanging in space."

She gives me a strange look. "We *are*. We're the ones they couldn't control."

"Who?"

She gives me another look. "Where are you from? And how did you make it through the Barriers?"

"I—I'm not from here. I'm not from *now*."

This seems to grab her attention. Her eyes light up. "Tell me."

"First tell me why you're here."

Her face falls. "It's him," she whispers. "I know he's watching. He must not see you because you're not from here." Her eyes dart around. "Or maybe he knows you're here. Maybe he *wants* you here!"

I follow her eyes and see nothing.

Her voice gets soft. Sad. "We were great once."

The space in the bubble begins to fill with trees, grass, translucent people walking by with smiles, a vibrant blue sky, color everywhere. Happiness and joy. Everything is so real, but when I reach out to touch, my hand moves right through the mirage.

"Somewhere along the way we got lost," she says, and everything begins to flicker, then disappear. "We began to believe the wrong people. We put our faith in this family that promised to lead us out of despair."

I see the family, a dignified and obviously wealthy one, in some sort of vacation home, then gathered in front of a stately mansion. I see news headlines announcing members of the family as winners of elections and landslide victories.

"Over the years, the family began falling apart—in-fighting, deaths, disputes. Eventually, they dwindled down to two siblings who outlived everyone." She lowers her voice. "This is not the official story, you know. This is the story they don't tell you."

As if to emphasize her point, she squeezes her eyes shut and a stream of official documents scrolls past me. And then, immediately after them, there is a stream of alternative news media articles, painting an entirely different picture—rigged elections, corruption, lies.

"We were becoming strong, teaching others to awaken latent abilities. We were building nations again like we once did, hundreds of thousands of years ago..."

I lean forward. "What happened?" I'm fully revived now, and hanging onto this strange, ethereal girl's words. Two siblings – Mantel, Haram's future incarnation, and his sister?

"They were better at killing," she says.

Grief and overwhelming sadness envelope me, pressing in from all sides and squeezing the air from my chest. Around me is rubble, screams in the distance, wailing women holding the limp bodies of children to their breasts, infants crying next to the bodies of caregivers who died sheltering them, grown men crumpled helplessly to the ground.

Her voice is empty. "We fought them as hard as we could, but they took everything. Left us with the worst plots of land and no food. 'Progress,' they said."

A news heading scrolls past: *A Million Empty Promises*. The video playing underneath is of an emaciated child drawing water from a roadside puddle. The water hovers in midair in front of him until he sips from the invisible vessel he's created for it.

"They took everything, draining the life force from every Able in sight. The ones they couldn't control, they captured and—and did horrible things to them. The most powerful ones, the ones they couldn't control *or* torture, they sent out here. But—" she stops abruptly.

"But what?" I feel her slipping away.

"We were the ones he couldn't control." Her voice takes on a dreamy quality. "He sent us out here forever so we couldn't help the ones who were dying. We were his biggest threat, but he had *her*, and she could surf. She sent us out here." She laughs, an eerie, tinny sound. "Unable to die and unable to live. Just watching the horror unfold."

"But... why?" is all I can manage.

"What?" Her face becomes wild. "Who are you?" she screams.

I stand and take a step back. "I'm friendly, remember?"

"No!" she screams again. Her face is contorted with rage and she's crouching like a cat about to spring on its prey.

I fight to contain the panic that's expanding and filling my insides. I remind myself that I'm not alone out here, that Gayla is only a thought away.

But what could she possibly do to help me?

My eyes dart around, looking for a way out—anything at all. The air seems to be getting thinner.

And then her voice goes calm again. She points to a cluster of stars to the left. "That's where you came from, right?"

I look in the direction she's pointing and see nothing different from every other direction. "I don't know."

She laughs. "You don't know? How can you surf the Dark and not know?"

"How do you know about the Dark?"

"Everyone knows about the Dark. You can only surf if you know about the Dark. He can't surf. Only she can."

For a moment, I see a spark of sanity in her strange, metal-colored eyes. *She's trying to tell me something.* But almost immediately, the suspicion comes back. "How can you know about the Dark and not know about surfing?"

I rub my temples to soothe the throbbing in my head. "I've never surfed in my life."

I look beyond the space we're in and panic floods my limbs. It's too much space. And we are the only ones in it for what looks like forever in every direction.

When I raise a finger to touch the thin barrier surrounding us, she screams. "Stop!"

But my finger connects with what feels like several thousands of volts of electric current. And then I'm sucked through the membrane of the bubble and into another one just like it that appears out of nowhere.

"They know you're here," she says flatly. "You showed them exactly where you were when you touched the skin and they pulled you through. You'll start floating away."

She's right. Already, my bubble is beginning to glide away from hers. I clutch my head, reeling from the pain that suddenly shoots through, temple to temple.

"You can think up anything you want in your own skin," she says. "Whatever you think up is what will appear. But be careful. Whatever you think up tells them something about you. Everything they learn they use against you."

A groan escapes from my lips as I try to sit up. Every bone in my body feels smashed. "How do I get out of here?"

"The same way you got in," she says. Again, there is a brief flash of intelligence in her eyes. And again I get the sense that she's trying to tell me something. But I'm in too much pain to try to figure it out.

Then she turns to stare at a bright, bluish light in the distance. "It's not over yet. That's Luda. She was a simple Able. She visited me once, too. You'll keep floating farther and farther away until you look like that. Unless you get out."

I squeeze my eyes shut and try not to imagine what it would be like to be stuck here forever. I listen for Gayla, reach out to her with my thoughts, but... nothing.

There's movement underneath me. When I open my eyes, I see grass sprouting up and trees forming around me. They are hazy and transparent at first, but then they become real, solid. Then there's a large building beyond the trees.

The orchard.

I must have thought it up and made it real. Her words come back to me. *Whatever you think up tells them something about you.*

Wonderful. I'm giving them a roadmap to Miss Maggie's. Just like I brought the enemy directly to Zanum.

I slash the images in my head. The trees waver, then tear and begin to drip with what looks like blood. I can't help the images of death and destruction that flood my mind. Thoughts of Dhan.

The landscape becomes real and I'm on a battlefield. There is smoke and severed limbs all around. Lifeless eyes stare at me from disembodied heads.

I look desperately to the girl. "Help me!"

"It's you," she says, with a ferocity that yanks me out of my despair. "You have to control your thoughts. But you better figure something out fast," she adds. "Because they're coming. You're not supposed to be here. But you let them find you."

I clench my fists and do my best to tune out the sounds of violence and bloodshed around me. I breathe the way Miss Maggie taught me. For a moment, she glimmers in front of me and I immediately shove aside any further thoughts of her. I close my eyes and focus, instead, on the Dark.

But I can't. I hear a moan that sounds like Dhan and my eyes flutter open, searching for him. Soon, I begin to hear something in the distance.

Sirens.

A few seconds later, there are blinding lights. So bright that even closing my eyes doesn't help shield them from the glare.

Everything happens in slow brutal motion. A screaming siren sound cuts through the space in front of my bubble and a laser-like beam strikes the girl in the center of her chest.

She looks like she's expecting it—wants it, even. She turns to me to say something, her mouth forming a limp 'O.' But her body blasts into a million pieces before any sound comes out. Her bubble turns deep red, dripping with opaque bits sliding in pink rivulets down the membrane.

And then my own body implodes.

When I open my eyes again, I can't move. At least not without excruciating currents of pain slicing through the length of my body. There is screaming everywhere.

I feel my body convulse, then lie still.

The screaming is me.

I'm alive.

My heart is beating in my chest. Relief rushes through my veins like ice water, soothing the burn I feel everywhere else.

The girl. What happened to the girl? She was trying to help me, trying to tell me things. I bite back the bile that threatens to send my body into convulsions again and switch off that line of thought.

I lift my head slowly and see that I am lying on a kind of hospital cot that seems to be suspended in midair. The room is dark, but there's a blue glow. Where it's coming from, I have no idea, but it allows me to make out the different shapes in the room.

I cast around in my mind for Gayla, or any sign that I'm not alone.

Nothing.

I am alone.

"Ah, she wakes," says a voice from the corner.

What looks like a pile of laundry—no, more like a mound of garbage—elongates into something with tattered skin and oozing sores, and moves toward me.

I try to scramble back, but I'm immobilized.

It laughs, this thing, in a voice that is neither male nor female.

"What—who are you?" I ask.

It stares at me, bending over the cot and leaning close to my face. The eyes are deep vacuous pits. Not human or animal—not alive.

"I take many forms," it says, studying me. "You don't *look* like you're anything special. I don't see why we had to launch an all-out hunt for you."

I follow its eyes and, for the first time, notice the small, sharp triangular peaks jutting out from just beneath my skin on my forearms. I jerk my arms without thinking, and bullets of pain whiz through my limbs.

I scream again.

"No, no," It soothes, stroking my fingers. "Hush."

I quell the impulse to jerk away, the pain from the last movement still strong.

"Those are very important and *must* stay," It says. "They monitor your thoughts, let us know how much force is present. Right now it is strong." It raises one tattered eyebrow in mild surprise. "The strongest I've seen, in fact. Now I can see why Master would want you." It opens its mouth in an empty grin. "After all this time, you led us directly to you. Now we begin harvesting your serpent fire. This is what Master has been waiting for. He will be very happy."

I swallow hard and steady my voice. "Why? Why does he want me?"

It raises an eyebrow. "Mace couldn't neutralize you. He has always been able to neutralize Ables, even the most difficult ones. But *you*." It squints its gaping eyeholes. "You kept wriggling free. Master thinks you have some sort of potent serpent fire from living among the Zanumites, and he wants it. But he has other plans for you, too."

It leans closer to me, its voice rising in excitement. "And I will sip from your fire, too, increasing my own power exponentially. Nothing will stop us then." Its voice drops into a whisper. "Master and I will do as we've planned for so many years! We will move through time as effortlessly as you, materializing wherever and whenever we wish! And I will take back what belongs to me. I will be *free*."

I struggle to keep up, to understand what I'm hearing. "How will you take my... serpent fire?"

It seems to have lost interest in me and turns to the peaks jutting up under my skin. It touches one on my left wrist and a searing pain blazes up through my shoulder.

I open my mouth to scream, but can only wheeze as beads of sweat wriggle down my face.

It doesn't seem to notice. Instead, it keeps poking different peaks, moving on to my ankles.

Each peak seems to correspond to something inside me. I feel little balls of fire detonate inside me and I can't breathe. Can't breathe enough to scream, to move, to think.

I'm relieved when darkness blots everything out and I fall. Fall. Fall.

Into the lap of nothingness.

Chapter 13

When I open my eyes again, I have to squint against the brightness. Slowly, my eyes adjust.

I am in a painfully white room. There is no furniture, no walls. Or at least it looks like there are no walls. It just seems like a room that extends into forever. White, bright forever.

I'm sitting on some sort of light-chair that reminds of the molded, brightly-colored plastic chairs I used to see at my pediatrician's office. Again, I'm secured to the spot with some kind of unseen restraints.

I look at my wrists. The spikes under my skin are still there.

A woman with thick, wavy red hair and bright pink lipstick materializes through the light-curtain. "Hello, Pammi," she says cheerily. There is an echoey sound to her voice. "We've been waiting for you to wake."

"Who are you?" I ask. My voice is hoarse and my throat feels raw. From all the screaming the other night, probably.

Was it the other night? How long have I been here?

"You would probably know me as Mantel," she says with a smile.

"But... Mantel's a *guy*. He's—" I stop myself from saying anything more.

She smiles wider and spreads her arms out. "He is! This is my favorite glamour, but if it unsettles you I am happy to take another," she says, morphing into an old man with a shock of white hair, then into a little boy with sesame-colored skin, and again into an old woman who looks like Vinta, before returning to the form of the redheaded woman.

"Why am I here?"

She pouts. "Oh, come now. You're a smart girl! Surely some of your little friends have filled you in? Or the lovely folk of Zanum?"

I keep my face as blank as possible.

She throws her head back and laughs. "Delightful!" She looks back at me with a twinkle in her eye, a twinkle that chills me to the bone. "This is why Mace had such a hard time with you. You're smart *and* beautiful." She tips my chin up with an impeccably manicured finger. "And powerful."

She speaks to the presence behind her. "Come, pet."

The thing that had been in the room with me the other night, or whenever that was, slips closer.

I shudder. I can see it better under the brightness of this light. It looks like it's wearing its insides on the outside.

I grit my teeth. I will not throw up I will not throw up I will not throw up.

"You've met my sister, Dyal?" she drawls. "Isn't she gorgeous?" She beams, like the proud owner of a rare animal. "The perfect combination of obedience and power."

The urge to hurl becomes stronger.

"Yes, I see you have met." Her voice becomes more business-like. "As Dyal may have mentioned, I would like your serpent fire. Yours is quite potent, indeed. It's a simple process, really," she says, as if we're discussing where to go for lunch.

"A small incision at the base of your spine to draw the energy up. In the old days, the days of your Zanum, the serpent fire could only be awakened by priests and priestesses through ceremony and ritual." She rolls her eyes.

"They wasted everything. Such tremendous energy! Wasted on praying to the dirt and grass and trees," she says, her mouth twisting with contempt. "Those dimwits were leading us nowhere fast."

She smiles. "And look! We have their greatest hope at our fingertips! She's putty in our hands, even if Mace failed. *We* will create the future of this world, and all others we come into contact with, won't we, pet?"

"Yes," her sister agrees. "You will be the Master of all Masters."

Mantel's glamour begins to fade and wane as her voice rises. "Morons. I knew they were up to something," she says, clenching her fists. "My idiot brother may have fallen for it, but I could see through their false promises!"

I lick my parched lips. "Brother? But Dyal's your sister, right?"

She glares at me. "Oh, don't play games with me. The brother who stabbed me in the back at that deplorable ceremony! You were there. I gave everyone in your time a description of you, and girls looking like you flooded my clinics, but could they find *you*? No. Even Mace assured me you couldn't be The One."

Now her voice brightens. "It wasn't until the ceremony that I knew we'd found you. Your mother made it much easier, calling my people each time she suspected you'd had a relapse. Such a good mother!"

"I don't know what you're talking about," I whisper.

"Smart girl," she hisses. "Never give up what you know, hmm? But it was only once you began crossing on your own that you became accessible! I'm sure they told you not to do that?"

Dyal grunts in agreement.

"You see," she says in a conspiratorial whisper, "you breached one of their shields without being detected. Those idiots were not even smart enough to tie up their loose ends! You left an opening for my Dyal, then, but she couldn't materialize. She can only shadow others through the Dark. That is why we needed to bring you here, my dear. Harvesting your fire is what will keep you here. It is the tether that will bind you to me."

I keep myself from railing against the restraints. The pain is a huge motivator to keep still. "How long do you plan to keep me here?"

"Why, for the rest of your natural life! Live serpent fire is the only thing keeping me this stunning and youthful. And keeping Ables on a tight leash to me is the only way I can manage entire nations, my dear."

She stands and walks just beyond my line of vision. "Your Zanumites sought to make a mockery of me. Vinta humiliated and publicly shunned me. I will go back there with you and eliminate him first. Then Zanum will be mine! No kings to placate, no battles to wage... simple and easy." She grins. "And then you will take me to your time so that I can harvest the serpent fires of that impressive group of Ables you've been spending time with. They're shielded and protected, but with you to take me through that hideous darkness, I will locate every powerful Able in history!"

The shock I'm feeling must show on my face. She comes back to where I can see her and pouts in mock pity. "Emotions make us do regrettable things sometimes, don't they? That wretched old priestess thought she could humiliate me and then banish me as if I were a mongrel." She narrows her eyes. "But she didn't know who she was dealing with. I will be more powerful than that old hag could ever dream of becoming."

I bite the inside of my cheek. This is a nightmare. If only I had listened to Pasea! She and Atesu knew more than I did. They knew what the dangers were, and they tried to warn me. But I didn't listen.

I look at Mantel, whose glamour has almost completely vanished now, and something begins to rise inside me, at the very core of my being. A kind of venom. My mother once said that when you're dealing with a madman, you have to become a little mad yourself. She was talking about Biodad, but I draw on those words now.

"I... I don't understand," I say. "I can't take you anywhere."

She leans so close I can smell death wafting from her pores. "Oh, but you can. That's why you are here. You can take things through that darkness with you. I've seen you do it. You have no idea how excited I was when Dyal—my darling, sweet Dyal!—saw you pull that branch through. You managed to take it from your time to thousands of years in the past." She shudders. "Now that is power."

I struggle to control the thing that is building inside me, threading through tissues and weaving in and out of my bones.

She doesn't notice. "You are my very own time machine! I've never seen anything like you. With you, I can go anywhere, to any time—with you, I can soar! But first," she says, turning to Dyal. "We must get her fire, pet. Why don't you start on that now? Soon, she will be our little captive forever."

"But—"

She whips around in a fury, and the glamour falls away completely. "*What is it?*"

Mantel the man is beyond ancient. Papery, loose flesh and skin on yellowing bones. But there's something else that makes my skin crawl, something that has nothing to do with the way he looks. It's the vacuous chasm that seems to open up when he's in his true form. A kind of magnetic black hole that pulls everything toward it. Including me.

As vile as he is, I want to move toward him. Toward the velvety darkness, the tortured vortex that is his soul. There is a sadness there, a longing, that pulls at me. I want to curl around it, protect it and soothe it until it becomes whole again. I struggle to keep my eyes from drooping, from allowing myself to be sucked in.

But the thing inside me, the thing I cannot name or picture, is still rising. It's like the eye of a hurricane, this thing. Calm, quiet, deadly, with madness and chaos all around it.

"But you said we should do the boy first," Dyal says.

The glamour settles back slowly, bit by bit. Once again, the woman before me looks like a solid, warm, living body.

"Ah, yes. He is an important one, too," Mantel says. "There's no rush. This pretty little nugget from the past isn't going anywhere. Bring the boy in."

As Dyal shuffles off, Mantel's eyes sweep over me. "Besides, watching this might help placate you."

Dyal returns with a pale blonde boy wearing what looks like a hospital gown. When I get a closer look, I see that the boy is actually a young man, probably not much older than me, and either passed out or sedated.

"Let's get on with it," Mantel says. Dyal turns the body over so that the man is slumped forward, straddling what would be a bench if there were anything underneath him. He looks like he's sitting on one of those mall massage chairs.

"Yesssss," Mantel says. Her voice is raspy. "Do it now, Dyal, *now*."

Dyal pulls the flaps of the gown aside to reveal the ridge of vertebrae along the man's back.

An old lesson from one of Dhan's classes flashes through my mind and everything makes sense. The serpent fire is the ball of energy that sits at the base of the spine. It's our very essence, the seat of our power.

Suddenly I remember what bubble girl said. If there are some he can't control, there's a way to stop him. He can't surf, she'd said. So his power is limited. *There has to be a way out.*

I fight through the terror, trying to get to the stillness that is rising inside me. I know it's there, I can feel it. Strong and solid and dark and steady. Climbing.

With the touch of a sore-covered fingertip, Dyal burns through the man's flesh at the bottom of his spine.

The pale body jerks in the chair and the man awakens. His shrieks of agony echo through the white chamber.

Beads of perspiration run down my ribs and I tremble. I keep my mouth clamped shut. The battle raging within the bounds of my skin is epic. But my face has to remain expressionless.

Mantel is watching my every move. "Don't even think about escape, sweet Pammi," he says. His glamour has all but disappeared again and I feel his excitement mounting, filling the room.

I try not to cringe from his decaying face.

"I need you here, in your body and awake, in order to harvest that delectable fire of yours."

I hear him, loud and clear, even above the man's now-hoarse shrieks. Everything becomes sharper and I'm sensitive to the tiniest movement.

"You're sick," I whisper.

He laughs. "On the contrary! I am the embodiment of countless serpent fires. I have outlived generations of my own progeny. Once I harvest your fire, you will belong to me. You will do as I say, just as my Dyal does. Your ability will remain as strong as ever, but it will be mine to control. I am about to hold the fate of the entire universe in the palm of my hand, young Pammi. I, Haram, an exile of Zanum!" His delighted laugh clangs throughout my entire being.

"There is no god," he says. "But if ever there was, I am he."

Dyal pulls a crackling stream of white light from the man's spine as blood splatters onto his fingers. The man's body rattles and jerks.

I grind my teeth together to keep from moving, from lurching away in horror.

When the last of the serpent fire is drained out of the man, he slumps in the chair. A deflated lump of bones and flesh.

Dyal shapes the crackling buttery, yellow-white energy into a sphere and walks it to Mantel. Glee lights up Mantel's face as he reaches for the ball and eagerly sips from it.

The young man stares with empty eyes, muttering incoherently. His skin is ashen and he looks barely alive.

There is no way I can calm down and relax enough to breathe. I have no access to the girls at the center and there is no sign of Gayla anywhere in my thoughts.

I close my eyes and search desperately for the calm thing—the quiet dark rising.

But I'm snatched back. "Oh, no you don't," Mantel growls above me. "I saw you slip through before. I need you here to harvest your fire. I will not lose you now that I finally have you in my hands! You are the key to everything I've been working for." The rage in his eyes billows like wildfire.

He's holding fistfuls of my gown and shaking my body like a dust cloth.

But his voice is fading away. I avoid making any skin contact with him. Somehow I know that is the key to keeping him here. Dyal has no skin to touch, or not enough, anyway, so I don't worry about her.

I reach out and make contact with the Dark that is within my own soul.

It is the serpent, it is the fire, it is the Dark, it is eternal night and eternal life. It is me.

I hear him shouting to Dyal in the distance. "Don't let her slip away—I need her fire first, you moron!"

And then I'm caught, suspended somewhere between there and here, never and always.

I'm at the door to the Dark, but something is keeping me from going through.

There is a man, but I can't see him. Only his shadow. Mantel. But I am real here and he is not. The clutches I'm in are not his. They are Dyal's. Somehow, Dyal is stopping me from merging with the Dark.

I look to one side and see a shallow pool full of bodies. Mantel's doing. I don't know how I know this, but I do. To my left, the sun lights up three golden temples, their domes shining like dazzling beacons. When are they from? In front of me, a giant eye is painted in blue on the wall of a red brick building.

And to my right is his shadow. He's searching for me—the one who got away. Trying to find a way to bring me back, or keep me here, in this crack between past and present and future, forever.

He doesn't want to kill me. No, what he wants is worse.

The bodies lie at the bottom of the pool, limbs entwined, eyes staring lifelessly up into oblivion. They are bloody and bruised. Many are battered beyond recognition, but not dead... they are in storage.

I hesitate for only a fraction of a second.

The shadow moves swiftly, coming into the light—coming directly toward me.

I turn and dive into the pool.

Chapter 14

I wake up screaming and clawing at the air. Hands hold me down and someone pushes me back onto a bed.

I scream and kick. I fight with every ounce of strength I can muster until a familiar voice shouts into my ear. "Stop!"

That stills me. I open my eyes and look around.

I'm back at the center. My body goes limp as relief and exhaustion flood my limbs.

Miss Maggie has one cool hand on my forehead and is checking my pulse with the other. The girls hover nearby.

She sets my hand down and pats my cheek. Her face is etched with worry. "How are you feeling, dear?"

"How long was I gone?" I ask. "My mom's going to freak! Did anyone get in touch with her? Has she been calling?"

Etienne looks at her watch. "You were gone about seven minutes."

My jaw drops. "No—it was, like, *days!*"

Miss Maggie smoothes my hair down. "Our experience of time shifts when we are projected into the past or the future—a natural distortion. You should know that, Pammi." She turns to Sharlene. "Bring her a damp paper towel, won't you?"

Gayla takes one of my hands. "You scared me. I was with you all the way until you left that space bubble thing with ghost-girl—and then I couldn't find you *anywhere.*"

Sharlene presses the damp paper towel against my forehead. "Does that feel okay?"

I close my eyes. "Yes. Thank you."

She squeezes my other hand and pulls up a stool.

"Pammi," Miss Maggie says, "do you feel strong enough to let Gayla go through the memory of this experience?"

I stare at her. I don't ever want to relive that horror.

"He came very close to you, dear," she says gently. "If he did it once, he will do it again. And the next time, he will finish what he started."

She's right. I nod my permission.

Miss Maggie pats my hand and turns to Gayla. "Share it with us. We will experience it as Pammi did. I need to know what she has seen."

I close my eyes again and relive my experiences. The room is silent as Gayla relays the memory.

Sharlene is the first to speak when I've finished. "Whoa."

Etienne moves behind her and runs her hands up and down Sharlene's arms, as if trying to warm her up. Her own face is grim and sober.

"He's crazy," Gayla whispers. "Like, really crazy."

Rage simmers in Miss Maggie's eyes, but she's otherwise calm and composed. "No. He is far from crazy. He is focused and intelligent, and full of pure, unmitigated loathing."

She clenches her hands into fists and paces to the window. "So he plans to use you as his own personal time machine, does he? He thinks he can shape and control what is not his to own? He has no idea what he's playing with, nor does he care, that arrogant—"

She stops pacing to look at me. "We can use that to our advantage. Pammi," she says, pausing as if she's drawing up plans in her mind. "You need to find a way to protect yourself as you Travel."

"He wants to kill Vinta," I say. My chest tightens at the thought.

"Wait—*the* Vinta?" Gayla asks, her eyes wide. "From our Hidden History class?"

Sharlene gapes. "I thought that was a myth."

I stare at them. "What are you talking about?"

Gayla looks at Miss Maggie for permission before continuing. "We have a class called Hidden History of the World. The Vinta-Haram story is one we learn early on."

"You should not have been there, Pammi," Miss Maggie says quietly.

I stare at the rug. "I know."

Her voice has a hard edge to it. "You disobeyed your guardians."

I can't keep the note of defiance from my voice. "No one was telling me anything! All of this involves me, but I had no answers. Everyone was talking about all this important stuff I'm supposed to do and no one was telling me *what*."

She doesn't let up. "The elders of the past knew which events and energy patterns outsiders needed to stay clear of. That's why certain activities are restricted. They knew that having a Traveler present could change the outcome of events in drastic ways. You being at that event led Mantel directly to you, and to *them*. You couldn't have made it easier if you'd given him a roadmap."

"I didn't know," I cry. "If someone had explained it to me, maybe I would've listened!"

At that, her eyes soften a little. "You managed to retain your abilities under the harshest pressure Mantel could apply through his doctors. And there are others like you, strong-minded Ables with a powerful will to survive intact. Mantel is angry, perhaps because he was never recognized as important and powerful like his brother. Perhaps he felt robbed of that at the Blesseds ceremony, and he has blamed his brother and the Zanumites all throughout the ages."

Etienne shakes her head. "Why couldn't he let it go?" She looks at Miss Maggie. "I mean, who cares if some people don't think you're important? Just move on and find people who do."

Miss Maggie smiles gently. "It does seem that simple, doesn't it? But look how long it has taken you to trust, Etienne. Some experiences, painful ones, teach us that the world can be a frightening and cold place." She shrugs. "Some people move through those experiences and become stronger, more loving. Others... others become filled with rage and vengeance."

"So, the Vinta story is for real?" Gayla asks.

Miss Maggie purses her lips. "They are all real, dear. Why on earth do you think we teach them to you, for heaven's sake?"

Gayla shrugs. "I just thought they were stories."

"Me, too," Etienne says.

"How did the story go?" I ask.

"Vinta offers himself as a sacrifice," Gayla says. "But his brother doesn't want to. Vinta tries to convince him, but the brother starts to question the entire governance of the city."

"And the religion and beliefs everyone has followed for, like, centuries," Sharlene adds.

"It splits the city into two camps," Gayla continues. "Those who believe in the old ways—"

"And those who are exiled and join the invaders in trying to obliterate everything Zanum is about," Etienne finishes.

"That's almost exactly what happened." I look at Miss Maggie. "Nothing's been changed, then!"

"Not quite," she says. "Your presence was like an open doorway to the Dark. We won't know the exact ramifications for a little while."

I recall something one of the Council members had said. "But they said they had secured it..."

Gayla seems to be sifting through memories—mine and hers. "Mantel said they probably didn't detect the breach because you'd been living among them for so long."

Miss Maggie confirms this. "You blended in as if you were one of them."

"But by the end of the ceremony," I say, "Haram knew I was there. As Mantel, he sent Dyal back." Things are beginning to make sense now.

"Yes," Miss Maggie says, "to see if Dyal could breach the shield through your presence... and she did. But she can only materialize if you take her with you, as you did with that branch."

"The branch," I repeat, trying to absorb everything. "Pasea was pretty freaked out that I brought through organic matter."

A silence settles over us. I'm reeling with everything I've learned—the immensity of it all.

Etienne is the first to speak. "So he wants to kill Vinta to prove something."

Miss Maggie's face looks grim. "He wants to show Vinta and the Zanumites that he is just as good as they are, if not better." She shakes her head. "A little boy's tantrum that will leave a lasting, possibly catastrophic impact on humankind."

Once again, we fall silent, each of us lost in her own thoughts. I feel like someone is sitting on my chest.

Again, it's Etienne who breaks the silence first. "Great. That's just great."

When I get home, my mother is in my room.

Sitting at my desk.

On my computer.

The look on her face says it all. "Why've you been looking at websites about time travel, Pammi?"

"Uh…" I drop my backpack and stare at her for a few seconds. A few seconds too long.

Her voice goes up a notch. "I asked you a question."

"It—it's for research." I scramble for an excuse she might believe.

"What research? You're not in school, remember?"

No. I don't remember a damn thing right now. "Why were you going through my browsing history?"

"That is not the point!" she says, slamming a hand on my desk and standing up. "Do you believe you are time traveling again, Pammi?" Her voice is a mixture of anger, dread, and concern.

"*No*, Mom," I say emphatically. This is the last thing I need right now. I try to calm her suspicions. "That's impossible. I was a kid before, and—and under a lot of stress."

I can tell she's trying to decide whether she should believe me.

I pull off my sweatshirt and toss it on the bed, trying to act like any normal girl on any normal day. "Mom, come on. Give me some credit, please?"

"I've put in a call to Dr. Mace, in any case," she says.

I freeze for a moment before forcing myself to move naturally again. I reach for my backpack and pretend to look for something. "I don't need to see Dr. Mace, Mom."

"It can't hurt to touch base, Pammi."

Her voice is calmer and I close my eyes for a moment, willing my heart rate to slow down. "Mom, seeing Dr. Mace always takes me back to that terrible time in my life." I look at her, letting all the emotions I'm feeling finally show on my face. "Please don't make me walk back into that office. I have to go back to memories of—of Biodad and England and…" I let the rest of it hang in the air between us.

She looks taken aback for a moment. Then her expression softens. "I never realized. I'm so sorry." She puts her arms around me and I bury my face into her shoulder, holding on like I used to when I was little.

"You don't ever have to go through those memories again, darling. I'll cancel the appointment," she murmurs into my ear. "I'm sorry I'm so jumpy around this issue. I know you've made tremendous progress and things have been going well." She pulls back to look into my eyes. "I'm very proud of you."

I breathe in the smell of her, wanting to stay in the comfort of her arms, to believe that everything has been going well and will be just fine.

Chapter 15

Mom promises to leave my online browsing history alone. That's a relief, but she also takes it upon herself to help me with my social life.

There is an upcoming Indian family function and she decides the two of us *must* attend. This, from the woman who avoids Indian family functions like raw sewage. Being divorced is still a stigma in our Punjabi and Indian circles. And having a boyfriend? Forget it. We're not exactly upstanding role models.

"Why exactly are we going to this thing?" I ask as she rummages through my closet for the few salwaar kameez suits I own, almost all of which were sent by my grandparents in England.

"It's your cousin Pinky. Because the girl is from our side of the family, our presence is required. She's marrying into a very wealthy family and it's important for as many members of her side to show up as possible," she says, her voice muffled as she reaches deep into a corner of my closet. She emerges triumphantly, holding up a dry-cleaning bag of peach-colored silk.

"I forgot I even owned that," I say, taking it from her outstretched hand. I do love my salwaar kameez suits. They're gorgeous and comfortable and remind me a little of the wraps the women wear in Zanum. "*Pinky*? With the skull tattoo on her back? *She's* getting married?"

Mom nods. "The very one."

"But she's only twenty-one!"

Mom gives a curt nod. "You know how these things are. Your Naniji called and strongly urged us to attend. She said it is a matter of family honor and our good name."

I groan. "But I thought we already ruined the good name? Now we can relax and be who we want to be, can't we?"

Mom smirks. "Not exactly. Your Nani went so far as to remind me that I have a young, almost-marriageable daughter. It's my duty to repair our family name so that you can find a suitable match and marry into a good family."

I stare at her.

She tries to keep a straight face, but soon bursts into laughter.

I shake my head. "But she's urged us strongly a million times before."

She goes back to her stern look as she takes my outfit back. "I'm ironing this, and you will wear it tonight."

"Is Dr. B. coming?"

Her nostrils flare. "Pammi. You know it is inappropriate for two unmarried adults to show up together at something like this. I'm supposed to be repairing our reputation, not *obliterating* it. Not to mention, this is my side of the family and there are still plenty of members who believe I've effectively marred their own children's chances at landing a good marriage match."

"Again, we're going to this thing becaaaaause...?"

"Enough questions," she says, pulling herself to her full height of five feet and three inches. "I can handle those people, Pams. I don't give a hairy rat's behind what they think of me and they know it. I'm happy as can be in my life with my gorgeous, smart-as-a-whip future psychologist daughter and my famous man-friend." She pauses and grins for effect before continuing. "And they won't say anything to you, so you have nothing to be concerned about."

She turns to head out of my room, but stops to look back at me. She sighs. "You've been tense lately. There will be young people at this affair and I want you to get out. Mingle a bit with people your own age, people you don't work with."

"I'd really rather just stay home."

"I know, Pams. But you might actually enjoy yourself... and you never know who you might meet."

The event is an engagement-slash-henna party for the bride-to-be. The wedding is in a week. "Gotta love those long engagements," I muttered when Mom told me.

She gave me a warning look, so I kept the rest of my thoughts to myself on the subject.

When we arrive, the house is overflowing with guests. Most of the family members are outside in the enormous backyard, where several canopies are set up—one for the soon-to-be couple, one for the food table, and another for the bar.

The women are all draped in gold and jewelry and wrapped in silks or chiffons. Their immaculately pedicured toes peek out of silver or gold strappy sandals. Most of the men are in suits and ties, though the bride-to-be's brothers are wearing intricately embroidered kurta pajamas.

"Oh, there's Pinky," Mom says, heading for the bride-to-be. "Doesn't she look stunning, Pams?"

"More like *stunned*."

She gives me another warning look before we get to the canopy where Pinky and her fiancé are sitting. They're huddled together in a swing chair that has fresh flowers covering its back and sides. A woman is putting the finishing touches of an elaborate henna design on Pinky's feet.

Mom air kisses her cheek. "Congratulations, darling!"

"Thanks, Auntie," Pinky says. "Hey, Pams."

I lean down and give her a hug. "Hey, Pinks. How's it going?"

"Great!" she says, in a too-bright, too-cheerful voice.

"Well, congrats." I wonder how long she has had to hold that smile in place and how many other ceremonies she has had to endure in the past week. Not to mention the ones coming up in the *next* week. And I wonder if she loves this guy.

I look him over and try to see if there's anything between them, but all they seem to be doing is presenting similar smiles. *Ugh.*

"Mom, I'm going to get some juice. Want something?"

She shakes her head. "No, darling. You go ahead. Mingle. I'll say hi to your bhua—oh, my goodness, is that Bunto? I haven't seen her in years!" And with that, she's off.

"Pammi? Is that you, girl?"

I'm face-to-face with a Bollywood magazine model. I squint into her face. "Bubbli?"

She squeals and throws her arms around me. "It's me! Ohmigod, where have you *been?*"

I shrug. "Same old. *You* look like you got one of those massive makeovers." As soon as it's out of my mouth, I realize that could totally be taken the wrong way. "I mean—"

She laughs. "No, totally. My braces are off, I discovered waxing, and Antonio does magic with my eyebrows!" She looks me over. "*You* look exactly the same."

I chew on my bottom lip, not sure whether that's a compliment or not.

"That's a good thing!" she says, touching my arm. "You were always one of those natural beauties! I was always so jealous of you."

Just then, two other girls swish across the lawn, the fabric of their long skirts clinging to their hips and falling gracefully to just above their perfectly done toes. The powder dusted across their bared bellies shimmers in the sunlight. "Bubbli!" they screech, almost in unison.

"Milli! Ritu!" Bubbli joins them in a group hug before turning to me. "This is Pammi. I haven't seen her in a million years, but doesn't she look ravishing?"

The girls smile and nod. Milli, the shorter of the two, has red highlights in her hair and flowers pinned up on one side. "I love that color on you!"

"Me, too," Ritu gushes, stroking the silk of my sleeve. "They really should bring some of these old styles back, don't you think?"

"*Totally*," Milli says. "I loved that when it came out." She turns to Bubbli. "*Where* did you get your nails done?"

Bubbli holds her hands out, fanning her fingernails for the other girls to admire. "Antonio's! They do everything. Go to Ilsa. She does an amazing Brazilian—"

I cut in before the conversation gets any further out of my range. As if it ever started in my range. "Bubbli, it was nice to see you. I'm going to go get something to drink."

"Oh, Pammi, it was amazing to see you, too! I'll see you again before the day's done, I'm sure!"

I nod, silently swearing to find a spot where I can remain safely hidden until it's time to go home.

I make my way to the bar and grab a cup of orange juice from a tray.

"That has vodka in it," a voice says behind me.

I put the cup down. "Thanks."

"I'm Bobby, your bartender for the afternoon."

I turn to look at Bobby the Bartender. He's cute. "Do you have plain orange juice?"

"Mango-peach okay?"

"Perfect."

He walks around to the other side of the bar, pulls out a pitcher, and pours some into a cup. "Here you go," he says, handing it to me with a wink. "Matches your outfit."

I look down. "True." I start to walk in the opposite direction of Bubbli and her crew. I can't help but notice that Bobby the Bartender is still watching me. I might be annoyed if he wasn't so cute.

I walk around the periphery of the yard, nursing my cup of juice and wishing I could be anywhere but here.

A soft breeze whispers against my skin, raising the hair on my arms.

I know what that is, that shift in the whatever-it-is of the atmosphere. It's what I feel when Sharlene's around. It's what I felt the night of the Blesseds ceremony.

That's what Pasea was talking about when she said the presence of an outsider alters things. Someone is here who shouldn't be.

I look around, but don't see anyone who looks out of place. This must be how Haram felt when he was looking around the night of the ceremony, wondering who the interloper was in their midst. Or did he already know?

I head toward the flowerbeds near the back and lean against the wooden fence, under the shade of a large maple. From here, I have a solid view of the entire gathering. If anything happens out of the ordinary, I'll see it.

What I will do once I see it is a whole other question.

There's a rosebush next to me. On it are some of the most exquisite blooms I've ever seen. It almost glows, but it feels set apart somehow from the rest of the garden. I feel an inexplicable urge to pluck one of the gorgeous buds and tuck it into my hair. I lean over to touch the petals of one of the flowers, and an electric charge courses through my fingers as I cross some sort of barrier.

As soon as my fingers make contact, the buttery yellow of the rose begins to leach into me. It spreads slowly from my fingertip to my knuckles and up toward my wrist.

I jerk my hand back with a gasp, but can't pull away—my fingertip has flattened and become a glowing yellow, indiscernible from the flower I was touching. The powdery yellow light spreads to my elbow.

I try not to panic. I'm in a very public place with my mother, engaged in a tug-of-war with a freaking rosebush.

The yellow spreads faster, up to my shoulder, creeping into my chest. I feel my heart being squeezed and I'm gasping for air.

I fight, stumbling back and pulling my arm away from the bush. The entire bush strains. It's growing with every new inch it claims on my body.

From behind me there is a rush of air and, suddenly, I'm free, tumbling backward to slam against the chest of Bobby the Bartender.

"You okay?" he asks.

I can't keep the tremor out of my voice. "I, uhh—um—"

"Who was that?" he asks.

I stop fumbling for words. "Who was what?"

"Never mind. What just happened?"

"No," I say, grabbing his arm. "You saw someone?"

He stares at me for a moment. "A woman. With torn-up skin and gashes on her face."

Blood pounds in my ears. "I didn't see anyone. I bent down to touch that—" and just as I point to the rosebush, I see that it's gone.

He looks into my face. "Who are you?"

"Who are *you*?" I ask.

He takes me by the elbow and leads me around to the other side of the maple tree where we're a little more hidden. "I saw a lady trying to drag you away from here," he says. "Normally, when I see people who aren't there, other people can't see them."

"You can see people who aren't there?"

He ignores me. "But you were fighting with her, which means you could see her."

"I didn't see anyone. I saw a rose bush. I reached out to touch one of the flowers and this thing—this kind of light—started creeping into my hand. But you got rid of it. How did you do that?"

Something seems to occur to him. "Shit," he says. He leans over the fence and grabs a shiny object, half-buried in the dirt where the rose bush was.

"My grandmother gave this to me," he says, shaking soil loose from what looks like an old wooden wheel that's been painted gold. "When I spin it properly and say the right words, it cuts contact with the dead and sends them back to wherever they came from."

I inspect the wheel. "Tell me, exactly, what this woman looked like," I say.

"Why?" He wipes the spokes clean, takes out a square piece of black silk and wraps the wheel back up.

"If she was who I think she was, she's not dead. She's not even born yet."

He stares at me for a moment. "Okay, now you have to tell me what the hell is going on."

"And you have to tell me who the hell you really are."

He grins. "My name really is Bobby. I moved here from Delhi a couple of years ago, to go to university. I'm studying engineering at Withrow Tech. My parents both died when I was young and I was raised by my Dadi. She was the only one who believed what I saw and helped me not be afraid. She also taught me how to get rid of the ones who meant me harm."

I hadn't noticed his slight Indian accent before. It's kind of sexy. "That's quite a story."

"Yeah. Now you."

I take a deep breath and explain going to Zanum as best I can. I tell him about being an Able and about the girls at the center. Then I give him a quick summary of my last visit into the future.

For some reason, I trust him. I know this could blow up in my face, but my gut feeling is that Bobby doesn't want to hurt me.

"Talk about a story," he says. "Dyal definitely sounds like the same one I saw. I always thought the ghosts I saw were dead. It never occurred to me I could be seeing impressions from the future." He looks up into the branches of the maple. "Dadi never mentioned anything about that."

"My mom freaks if she thinks I'm 'hallucinating' or even *talking* about time traveling."

He shakes his head. "In India, too. There are those who ignore or deny these things, but I think even they still believe there is more to everything than what they can see. Spirits and the unknown are so embedded in the psyche and mythos there."

"What would have happened if you hadn't broken that contact using your grandmother's wheel?"

"You would have disappeared. My grandmother used to tell me stories about things like that. People who went missing and were simply never found."

"So Dyal can just come and *take* me whenever she wants? But she's not supposed to be able to materialize in any time period other than her own."

He considers this for a moment then shakes his head. "She didn't. That rose bush wasn't here. It was slightly removed from this plane. In other words, no one could see it but you. This... Dyal must know that you can see things in the half-plane. That's what Dadi called the space in between, where I can see, but others can't." He looks thoughtful for a moment. "My guess is that Dyal wouldn't have been able to take you into the half-plane without your consent."

"My *consent*?"

"You reached out and touched the flower."

"So I have to go around and not touch anything?"

He sucks his teeth. "Of course not. Was there anything that was strange? Or something you noticed that was out of the ordinary?"

"There was this shift in the air. The temperature or the feel, I don't know, but something that made me feel like there was another presence here."

He points to me. "The half-plane. Whenever you feel that, you have to be careful. If there's something that seems to be drawing you to it, stay far away and be on guard."

"Is that how you feel it when there's a ghost or a spirit, or impression, or whatever?"

He nods. "I felt it right away. As soon as you walked off with your juice, I felt something hovering around you."

"Here you are!" My mother comes around the tree. She's lifting her sari up with one hand and giving both Bobby and I the eagle eye. "And who are you, young man?"

"Hello, Auntie," Bobby says, his face flushing with pink splotches. "I'm Bobby, a friend of the family. I'm studying engineering at Withrow Institute, but my family is from Delhi."

Smart guy, listing the education thing right off the bat.

Mom takes his outstretched hand. "Very nice to meet you, Bobby." Her face is all aglow when she turns to me. "I'm so sorry to interrupt, Pams, but we should go." Her grin threatens to eat her entire face. "I'll leave you two to say good-bye and such, but come out from around that tree. Doesn't look good for two young people to be hiding."

And then she *giggles*.

I cover my face when she's gone. "Please let me apologize for my mom."

He laughs. "Don't worry, I'm used to it. Ever since I started at the university, all I keep hearing about is marriage. Especially at these kinds of things."

"Just tell them you see ghosts," I say.

This time I notice the dimple in his cheek when he smiles. "I'll try that next time."

We stand there for an awkward moment before I turn to go. "I guess I should head out."

"Right," he says, clearing his throat.

I wave my hand toward the now-flowerless flowerbed. "Thanks for that."

"Anytime."

"Okay, so... bye."

"Wait."

I stop and realize I'm holding my breath.

"Pammi, right?"

I smile. "Sorry. Hi, I'm Pammi."

"Can I maybe call you sometime?"

I bite my bottom lip.

"I'm sorry," he says quickly. "If you have a boyfriend or something, I understand—I didn't mean to—"

"I do have a boyfriend. In Zanum."

"I should've known. But isn't that hard, with him all the way there and you here?"

I cock my head to the side and notice that Bobby's eyes are like open blossoms. "Sometimes. But it wouldn't hurt to have a guy my mom heartily approves of calling me. It would get her off my back and give me some breathing space. And it wouldn't hurt to have someone outside of the center to talk to about everything I can't talk about."

He pulls out his cell phone and punches my number in as I rattle it off, ignoring the pangs of guilt in my belly.

"I enjoyed talking to you, Pammi," he says, before heading back to the bar.

On the ride back, Mom talks nonstop. "It's so healthy for you to be out and about, darling. You are a beautiful, smart girl; it's completely natural for boys to be drawn to you like that young man was! From where I was sitting, it looked like he was hanging on your every word! You need to be around young people your own age. I saw you chatting and laughing with those girls..."

I let her go on and "uh-huh" in all the right spots. I have other things on my mind. Like the fact that Dyal and Mantel are after me now with all their might. And they plan to use me to destroy a place and people I've come to love. Including Dhan, the absolute love of my life.

But the one thing that keeps niggling its way into my thoughts is Bobby the Bartender, who sees people who aren't there.

Chapter 16

The next day, I wake up with a headache. Mom's already gone and the apartment is quiet as I get ready to go back to the center.

I kept waking up during the night in a cold sweat, terrified to return to the nightmare I'd awoken from. All I saw was the face of the girl in the bubble, her eyes beckoning to me. And then bits of her flesh as they slid down the clear membrane.

At one point, Etienne's face became Dhan's face, which morphed into Bobby the Bartender's. I don't even want to think about what that could mean. I miss Dhan so much my bones ache. How can I possibly be thinking about another guy?

But this isn't just any other guy. *Aaagh*!

I shove the thoughts aside as I walk into the center. Miss Maggie, the girls, and Celia meet me in the foyer.

"Good, she's here," Sharlene says. "Let's go."

"Where are we going?" I ask.

"Geneva Mall," Gayla says with a grin.

"The mall?" I stare at them.

Miss Maggie lowers herself onto a high backed chair and folds her hands in her lap. "I want you girls to go out into the world together. It will be your first time as a group. The only way to know the true challenges you'll face in the real world is to go out in it, beyond the protective arms of the mansion."

I wonder if now would be a good time to bring up the rose bush incident. I decide not to. One, I don't want to make anyone more nervous than they are already. Two, I don't want to make *me* more nervous. Three, I can't talk about it in front of Celia, anyway. And four, I don't want Miss Maggie to change her mind. I'm looking forward to going out into the world with these three. This group is the closest I've ever come to being part of my own crew.

We climb into Celia's hybrid SUV, wave good-bye to an anxious-yet-resolute Miss Maggie, and head to Geneva Mall. The ride there is about twenty-five minutes on the highway. Gayla, Sharlene, and Etienne sit in the back, and I'm next to Celia in the front.

Celia finds a parking spot close to the movie theater and we all pile out.

"I need a wallet," Etienne says. "Where was that place with the sale, Shar?"

"Sundress and a pedicure," Sharlene says in a singsong voice before answering Etienne. "Leatherbound, Inc. They have interesting outfits, too—with chains and stuff."

Gayla pipes up in a too-bright voice. "A movie!"

Celia grins. "Sorry, hon, not today. You are to mingle and interact with your environment. Those are my orders."

Gayla grumbles under her breath.

When we get inside the main entrance, Celia looks at her watch. "Okay, ladies, ninety minutes to do as you please, then meet back here."

She turns to me. "Is your cell charged up?"

I pull it out of my pocket. "Yep."

She dials my phone. "I'm calling you so you have my number. If there are any issues, any at *all*, ring me on my cell and I will drop everything, understood?"

"Yes, Celia," we say in unison.

Sharlene giggles as we watch Celia clip-clop away in her heels.

"Free at last!" Etienne says. "Leatherbound, Inc. first! I called it."

Sharlene leads the way, slipping her hand into Etienne's.

I can't help staring. How did I not notice this before? I go back and do a mental check for clues I could have seen, and then it seems obvious. The way they look at one another, the chemistry between them. *Duh.* If they had been a guy-and-girl couple, I wonder if I would have picked up on their relationship right away.

Gayla's already moved on to watching a family with three small children struggle with all their bags and a stroller. I act cool, but seeing the intimacy between Sharlene and Etienne renews that familiar gnawing pang. Images of Dhan flash through my mind. I shove the memories aside.

"Wait," Sharlene says, pointing to Muchly Music. "Let's stop here first. They have those listening stations and the section with old vinyl records."

Gayla and I get paired off by default. "So what about you," she asks. "Are you seeing anyone?"

"Just Dhan."

She nods. "Right. Your ancient dude."

I know she means no harm, but I can't help wincing anyway. It's not her fault Dhan lives so long ago.

"You?" I ask.

She shakes her head. "It's hard to meet anyone when you're living at the center," she says. "I mean, I'm glad I'm there and I wouldn't want to be anywhere else... but it would be nice, you know? Except I don't think I could do it."

"Do what?"

She shrugs. "Be in a relationship. I'm too shy. My tongue forgets what it's for when I'm around anyone I really like."

I laugh. "That happens to a lot of people when they really like someone, Gay."

She doesn't say anything.

"You get better when you know someone," I say. "When they're more familiar and you're not so scared to be yourself. That's why you're supposed to take your time." I don't know if that's true, but I want to say something to help her feel better. I know what it's like to feel that lonely, always wondering why everyone else gets to have someone to love and hold, and you don't.

Sharlene and Etienne head for the Eighties section while Gayla and I veer straight toward the Rock/Alternative aisle.

Gayla flips through CDs next to me. "The other thing is," she continues, "it's harder for me to control my ability when I'm emotional. I'm thinking that would make it hard to be in a relationship—since they're all about emotions and all."

Suddenly, my own boyfriend angst feels petty. I think about what it must be like to have an ability like Gayla's, where people are afraid to trust you—or worse, you're afraid to trust your own ability, always worried it might get out of control and you could end up hurting the people you care about the most.

A single teardrop slides down to the tip of her nose, dangling there until she wipes it away with the back of her hand.

I reach across and give her shoulder a quick squeeze. "You'll figure it out, Gay. I never thought I could do half of what I've been learning lately."

She wipes her eyes. "Yeah, that's what everyone keeps telling me." She takes a shaky breath and smiles, looking at me with still-watery eyes. "Ironic, isn't it? I can go into people's heads and sift through thoughts and memories that their most trusted friends and intimate lovers might never know, but I can't have that closeness in my own life."

The sadness in her voice plucks at me. I want to do something to help, but I know this is her path. Just like no one else can help me with mine.

This time I give her a big hug.

"Everything okay?" Sharlene and Etienne are standing next to us, holding Muchly Music bags.

Etienne puts a protective hand on Gayla's shoulder. "You all right, Gay?"

"Everything's okay," Gayla says, offering a wobbly smile. "Except I'm starving."

"Let's go to the food court now," Sharlene suggests.

Etienne laughs. "What about your pedicure?"

Sharlene shrugs. "I'll get a new color and paint my own toes. Let's eat!"

We make our way to the food court, debating the pluses and minuses of vampires versus zombies, tattoos we'd like to get, or not, and hair colors that work for our skin tones.

When we get to the food court, everyone gets her food of choice and we settle into the most private table we can find.

Sharlene and Etienne sit next to one another and Gayla and I sit across from them.

"What's that?" I ask, pointing at Sharlene's tray of food.

She pushes the tray toward me. "Hakka. Ever tried it?"

I shake my head and spear a deep-fried ball, popping the whole thing in my mouth. "Yum." I wipe the spicy dribble from my chin.

"I tried it the last time we were here and I'm addicted. It's a 'succulent blend of Indian and Chinese cuisines,'" she says, reading the carton.

I nod. "Of course. No wonder I love it."

Etienne is chewing a huge bite of cheeseburger. "Aren't you Indian? Shouldn't you know about hakka?"

"Yes. Because being Indian makes me an expert on all things Indianish." I give her a deadpan stare until she snorts.

"Whatever," she says, taking another bite of her cheeseburger.

"I was born in England," I explain. "I lived there until I was five. My mom and Biodad were born in India."

Gayla raises her eyebrows. "*Biodad*?"

"Biological dad." I try to keep my voice light, but it falters. I clear my throat. "He used to beat my mom. When he started practicing on me, my mom took off and came here. Once we got here, everything was fine until I started having 'hallucinations.'"

It feels so good to talk about this with people who understand. To say some of these things *out loud*.

We eat in silence for a few minutes.

Sharlene sops up the last of her curry sauce with some naan and pops it into her mouth. "Born in China, adopted to America. Raised as a nice, Jewish girl. Except I turned out to be a freak."

"Freaks're gonna take over the world," Etienne says through a mouthful of fries stolen off Gayla's tray. "Barbados. My grandmother was like me. She said it was passed down in our family. My uncle was living in Brooklyn and sent for us. My mom got pregnant with me at fifteen, left me with my grandmother and took off. Never came back. My grandmother said she could do what we could, but couldn't handle it."

"How did you end up at the center?" I ask. "Why didn't you stay with your grandmother, or your uncle?"

"Grandmother wanted me to have more opportunities and, as we all know, America is the land of opportunity! My uncle knew I was like my mom, but he wasn't strong enough to handle the more powerful people who wanted to come through me. They would take over sometimes—destroying property, hurting people, animals. He got fed up when the cops brought me home one too many times." She shrugs. "Foster parents couldn't handle me either and, later, neither could the juvie staff."

Sharlene takes a sip from her water bottle and recaps it. "Miss Maggie found Tee at a hospital after someone came through and wanted to hurt *her*. They thought she tried to commit suicide."

"And here I am," Etienne says. "Your turn, Gay."

Gayla cocks her head to one side. "Not so exciting. Born and bred in the U.S. of A.—New Mexico. My parents were hippie-dippie, artsy-fartsy types, but they freaked out when I started climbing into their brains at night instead of their bed like a regular kid. They thought they were going crazy. Eventually, they figured out they were both having the same thoughts, put two and two together and came up with 'she's crazy.' Then, the usual—hospitals, psychiatrists, tests, drugs..."

"How old were you?" I ask.

"Seven." Sharlene answers for her. "We were all seven."

Etienne crumples up her wrapper. "Something about that age opens up whatever latent ability you have. And then it's up to you. It's like one of those things where, if you choose to see it, it's there, but if you don't, it never grows."

Gayla lays her napkin over her uneaten food. "For some reason, our abilities started out a lot stronger than most and we managed to keep them, even through all the testing and drugs."

"You know what's funny?" I say, "In Zanum, people like us are just accepted. We're no big deal."

Etienne nods. "There are people in the Caribbean who believe in the old ways too."

Bobby's words flash through my mind. "I met a guy this weekend," I say. "He's here from India. He said he can see spirits and that his grandmother showed him how to deal with the angry and harmful ones. He says in India there are people who believe in unexplainable stuff, too." I don't know why I'm so nervous. "He's going to Withrow Tech for engineering and Dyal tried to suck me back somehow through this rose bush and then Bobby the guy who can see spirits threw this wheel thing and chanted some phrase his grandmother taught him and then Dyal was gone." All of that comes out as one long word.

They all stare at me.

Gayla speaks first. "Who is this guy? Is he from our sibling residence?"

"Sibling residence?" I look at her in confusion.

"There's a center for boys with abilities. Miss Maggie started it with the help of her 'longtime man-friend,'" she makes finger quotes around that phrase, "around the same time she started the center."

I shake my head. "I don't think Bobby even knows about it. He didn't mention anything to me, anyway."

Etienne holds up a hand. "Wait. Dyal did what? I thought she couldn't materialize here?"

"She can't," I say. "But she can bring us into the half-plane with her."

"The what?" Etienne looks at me like I'm speaking Kabardian. "What the fuck is a *half-plane*?"

"So it's true," Sharlene whispers. "I've been feeling like we're being watched since we got here." She pushes her tray aside. "I'm going to check out the rest of the mall."

I grab her arm. "No! What if Dyal sucks you through?"

Etienne grabs Sharlene's clasped hands. "Jesus, Shar. What if she tries to take your snake energy, or whatever?"

"I don't think she can," Gayla says. She looks up after a moment. "Shar travels through space, here and now. But Pammi travels through the Dark, a kind of highway that takes her from one point in time to another."

"So, maybe I'm safe because I'm not traveling through the same material as Pammi?" Sharlene asks.

"I think so," Gayla says in a tone that does nothing to inspire confidence in any of us.

Sharlene draws a deep breath. "Well, there's only one way to find out."

Etienne grips her hands. "Don't."

"I might spot something, Tee. It could buy us time, or give us an advantage if there's danger."

"Shar—" Etienne half gets up out of her chair, but Sharlene's head is on her hands and she's gone.

"Shit!" Etienne says.

"She's going to be okay, Tee," Gayla says, stroking Etienne's arm.

Etienne massages her forehead with the heels of her hands and says nothing.

I get up and hover over Sharlene, as if I can protect her somehow, and pray that Gayla's right.

A few long minutes later, Sharlene raises her head. "All clear," she says with a smile. "Or at least everything *looks* clear."

"Don't you ever fucking do that again," Etienne says.

The hair on my arms stands on end. I look around. "She's here."

They all freeze.

"I guess I'm not such a good scout," Sharlene whispers.

Etienne wipes her mouth and pushes back her chair. "I feel it, too. Like some shit is about to go down. Let's go. We're easy targets sitting here."

"Hold on," I say. "Bobby said I should be careful when it feels like this. That I shouldn't touch anything unusual or anything that seems out of place."

Gayla gives me a look. "A rose bush would hardly seem out of place in a garden, Pammi."

"No," I agree. "But it had this magnetic pull. I couldn't keep myself away from it—almost like I was being hypnotized."

She nods. "Okay, so we avoid the magnetic pull."

We get up, dump our trash and pile our trays, and start weaving back through the mall.

"Hey, I'm going to run into Leatherbound, Inc. to get that wallet," Etienne says as we near the store.

"Now?" I say incredulously.

"I swear I will stay away from all magnetic pulls and rose bushes. I am not scared of mummy-lady, especially when she can't show up here. Are you?"

I glare at her. "Scared, no. Being smart, yes."

She looks around and lowers her voice. "Says she who went to the Blesseds ceremony when she was supposed to be going home."

I grind my teeth to keep from yelling at her. But she's right. Like her, I'm not one to run from anything. I sigh. "We'll all go with you."

Gayla and I follow Etienne and Sharlene into Leatherbound, Inc.

"This feels like walking into a dungeon," I say under my breath.

Etienne and Sharlene head to a glass case with an array of wallets as Gayla and I hang back, checking out the offerings on hangers. I finger the leather outfits. Sharlene was right. They look like lingerie with chains and studs and grommets.

Just as Gayla says, "I don't remember this store having this kind of stuff before..." something shifts in the air. It's almost audible, like a *whoosh*.

I turn to her. "Did you feel that?"

Sharlene runs over, dragging Etienne behind her. "What was that?"

We scan the store, all of us tense. I have no idea what I'm looking for, but everything seems to have stopped. It's like we're encased in a membrane and the rest of the world has fallen away, drained of color. Like we never existed there at all.

The half-plane. We walked right into it.

And then Dyal is there.

Chapter 17

"You will not escape again," she says, coming toward me. Her breathing seems ragged. "I will not suffer another of Master's punishments because of you."

A searing pain knifes through my ankles and I drop to the floor. I see Etienne and Sharlene scream and clutch at their ankles, too.

Gayla is the only one of us not in pain. She's facing off with Dyal, and her body is tense with concentration.

Dyal laughs. "You cannot keep me out forever. Soon, your strength will give, and you will be hobbled just as your friends are."

I struggle to form a sentence. "Use your abilities," I rasp.

Etienne's face is contorted in an effort to bear the pain. "What?"

"She... can't... get to you..."

Understanding clears the fog of pain on Etienne's face. "I don't know if I can," she says through clenched jaws.

Dyal is still facing off with Gayla and I wonder why Gayla is not sending any thoughts to us. I shift my attention back to Etienne.

"C'mon, Tee," I urge, fighting through the pain.

She inhales a couple of shaky breaths. I see her arms tremble as she struggles to hold herself up on her hands and knees.

Soon, her eyes open wide. "Whose child are you?" booms a voice that is Etienne's and... not. Etienne stands, apparently feeling no pain at all now, and begins to walk toward Dyal.

Dyal looks mildly interested as Etienne approaches. "Ah," she says to me. "So you are more clever than you appear. You have sent your friends off, have you? But where will *you* go? I can find you in the Dark, as you know. And that is your only ability."

The edges of my vision begin to grow dark as she peers down at me, amused.

She's right—I have nowhere to go.

"What nonsense is this?" Etienne growls. "Why are you harming these children?"

Dyal turns to her. "You have no place here. You have not been summoned."

"You will not order a high priestess. In my time or not, I will not allow harm to come to these children."

"What will you do to stop me?"

In an instant, the priestess Etienne is channeling is by my side. She places a palm flat on the top of my head, and a flood of warmth courses through my limbs, my chest, my belly and legs.

Dyal's eyes widen as she lunges toward me. "*No*—I must have her!"

I hear the calm voice of the priestess as stars explode in my head. "You will not."

I'm on the outside of the membrane. In the black-and-white part of the world. Shades of gray all around me. Life is moving on, a normal day in a mall. No one can see me.

Do I even exist here? Am I in the half-plane? I look down at my arm and it's the same warm brown tone I've always known.

People walk into the membrane and out the other side, oblivious to the raging battle in this parallel plane. They walk through Etienne and Sharlene and Gayla as if moving through smoke. I watch Dyal toss my limp body aside, roaring at the priestess who is speaking through Etienne.

Think, Pammi, think.

Dyal can't get to me outside the membrane. That's why the priestess sent me out here, right?

Dyal and the priestess are still locked in confrontation. Dyal raises her arms. Little by little, things begin to shift. The air sparks around her and a small tear appears in the membrane.

The priestess looks up at the patterns of lightning and electric charge. The look in her eyes turns from alarm to rage. She begins shouting and waving her arms.

The membrane tears some more and color begins to seep into the black-and-white-world. Children nearby point to the crack of vibrant color shooting like rainbow rays from the bubble.

Dyal is about to merge two planes that aren't supposed to merge—trying to materialize in a time that's not hers. What that will do to everything, and *everyone*, I have no idea. But judging by the priestess's reaction, it's cataclysmic.

And then I feel it. The same searing pain that shot through my ankles earlier now slices through every inch of my body. I scream. I want to outrun this pain somehow. I claw at my skin, drawing blood. Tears fill my eyes.

That's when I see him—Bobby.

He looks directly at me and makes a motion with his hand.

"You can see me?" I gasp.

But he can't hear me.

"Stand up," he mouths, motioning for me to rise.

I'm on the floor with my knees buckled underneath me. Liquid trickles out of my nose and lands on the floor. A drop of blood so round, so dark and shiny, I'm amazed at its perfection.

It begins to blur slightly.

This is not good. I could die right here, in the crack between two planes of existence, and no one would ever find my body. Mom and Dr. B. would have to mourn without a proper good-bye. Zanum. Etienne and Sharlene. Gayla. Dhan. What would happen to them?

I close my eyes and pull from the area under my bellybutton. The dark serpent stirs there. Its ascent is quicker this time than last.

I hear Pasea's voice from somewhere far, far away. *It is your power source, the Sea of Energy. Draw upon it now, Mika.*

I look back at Bobby. His lips are moving and I know he's chanting something like he did the day I met him. He reaches into his pocket and unsheathes the sun-shaped circle. It glints in the light for an instant before he throws it toward me like a Frisbee.

I watch it whiz toward me in black and white, disappear for a flash, then land in front of me, in color.

I reach out with a trembling hand, trying to grasp it. Instead, I collapse onto the blade.

And then I'm in the Dark. I *am* the Dark. I'm everywhere. I know Dyal is right behind me. I feel her. I smell her outrage, her desperation. She wants my serpent fire, but she won't get it.

I refuse to die.

I feel no more pain. The one thing she was using to control me is gone.

I spread like a mist, not seeing anything—sensing my surroundings. I know where Bobby is, but he doesn't know where I am.

He thinks I am dying. I don't know how I know this. I just do.

Dyal slams into me, full force. I reel with the impact as we tumble, end over end, through an eternal void.

I smile. She's like a child. I reach out and feel something seeping into me. It feels good. I want more. I inhale, breathing deeply into my lungs. And then deeper still.

I am stronger with each breath. It's exhilarating. I feel like I can envelop the entire planet. The cosmos, even.

Somewhere in the distance, I hear a faint, wavering voice. It's so thin and wispy that I'm not even sure I actually hear it. But when I make out the words, I stop what I'm doing.

...You are taking not only my serpent fire, you are consuming me in my entirety. You have become my brother.

I ponder whether to continue, but only for a brief moment. Do I want to become Mantel? No, of course not. But this sweet, syrupy essence, the serpent fire, is addictive. It's like floating on a calm stream and the exquisite touch of first love and the comfort of a mother's arms and the promise of ultimate power over everything. How does one walk away from that?

I go back to sipping.

I find a shimmering thread—easily this time. In fact, it almost seems as if the thread appeared in my hand with just a thought. I know with certainty that it will take me back to the store.

Dyal is gone and Sharlene, Etienne and Gayla are back. It doesn't occur to me to question why I know this. How I can glean this information from the Dark, when before I could not.

Chapter 18

"Okay, what the fuck just happened?"

I don't answer Etienne immediately. Bobby is behind her.

"This is Bobby," I say.

Sharlene and Gayla acknowledge him with a nod. He nods back.

Etienne charges past me. "Let's get the hell out of here."

"What happened to not being scared?" I ask innocently.

She fires me a death glare, but says nothing. I grin. Bobby falls into step beside me and we follow the others through the mall until we're all outside.

"I repeat," Etienne says. "What just happened in there?"

Something occurs to me. "Aren't you supposed to be weak and drained after a channeling?"

She looks taken aback for a minute. "Yeah. But I feel totally fine."

"Something happened to you," Gayla says, searching my face. "I couldn't read anyone's thoughts while I was shielding myself from Dyal, but when you collapsed, I could. I could read everyone's all at once. It was almost like when I was a kid, only I could control it."

Bobby nods. "I felt it, too. Something pulled me to the mall in a way I've never felt before. I saw all of you, the mall... Dyal from the future," he points to Etienne. "I saw you channeling someone else—you must've been. You actually morphed into someone else. I saw *everything*, the past, the present, and the future." His voice is tinged with awe.

"Same here," Sharlene says. "I was flying around inside that bubble and then I could go anywhere. I could *smell* things. It's almost as if all our abilities became amplified."

"Okay, spill it," Etienne says. "Where did mummy-lady go? Where did *you* go?"

I look at the ground. "I have no idea what happened. It's like I absorbed her somehow."

"Like, you *ate* her?" Sharlene looks disgusted. "Ew."

"No," I say, searching for the right words. "It's like she became a part of me."

Bobby watches me carefully. "You did what she does. You took her power."

Part 3:

Return to Zanum

I am the Dark. It moves through me, with me, around me. It speaks to me. It speaks through me. It is the wisdom of the ages, the womb of all creation. Everything our myopic eyes see was once a part of the Dark.

Dyal was Mantel's younger sister. As a child, he had controlled her so thoroughly, so completely, with his power that she soon became an extension of him. But a critical part of him died when he refused to let his soul move on as it should. And Dyal became the life force, the essence Mantel imbued with the serpent fire of countless victims, to keep himself, and her, alive far beyond their natural life spans.

Mantel's only hold on Dyal was that she loved him. And this, Mantel manipulated like a snake charmer. When Dyal's every cell fused with mine, I understood vividly how that love was used to create the chains that bound her.

Mantel was still there, somewhere in the future, perhaps devising a new plan, or creating a new Dyal. But he was not in the Dark, and there was no one with the power to move through it for him the way Dyal could.

Without Dyal, Mantel could not access me, even with a thousand Dr. Maces. I was not afraid of them anymore, Mantel and his doctors. And that left me free to expand and spread my wings.

Chapter 19

I'm sitting on a bench at the statue park with Bobby.

"It's weird. I get these flashes of memory, or thoughts, that I know aren't mine."

He stops futzing with his bike helmet. "Are they Dyal's?"

I shrug. "I guess."

He looks out at the canopy of leaves that is at its darkest end-of-summer green. "You know, I didn't mention this before because I didn't want to scare you, but when I look at you, I see a kind of shadow behind you wherever you go. Even in the shade."

I almost drop my own helmet. "What do you mean?"

"It's not, like, an actual shadow. It looks like it's made of light, and when I try to get a better look, it goes away. I can't see it dead on, but I know it's there. Think it's Dyal?"

I shrug. "Maybe. I don't know how to get rid of her."

He places a hand over mine. "Do you want to?"

I don't know what unsettles me more—his hand over mine, or the fact that I know I don't want to get rid of Dyal. It's like growing a new body part. Like when you get boobs, maybe. Like they were meant to be there all along and then suddenly they're just there. Considering their removal is unfathomable.

I stand up and fasten my helmet snugly under my chin. "Come on. Let's ride."

I begin cycling hard along the bike path, alone with the breeze for a minute, knowing Bobby is not far behind.

That night, I'm restless. Being with Bobby today was discomfiting. On the one hand, I love his company. I can share things with him that I can't with the girls at the center. I've told him things I haven't even told Dhan.

Bobby is the one I've shared the most with about what happened at the mall. He could see both planes, like me. The girls couldn't. Neither could Dyal. He also grew up kind of like I did—with a grandmother who normalized what he could do, like what Pasea did for me. He was guided and taught as a child in India, like I was in Zanum. And he grew up now, in my time.

Being near Bobby, feeling comfortable and at ease with him, and being hyper-aware of his closeness makes me yearn for Dhan all the more.

Maybe the guilt I feel as Dhan's face takes center stage in my memory is the reason I form the plan. A plan that takes shape quickly. It's slightly crazy, but it's a plan I know I'm going to put into motion anyway.

I tiptoe out of my room and listen at my mom's door for a minute. Then I grab my jacket and the car keys, and slip out into the night.

I drive to the center. I don't park in the lot, though. I don't want anyone to know I'm here, especially Celia or Miss Maggie. I park the car down a narrow dirt path off the main road and walk through the trees, along the edges of the orchard, until I see the sleeping quarters.

I find a large oak tree and sit against its trunk. I close my eyes and focus on Gayla.

Gayla, are you there?

Yes! Stop yelling!

Sorry. I'm here. I show her the orchard and the tree.

Why? Shouldn't you be at home?

I ignore her question. *I need a favor. Can you ask Etienne to come out here?*

She hesitates. *She'll have to sneak out. It's not like she's never done it before, but it's late. She could get in big trouble.* She sighs. *I'll pass on the message.*

I relax against the trunk of the tree and wait to hear back. After several minutes of nothing, I begin to get worried. What if Etienne doesn't show up? What if she gets caught trying to sneak out?

But then I hear leaves rustling and Etienne pops into the small clearing.

I can't keep the relief from my voice. "Thank you!"

"This better be good."

"I know. I wouldn't have done it if it wasn't important."

"What is it?"

"I want to try something. I want to see Dhan."

She shrugs. "What's that got to do with me?"

I gather my nerve. "You need to practice calling people up at will."

She looks at me suspiciously. "And?"

"Aaand... you could try to channel Dhan."

"You're insane," she says.

"Wait—if I'm here, we could use both of our energies. I'm *sure* I could help you bring him here."

"Why? You're still working on your own ability." She's annoyed.

"I have a lot more control now."

More guilt. Bobby is the only one who knows how the mall incident has changed my ability. I push even harder. "I learned a lot of stuff last time I went through the Dark."

"So? C'mon, you're wasting my time."

I stand my ground. "The only thing standing between us and the super-powerful Ables we can become is our emotions."

She turns to leave. "You're making no sense and I have to go before someone catches me."

"It's the heart plus the will and the mind," I say quickly. "Shar keeps freaking out and flying out of her body, Gayla gets emotionally entangled with someone and loses control of her ability. I get scared and pick the wrong strand in the Dark, and you…"

She stops and turns back. "I *what*?" There's a deadly gleam in her eyes. I know I'm pushing it.

"You don't stop people who want to come tearing through you. It's your body, Etienne. *You* decide who gets to use it."

There's a moment of crackling tension between us. I actually wonder if she'll hit me.

"Come on. Isn't it worth trying? There's so much to gain, and not much to lose. This could actually *work*. Just try it with me, Tee. Try concentrating on making your feelings come together with what you want and what's going on in your head. I'll help you. If you lost Shar, wouldn't you want to see her?"

"Okay, don't overshoot it. You had at me at the will and the emotions and the head shit."

"And you let me keep going?"

A smile tugs at the corner of her mouth. "You're arrogant. Needed to bring you down a notch."

"*I'm* arrogant?"

"If this backfires, newb, I'm going to beat the crap out of you."

I believe her, too. "I'll tell them it was all my idea."

She walks over to the thick oak tree and sits down. "You won't be able to with your mouth all swollen up."

"You don't scare me," I lie.

She laughs. "It was all your idea," she says, right before she leans back against the tree trunk and closes her eyes.

I sit in front of her and take her hands. I focus on a single thought—Dhan.

I know I can do this. Something has changed inside me. I don't know how it happened, but it's there, clear as... having another person sitting inside me. I feel like I have a tool, or a weapon, that no one knows about.

Except maybe Mantel. Dyal is there, within me and around me. She's threaded through my every pore and cell. I'm the one who gives the orders and makes the decisions, but she whispers her thoughts and images and life force into those decisions.

After what feels like hours, everything seems to go still. Like not even the particles in the air are moving. It's familiar to me now, this feeling. We have stopped and stepped out of the normal continuum of time and space.

When Etienne's eyes open, they do so slowly, as if adjusting to the light. She begins to tremble and a low moan escapes from deep in her throat.

"Etienne?"

She looks at me like she's trying to focus. "Mika?"

"Dhan!" I grab her hands—*his* hands. "It worked!"

"Mika..." He looks around as if in a daze. "I felt a strange pull. The more I turned to it, the stronger it became." He looks down at Etienne's body and stands. "She is... I'm in her body?"

"I asked her to."

"You shouldn't have done this, Mika. I don't know how it will affect her, or me."

"I didn't do it. Etienne did."

"No, it was you. I know now that the pull was you. I could *feel* you, Mika. But you are different. Your energy has changed."

"I had to see you." Etienne, the oak tree, the center... everything falls away. "You're *here*. I can't believe it!"

He looks around. "This is your world?"

"Yes!" I whisper excitedly. "Come with me, but keep low so we're not seen."

"Pasea would have your head for this, Mika."

I giggle, giddy with having Dhan *here*, in my time. I take his hand and scurry just close enough to my car so that he can see it from our hiding spot.

I point. "*That* is a car."

He smiles. I can see him etching it into his memory. It's a little weird to be holding Etienne's hand, knowing that *Dhan* is in there. That it's Dhan who is looking out at me lovingly through those eyes—eyes that have fired hostility toward me more times than I can count.

We shuffle back to the oak tree, staying low to keep from being seen. "So hard to believe it's *you* in there." I place a hand lightly over his chest and close my eyes. The heat of his body and the gentle thud of his heart are reassuring.

He takes my hand in his and looks down at the back of Etienne's other hand as he does so, curling the fingers in and straightening them out again. "It's me. We have many high priestesses who do what your friend does. The spirit who channels through takes over completely. It's my command that wills her muscles to move."

Like me and Dyal. My heart skips a beat as the thought flits through my mind.

As if to prove his words, Dhan jumps for one of the lower limbs of the tree and pulls himself up into its branches.

"Dhan! Someone might see you!"

"Wait," he says, craning his neck to look through the leaves. He leaps back down. "I wanted to see your structures."

"The building?"

He nods. "Interesting, but not as spectacular as I'd imagined."

I grin and throw my arms around him. "You're *here!*"

He puts his arms around my waist. "I've missed you so much, Mika," he says, burying his face in my neck. "You have no idea."

"Kiss me," he whispers.

Suddenly, I want to laugh. A few minutes ago, Etienne was threatening to beat me up and now I'm thinking of kissing her mouth.

I close my eyes and lean in as Dhan softly brushes my lips with his. Then he pulls me in for a deeper, longer, more urgent kiss. The way he holds me, the places he puts his hands, the way he gently probes my mouth... it's Dhan.

Kissing him after so long, knowing that he's alive somewhere, opens up the gates to all the longing and yearning I've kept locked up. I press myself against him, wanting desperately to erase the divisions between us, to move beyond the bodies that are separating us.

When he pulls away, I lean my head against his shoulder. "I was afraid you were—that you had been..." I let the rest of my unspoken question hang between us.

"Things are not good," he says. "Our general has taken us deep under the earth to connect with Atesu and the Council, and to strategize. But we are losing many warriors and the invaders are making steady progress toward our villages." He tightens his arms around me. "We are losing, Mika," he continues. "Zanum is surrounded. Atesu can no longer protect us. Maybe it's right that we say a final good-bye."

I look into his eyes. "I'll see you again." I cup his face in my hands, close my eyes and press my mouth against his.

He kisses me back until I feel him trembling. My hands find his and we hold them up, palm to palm, fingers interlaced. His trembling becomes stronger.

"Dhan?"

He lifts his head.

"Dhan..."

"It's me."

Etienne.

"Can you bring him back?" I swallow the wave of grief that washes over me.

She shakes her head.

I reluctantly peel away, cold seeping in where Dhan's warmth had been.

Etienne is shivering almost uncontrollably and she looks ashen. I yank off my sweater and wrap it around her. I pull my sleeve down over my hand and wipe her forehead. "Are you okay? Can I get you something?"

"Water." Her voice is strained.

"Wait here."

I crouch low and run through the trees to my car. I grab my half-full bottle of water and race back to Etienne.

She drains it.

For several minutes, we sit next to one another in silence as she regains her strength.

"It worked," I say. But the victory is clouded with a deep sadness.

She stares straight ahead. "Must feel good to know you were right."

I look down at the ground. "Good isn't what I feel right now."

She looks at me and opens her mouth as if to say something, but shuts it again.

We hear the rustling of leaves at the same time.

Etienne clutches my arm and puts a finger to her lips.

Sharlene breaks through the trees, with Gayla behind her. "Hey," Sharlene says, "we couldn't help ourselves. We had to sneak out to see what was so urgent that—"

She stops abruptly when she sees us.

Gayla's eyes widen.

I suddenly see us through their eyes. Etienne wrapped in my sweater, me sitting close with my Honeybee Lip Dust smeared all over her face.

Sharlene's face hardens.

I scramble up quickly. "We were—"

"Tee, what the hell—" Sharlene begins.

Etienne cuts her off. "Pammi wanted to see her dead boyfriend."

I wince.

Gayla's mouth unhinges. "Did you channel someone? That's dangerous, Tee! What if someone else came through? What if you were too drained to recover?"

"I did it at the mall," Etienne says, annoyed.

"That was different!"

"He said we're losing," I say. My voice is as wooden as I feel. Even with all my newfound power, I have not been able to figure out how to help the people I love most. Haram, Mantel's earlier incarnation, is still leading a massive army right into the heart of Zanum.

"Dhan said the city is surrounded. We're too late. If they wipe out Zanum, everything changes for us, and everyone like us, who comes after. Mantel could still win, even without Dyal."

The tension disappears. "Oh, god," Gayla says, putting an arm around me. "You okay, Pammi?"

Sharlene pulls a tattered tissue out of her pocket and offers it to me. "It's clean."

I take it and dab at my eyes.

Etienne's voice is hoarse. "I need some more water," she says, shrugging off the sweater and handing it back to me.

"Come on. Let's get you back to your room," Sharlene says, taking Etienne's hand.

"Wait," I say, pulling Etienne back. "We need to do something."

"Tomorrow," Etienne says. "I'm done for today."

"*No.*" A sense of urgency pumps through my veins. But more than that, a sense of strength.

They all stare at me in disbelief.

"You're out of your mind," Etienne grumbles.

"The last time I visited, Pasea and Atesu were freaked out that I brought over organic matter. Pasea got really excited about it and I couldn't figure out why. But Mantel knew that meant I could bring him back with me."

Gayla gives me a look. "So?"

"That means that I can take us all across," I say. "I can bring you all with me. I *know* I can do it."

"But you haven't been able to find a way back to Zanum," Sharlene reminds me.

"No. But I know I can. You have to trust me," I plead.

"I don't know if it's a good idea. Something really bad could happen." Gayla says.

"Fine. I'll do it on my own, then. I can't stand here and let everything go to hell." I gesture around me. "All of this—us—everything Miss Maggie has built, every Able who comes after us, all of it left to whatever fate Mantel and his warped, demented brain has in store."

This seems to hit home. "Okay, wait," Gayla says, "I'll help. But maybe we should get one of the teachers involved."

"Are you kidding?" Etienne says. The color is back in her face. "Word would get to Miss Maggie before you can finish your sentence."

Sharlene looks up into the darkening sky. "Fine," she says, grasping Etienne's hand. "We're in it together. If anything goes wrong, we've got each other's back, right?"

Etienne drops her shoulders in resignation. "Shit. If anyone finds out, none of this was my idea."

"I'll take full responsibility," I say.

We sit down on the grass and look at one another, as if gleaning courage and strength from each other before beginning.

I take a deep breath and exhale. "Ready?"

Chapter 20

Once our breathing is in sync, I hold on tight to the hand of the girl seated next to me on either side, and I drift into the Dark.

Move carefully—not too fast and not too slow, Sharlene urges, repeating something I've heard Miss Maggie say to all of us at one time or another.

I'm jolted by the feel of her right next to me. So vibrant and clear, it almost throws me off. *I'm getting your thoughts straight, not through Gayla.*

Something's changed, Gayla agrees.

I don't respond. Instead, I try to keep the thoughts from flowing through my mind. How could I explain what happened, what I've become, when I don't even know myself?

I see faint outlines, each one representing one of the girls. They are a mix of color and light, unique to what each particular girl is feeling and thinking. *Wow, so this is what you can do in the physical world, Gay?*

Sort of, she sends back. *But I see more physical, concrete things. Memories, images, that sort of thing.*

This is SO awesome, Etienne says. She's all pinks and purples, with a spot of green popping up here and there. *It's like floating at night in the ocean.*

There is something about her colors and how she glitters with specks of stardust that draws me closer. I tear myself away and look at Sharlene's gold and apricot and lavender swirls. Calming, but with sudden bursts and blacked-out areas.

Gayla is a blend of forest greens and midnight blues. Solid, but with crackling oranges and reds in the deeper layers. They all have the same stardust glittering throughout.

I become aware of another energy, a warm, flowing light moving through and around me and all of a sudden I feel crowded, fighting for space to breathe.

I shake off the urge to kick them all out of what has always been mine alone. My quiet. My peace. My comfort.

But Dhan.

I force my attention back to what needs to be done.

I need to get to Dhan. Pasea and Atesu are out there somewhere. We have to save Zanum. The secrets of the Ancients rest there—secrets to gifts like mine, Etienne's, Sharlene's and Gayla's. So much I still have to learn, that could go up in smoke if those tablets are destroyed. Or worse, end up in the wrong hands.

Everything rests on whether I can do this or not. If I can't navigate this properly, I could do some serious damage *and* lose Dhan and Zanum forever.

The thought that I'm not up for it, that Dyal is now a part of me and I have no idea how that will affect this journey, almost makes me want to stop and give up. To just let things happen and be a regular, normal girl for a change. But that has never been an option for me.

I shove the fear aside. Can't stop now. I concentrate on the strands.

They all look the same. I peer closer, trying to see each separate color. I go with my gut this time instead of looking with my eyes.

I find the strand that feels right. And then I do something unusual. I pray. It's a little awkward at first.

Dear...um, Dark: please help me complete this task. A lot of people are counting on me. Really, really good people. I know you put me here for a reason, and you gave me this gift for a reason. I never believed that before, but I do now. I used to think it was a kind of curse. I didn't understand why I even existed—if I even should exist. But I see now that I can do something— something very important for the people who matter most to me. And I know that is why I'm here. To do Your will, whatever that might be. Please help me do it right.

I open my eyes and follow the strand. The combined energy of the girls surrounds me, flowing into me and out of me like the in breath and the out breath. We are silent and steady as we make the journey through the Dark.

After what feels like a long while, I see light in the distance. The light grows as we make our way toward it. Part of me wants to rush in because minutes—no, *seconds*—matter. But it would be worse if we step into this world and it is not Zanum. Gayla was right, something *is* different. It almost feels as if I'm *creating* something with each step. I can't quite put my finger on what is going on, but this journey is unlike any I've ever made before.

I listen to the sounds on the other side of the veiled world. The girls' energy envelops me. I step forward.

I open my eyes to the blinding light of the late afternoon desert sun. There are no thumb pianos in the distance, no Pasea to welcome me.

The girls materialize in front of me, open their eyes and look around.

"Is this it?" Gayla asks apprehensively.

"This is it."

I lead them up the dunes in the direction of the city. I'm amazed at how well I know the way. As we get closer, we hear the sounds of fighting—screams and shouts, the rushing of feet, the clash of metal.

Fear spikes through me. This is not a movie or TV show. These are real screams of terror. Real sounds of agony and pain. Real loss and devastation.

Smoke wisps up into the sky from several spots throughout the city. We continue until I halt in mid-stride.

The brilliant white guardian cobra is scattered in bloody pieces between us and the wall. The leg of an enemy warrior is in her open mouth, and half a dozen bloody bodies of the warriors she managed to kill, before she was felled, surround her.

Sharlene slaps a hand over her mouth as Etienne curses under her breath. I turn to the side and retch. Over and over until there is nothing left in my stomach.

Gayla's face is pale and she's trembling, but she can feel what I'm feeling and reaches out to rub my back.

"Let's go," I say, more determined than ever. I head toward the wall. The wall that every Zanumite worked hours under the heat of the sun to build, which now lies in rubble.

I move quickly, stepping inside the wall and slipping into a dark, narrow alley. The others follow behind me. I wait, scanning our surroundings until I'm sure no one is nearby. All of the action is on the other side, toward the river, which makes sense since that's the easiest travel route into and out of the city. If anyone wanted to escape, that's where they'd run.

"It's not safe to speak or be seen," I whisper. "Say everything through Gayla."

I look at Sharlene. *Can you find the best path to the Serpent Temple? It's the largest dome-covered building on the edge of the city toward the river. That's where Atesu and the High Council talked about taking everyone in the event of a crisis.*

Sharlene gives me a quick hug and sits cross-legged on the ground with her back against the wall of a hut. She closes her eyes and her body immediately slumps over to one side, as if she's sleeping.

I crouch down next to her and look at Gayla. *Gay, can you show me everything Shar is seeing?*

Gayla closes her eyes and transmits what Sharlene sees. It's not pretty. My stomach churns as I take in the sight of a broken and battered Zanum. Beaten-in doorways, shattered glass, items from homes scattered throughout the paths I've walked so often. Smoldering fires are all that's left of some of the huts. Warriors from the invading army scour homes for prisoners, or loot, I don't know which. And Sharlene doesn't slow down to find out.

I see all the places where Dhan and I kissed, held hands, joked with and teased one another, in ruins. The spots Pasea took me to point out small marvels, little delightful creatures... all rubble now. The sacred tree in Center Square has been chopped down, its branches cut off and scattered. The statue of Divine Mother is toppled, her head and breasts smashed into a fine powder.

My blood is boiling. A scream takes seed deep in my belly, growing roots that go deep into my legs, branches that rip through my arms and knife through my fingertips.

That will not help.

The words hit me like a blast of ice water. For a moment, I stand paralyzed.

Dyal.

It's the tiniest distinction. Like noticing the hair's breadth of difference between identical twins. I know those words were not mine. They came from somewhere just outside of me. Or just above me. I don't know.

Dyal is no longer. She is me. She is you.

I feel like I'm going nuts. Are those my words?

You must ignore your emotions—your fear, outrage, pain—if you are to succeed in your mission.

The words, wherever they originated, ring true. I don't have the luxury of falling apart right now. I drag my focus back to our mission.

When Sharlene's just about to turn the corner toward the less-defined path to the Serpent Temple, she stops and goes back the way she came.

I grit my teeth. *What is she doing? Gay, tell her we don't have time.*

But Sharlene ignores Gayla's questions. She moves into one of the homes, up the stairs, and into one of the tiny areas usually reserved for grain storage. There, cowering under a low shelf with a bunch of earthen pots, is a little girl about three years old.

She looks at Sharlene, terrified but dry-eyed.

It's all right, Sharlene says to her. Then to us, *She knows I'm here! She can feel me, or see me...*

The little girl seems soothed. She rests her head on one of the pots and squishes her body up into a ball.

Gay, can you reach this girl? Can you let her know we won't leave her behind and that we're coming to get her?

Gayla looks stricken. *I don't have her permission, or her parents' permission.*

You have my permission, goddammit! That thought is unmistakably Etienne's.

Just do it, Gay, I transmit.

Gayla hesitates for a second then squeezes her eyes shut.

The child widens her eyes. I don't know what Gayla's saying to her, but I can tell it's fast. Within minutes, the girl nods and sits up. She whispers something.

What is she saying? Sharlene asks.

Gayla comes back. *I can't translate the language, but the image in her head is one of a doll.*

Tell her we have to move, I send. *Now.*

Sharlene hesitates only for a second before moving on, much more quickly now, but still scouting other homes for Zanumites who might have been left behind.

When the Serpent Temple comes into view, my stomach drops. It is surrounded. The invaders are battering one of the doors with what looks like a large tree trunk.

Gayla's thought echoes my alarm. *How are we going to get in there?*

I have no idea. But we have to do something and we have to do it fast.

Ask Shar to come back, I send with as much confidence as I can muster. *We have to get inside that temple.*

How? Etienne asks. *Do you have a plan?*

Yes, I lie.

I know she doesn't buy it, but we have no choice.

Sharlene whizzes back. She sits up straight, opens her eyes and scrambles up. We all hold hands for a second, and then head down the dirt and stone paths of the city.

Sharlene's up front leading us, me behind her, Gayla and Etienne rounding up the rear. Sharlene keeps the pace quick and steady, until something stops her short.

We all collide against her.

Etienne curses. "What the f—?"

Sharlene motions for us all to back up. We catch the voices of warriors just a few feet away from Sharlene. They are not speaking Zanum.

We plaster ourselves against the side of a hut and I pray that the shadows will hide us. All of us hold our breath as the voices of the men come closer. I grab Etienne's hand on my right and squeeze it for strength. She squeezes back, leaning her head against the wall.

Soon, the men are right around the corner from where we are hiding. They stop there, speaking in loud voices. One of them bursts into laughter, backing up so that we can see him.

If he turns, or if one of us moves even the tiniest fraction, he will spot us. A bead of sweat forms at my temple and begins its descent along the side of my neck.

The soldier puts his arm up against the wall and leans against it. Just a foot or two from his arm, Sharlene trembles in the shadows.

Another man laughs, saying something in a taunting tone, and the one closest to us moves back out of sight.

Gay, I send, *we have to move. Tell Shar that we're taking another path.*

Sharlene: *I'm not leaving without that little girl.*

Shar—!

I mean it. She's one of us. I can feel it. If we leave her, and these Neanderthals get a hold of her…

She's right. *Okay*, I say. *There's only one way to do this, then.*

I motion for Etienne to slide toward the door to the hut closest to her and duck in. The rest of us quickly follow, single file. We're in a hut similar to Pasea's, but smaller.

I run to the upper level and look around for the steps leading to the rooftop. "We're going to have to crouch when we're up there and pray that no one sees us," I whisper.

I stay close to the waist-high walls of the rooftops and leap the foot-long gap between huts as we race toward the little girl's hut.

Bursts of adrenaline shoot through my limbs. I run faster, hoping everyone is keeping up. If we don't move fast, we'll be seen, and then, god—or whatever—help us.

When we get to the little girl's hut, we hear a shout from below. We've been spotted.

Hurry!

Gayla drops into the little girl's thoughts before she sees us to let her know we've arrived. Sharlene hurries down to get her.

We're moving with the superhuman speed of people running for their lives.

Gayla imprints Sharlene's image into the child's mind so she feels familiar to the little girl. Sharlene gathers the child up in her arms, forcing a feeble smile for her and putting a finger to her lips, just as the girl opens her mouth to speak.

Sharlene comes back up. "Let's go," she says in a shaky whisper.

We break into an all-out run. I have the advantage of knowing the city better than our pursuers, but I can still hear their shouts behind us. We crouch and duck through the simple homes of brickmakers and tailors. There is no one in these quarters. Less to pilfer here.

Amazingly, Sharlene is able to keep up, even with the girl in her arms. When we turn the corner to the narrow grassy path leading to the river, I realize that if we keep going we'll be headed straight for the warriors surrounding the Serpent Temple. I have no alternate route. Each step fills me with dread. Am I running all of us straight to our deaths?

Behind me, Etienne yelps.

I turn. She's rooted to the spot, yards back from the rest of us. The sounds of the men chasing us are not far, but we scurry back.

There, staring straight into her eyes, is one of the largest brown cobras I've ever seen. It is up and swaying, its hood fanned out. Its tongue darts out to feel the air.

My voice comes out as a gravelly whisper. "Don't. Move."

The little girl giggles and squirms out of Sharlene's grasp.

Sharlene grabs at the hem of her wrap. "No!"

The girl tears away and heads straight for the snake, cooing in Zanum and giggling.

She stops in front of the snake, whose head is actually higher than her own, and asks a question. The serpent hisses, darting its tongue out again. It sways, pulling its lips back to display an impressive set of fangs.

The little girl giggles again and puts her hands on her hips. She shakes a finger at the serpent, saying something in a stern tone.

The snake unhoods, lowering itself back to the ground.

"See?" Sharlene says with a small, satisfied smile. "I *told* you she was one of us."

Etienne rubs the back of her neck. "Huh. She talks to animals."

"We have to go," I say. The shouts behind us are closer.

Sharlene grabs the little girl's hand and begins to lead her back along the path. The cobra keeps pace with the girl until we reach a fork in the path. One side goes to the temple, the other to the river.

The two men we'd seen in the upper city are in sight now, coming quickly toward us. I set off toward the Serpent Temple.

"Wait!" Sharlene says.

The little girl has let go of her hand and is off chasing the snake down the fainter, more wooded path in the opposite direction of the temple.

Sharlene runs after her and the rest of us follow. When Sharlene finally grabs the girl's arm, the snake is gone.

"Come on, you guys, let's hurry!" Etienne says, turning to see how close the men are.

"I think we lost them," Gayla says, struggling to catch her breath. "I dropped into their thoughts for just a second—to confuse them."

Sharlene grins. "What happened to permission?"

"I think she gets a pass, this once," Etienne gasps, slapping Gayla on the back. "Good work, Gay."

I survey my surroundings. "Hold on. I know where we are." Beyond the leaves, I catch a glinting reflection from the moon.

Gold.

I stumble toward the stone slabs that Dhan took me to that day that seems so long ago now.

"Wow," Sharlene breathes, breaking through the haze of my thoughts. She looks up at the rise of gold and stone in front of us. "They're amazing."

"Who made these?" Gayla asks.

"The people of Zanum," I say, finding my voice. "Over many generations."

"Is this going to help us?" Etienne asks, using two of her front dreadlocks to tie the rest of her hair back.

I run my hand along the surface of one of the giant slabs.

"Where's the girl?" Sharlene says, frantically looking around. "Oh, god, please don't let her have turned back to where those men are!"

"Um, you guys?" Gayla calls.

With Sharlene and Etienne at my heels, I walk to where Gayla's crouched down, examining something at the base of one of the center stones. There, hidden by the tall grass and bushes, is an opening with steps leading down into the ground.

The little girl stands just inside the opening, an elfin grin on her face. Next to her, the hooded cobra sways.

Without another word, we follow the snake and the little girl into the ground.

Chapter 21

The steps are narrow and made of crumbling dirt and brick. They wind at points, and periodically stop at landings with doors. So far, we've passed three doors and they have all led to another set of steps. The only difference is that, instead of being dug into the ground and laid with bricks, the steps are now chiseled straight into the deep subterranean rock of Zanum. It's warm down here, and the path going deeper underground is lit with glowing stones that are set on small shelves carved into the walls.

The cobra slithers soundlessly down with the little girl not far behind. I wipe the sweat from my forehead with the back of my hand.

Gayla whispers, "It's getting hotter, isn't it?"

"I don't know about you all," Etienne says from the rear, "but I feel like a total moron following a snake and a kid down into the bowels of the earth."

"Shh!" Sharlene says from somewhere behind me.

Etienne says nothing more.

The girl skips down the stairs. The snake must be moving faster.

The steps have gone from a dank and narrow stairwell to wide, smooth stone slabs, intricately carved with symbols. There are also more of the glowing stones, so it's less claustrophobic and dark.

We come to a large door with the same detailed scenes from the stones steps etched into it in gold, lapis, and turquoise.

"It's so gorgeous," Gayla says, looking up at the different images of women gathering water at a well, lines of people marching, the weighing of symbols.

I tug at the door and it doesn't move. Opening the doors at each level has become increasingly difficult, and this one is almost impossible.

Etienne grabs part of the handle. "Pull harder—on three. One, two, *three*."

We give it everything we have, but the door doesn't budge.

"Maybe it's a push door?" Sharlene asks.

Etienne and I lean our shoulders into it and push on the count of three. Still nothing.

I look at the little girl. "Well?"

She giggles, but says nothing. The snake is coiled on the ground, keeping a wary eye on us.

"We have to do something," Etienne says. "I feel like I'm losing oxygen."

Sharlene nods. "The enemy could be in the temple already, Pammi."

I begin to doubt myself. Maybe I should have gone toward the Serpent Temple instead of following this kid. I want to shake her. What did she and her snake lead us into? Everything in my gut had told me to follow them. But now...

"Shar," I say. "You have to go through and see where we are—if we're even anywhere near where the Zanumites are taking refuge."

She nods once, than sits on a step, leaning against the smooth rock wall.

Gayla goes and sits next to her, closing her eyes to relay what Sharlene is seeing.

I wait for the images, but nothing comes up. I open my eyes. "What's going on, Gay?"

She shakes her head. "I can't get to her." She squinches her eyes tighter, but opens them again, looking panicked. "I don't sense her *anywhere*."

Etienne slams her fist against the door. "We're at a dead end!" She goes to Sharlene's side. "Come on, Shar," she pleads. "Come back."

Suddenly, the snake rises and fans its hood. The little girl stands next to it.

The door begins to open.

Sharlene opens her eyes. "Did you guys *see* all that?" Her face looks flushed.

Etienne hugs her. "You're okay! Gayla couldn't get through to you."

I'm staring at the door, not sure who's going to come out, wondering if we need to turn tail and run the other way. I move to put my body between the door and everyone else.

But Sharlene is smiling.

A silvery-white head pokes out from behind the door.

"Pasea!" I squeal and run to her. I throw my arms around her and almost collapse against her in relief.

She gives me a brief smile, enveloping me in a tight hug. "Quickly, Mika. We have been waiting for you." She looks at Sharlene. "We felt your friend when she entered the space and knew you had arrived at last."

She ushers us all through the door and it shuts behind us on its own. We walk down a narrow hall glinting with gold and gems embedded in the rock walls. Pasea is holding one of the glowing stones wrapped in bright, colorful fabric.

"The enemy has breached the first seven gates," she says, leading us through the winding paths. "There are only two more. We do not have much time, Mika." She looks over her shoulder at me.

"I thought you'd be upset that I brought—"

"It is not for me to decide. You are here because it is the will of That Which Is Unknowable."

I'm trotting to keep up with her. She descends a set of three steps and opens another door.

I'm the first to gasp when I walk in.

Thousands of Zanumites are assembled in a large, square, auditorium-sized space. There's a stream burbling through one side. The space is lit up with the same glowing stones that lit the steps on our way down. The walls are thick glass in this room, and behind them are painstakingly perfect images carved into the rock walls. The images glow behind the glass, casting a bluish light into the room. They seem to move and flow, telling stories.

"The Sacred Tablets," I say, unable to take my eyes off them.

Pasea nods. "This is our library. And these," she gestures to the large story-slates behind the glass walls, "are our Sacred Tablets. They contain the collective wisdom of our ancestors. When we are transported, they, too, shall be transported along with all our secrets and truths."

"Holy wow," Gayla breathes. "It's amazing."

The Zanumites are sitting in a circle. Small children, pregnant and nursing women, the sick and the most elderly are at the very center. After that, the children spread out in rings from youngest to oldest. The women of the city are around them, and the men, including the warriors who have returned, form the outer ring.

There is another, single ring around the warriors, and that is formed by the High Council members. They each greet us with a nod. Atesu sits in a throne carved directly out of the rock face. I look at the Three Blesseds—Vinta, Ghera, and Maitreyi—and they each give me a nod of welcome.

"Bahari," Atesu says. Her voice is calm, but the thread of urgency underlying it is unmistakable. "Let us begin."

A woman squeals and runs out of the circle, gathering the little girl who led us here into her arms and speaking excitedly to her through tears.

Armenra. My heart fills as I remember that night she gave birth. It seems like eons ago.

Pasea ushers her into the circle, shooing the child in with the others. "Maja forgot her doll and ran back just as the doors were closing behind us," she explains. "We thought we had lost her." She smiles into my eyes. "But clearly she had another purpose."

There are four empty thrones in the outer circle. Atesu points to them, indicating that we are to sit.

I turn to Sharlene, Etienne, and Gayla. "This is it." I keep my voice steady. "I'm going to take us all out of here. The only way I can do it is with you. You all have to focus with me."

We grasp hands and touch our heads in the center of our little foursome.

Sharlene hugs me tight. "You can do it, Pam," she says. But her voice wavers, betraying the certainty of her words.

"*We* can do it," I answer.

Etienne gives my shoulder a quick squeeze. "We're right here with you."

"I'll stay linked to you," Gayla says, hugging me. "I'll be there the whole time."

We each walk to a seat and sit down. I look through the warriors. *Dhan!*

He's looking every inch a Zanum warrior in his waist-wrap and hammered gold cobra headband. His skin is dark and his spear and shield lean against his seat. His body has become leaner and stronger than what I remember.

Every muscle in my body hurts with longing. Before I know what I'm doing, I'm running across the room.

Dhan stands up, takes two long steps, and wraps me up in his arms. "Mika."

I pull his head down for a kiss.

"Atesu said I am to sit directly across from you to generate the strongest force we can," he whispers in my ear. "I know you can do this, Mika. You are a warrior. I have complete faith in you."

As if on cue, Atesu's voice slices through our cozy moment. "Please take your seat, bahari. *Immediately.*" She watches me with heat-like intensity as I tear myself away from Dhan and do as she commands.

"Mika'Arini," she says, "this is part of your destiny." She points to an image on the wall behind the thick glass. The image is of a large circle of people in a square room, with nine thrones on the outside of the circle. One of the thrones has lines radiating out from it.

The tablet next to that one is empty.

"The four of you," Atesu continues, "together, can generate half of the energy force necessary to transport all of our Zanumites, this library, and our Sacred Tablets. The rest of the energy force will come from my High Council members. Where we go, Mika'Arini, and how—*if*—we get there is up to you. You have the support and guidance of the High Council as you navigate the Dark, and the power and force of your fellow bahari.

You are not the same person you were when you were last here."
She looks deep into my eyes and I know she knows about Dyal.

And here I was worried about taking three others through the
Dark. Right now, I would be thrilled if it was only three. But these
Zanumites are my family. I set my jaw and straighten my spine.

Atesu holds her arms out. "The army has breached the eighth
gate. It is only a matter of minutes before they find the path that
will lead them into this room."

She looks at me, then at the others. "Now," she says.

Everyone holds their arms out in front of them, palms facing
the circle of Zanumites.

Sharlene, Etienne, Gayla, and I do the same.

I go into myself, breathing deep into my stomach the way I've
been taught, directing the breath to just an inch below the belly
button, the power point. The Sea of Energy. I feel the dark energy
stirring at the base of my spine, and I feel Dyal's silent warmth
moving around me and through me.

Within minutes, everyone in the library is breathing together,
creating one single energy field emanating from our bodies and
surrounding the Zanumites.

I venture into the Dark, hesitantly at first, then gaining speed.
I didn't realize I would be moving so fast, but the energy from
everyone else must be propelling me faster than I am used to. It's
like trying to swim with thousands of people on your back, just
being driven down into the depths of the ocean.

Soon, I'm spinning and tumbling. Every so often, a jolt goes
through me like a ton of electricity pumped through my limbs. I

look around and see that the others are with me—all holding on, trusting me to get us to where we need to be.

I start to feel out of control, like we're zipping through the layers of time and space and I don't know where I'm going. I hear Dyal's whispers in my head, tinkling like chimes in a strong wind. Syllables made up entirely of sound rhythms that feel at once ancient and eerie. I know these are the voices of the far, far, distant past. I look around for markers, some sort of signs... anything.

The mind, the heart—the heartmind—and the will have to be one. I no longer know where the voice is coming from. Whether it is my own, Dyal's, or someone else's entirely. And I don't care.

I listen.

They are the sacred Trinity of Creation. The mind and the heart and the will have to be one.

The mind and the heart and the will have to be one. The-mind-and-the-heart-and-the-will-have-to-be-one, themindandtheheartandthewillhavetobeone...

Just when I feel like I'm on one of those upside-down roller coasters, searching for the OFF switch, I see strands waving just to my far left, and I will myself to move toward them. It takes everything I've got, but I keep pushing until I can see them better.

There are many. The Zanumites' energy is jittery and unsteady. It's hard for me to decipher which of the strands to grab hold of. I want to scream or cry, but I force myself to look carefully. Deeply.

Dyal continues to whisper, a sound like the waves of the ocean.

There is one strand that has a different feel to it, a different kind of glow coming from it.

The mind and the heart and the will have to be one.

I remember Atesu's words. *Have faith in the Wise Dark, and let it guide you.*

Please let it be the right strand.

I study it, taking my time. *Never rush forward*, is what Pasea always said.

When I'm as certain as I can be, I reach out and grab the strand that is calling out to me, and I hold on for dear life.

I begin to walk, with the crackling, zipping energy of the Zanumites, the Sacred Tablets, Etienne, Gayla, Sharlene, the High Council, and Dhan. I feel his energy as if it's right next to me. He has complete faith in me. It spurs me on. A small bud of confidence blooms in my chest.

Then the strand sizzles at my touch and begins to twist and turn as if it is alive. I grip it with both hands, but it whips me around. I hang on as all of us, every particle of energy in the Dark, lights up and shatters, exploding into a shower of tiny pieces.

Chapter 22

My eyes are sealed shut. I struggle to move my arms, but they are dead weights. There is a fog behind my eyelids and I know I'm not in the Dark anymore. I take in the sounds around me: beeping, voices, a hum.

I drift back into the large square room deep in the earth where the Zanumites were gathered. Blue light radiating from the images—the story in the walls. A story depicting the history of a people from the beginning of time to...

I push up, willing my arms to move and my eyes to open, but... nothing.

I don't know how long I've been out. The fog is still there, but I can open my eyes now. Just little slits. The light is unbearable and everything hurts. I hear voices, some shuffling, and a sort of whimpering, mewing sound.

That sound, I realize as I drift back into the merciful nothingness, is me.

I open my eyes and wince against the blades of light slicing through the blinds.

Everything starts to come back. I try to sit up, only to grab my head and lie back down from the throbbing pain in my skull.

A woman's face comes into view, hovering above me. "Easy does it, honey. We're glad you're back, but no marathon for you just yet." She smiles, checks something on my wrist, then moves aside.

I turn my head slowly to the right.

My mom is sitting in an armchair with Dr. B. next to her. Her face is drawn and pale. "Pams," she says. Her eyes tear up. "My darling."

I lick my lips and discover how very parched my throat is. My voice comes out as a croak. "What happened?"

"You were found in the field by the center, sweetheart," Dr. B. says, smoothing my hair back. "Miss Maggie had you rushed to this hospital. She put you under special care in one of her wings." He places a light kiss on my forehead. "Just a case of heatstroke— nothing worse, thank god."

I search about the room. "What about—" But the pain in my head starts up again and I can't finish.

"It's all right, love," Mom says, squeezing my hand.

"But—" I want to ask about the others.

"Shhh, sweetheart."

I call for Gayla. *Gay! Are you there? Can you hear me?*

There is no response.

The blankness rolls in and swallows me up again.

The next time I wake, it's easier to open my eyes. My head moves with less pain, too.

"Ah, there she is."

Miss Maggie!

"Your parents have gone downstairs for a bite to eat."

"They're not my parents," I say wearily. "It's my mom and her... partner, Dr. B."

"But he parents you, does he not?"

I look at her and, after a moment, nod mutely.

She smiles. "Indeed," she says. "He was quite concerned about you."

I shift to a more comfortable position.

"You're looking better. How are you feeling?"

"Like somebody put me in a blender and pressed 'liquefy.'"

She purses her mouth. "That was one of the most foolish stunts ever pulled at my center," she says, anger glinting in her eyes. "We could have lost you all, Parminder. What on earth possessed you to go ahead without supervision? Of all the—"

I try to sit up. "Where are the others?"

"Oh no, you don't," she says, guiding my shoulders back to the pillow. "You must rest." She grabs an ice pack from a nearby container, cracks it to activate the ice and presses it against my forehead.

I take it from her gratefully, and move it to my throbbing temple. "Gayla. I can't feel her." I search Miss Maggie's face in panic.

"They are all as badly torn up as you."

"But they're *alive*?" Relief floods through me.

"You did a real number on everyone, Parminder," she says, the anger surfacing again. "All of you are fighting for the health of your organs—the result of the particles of your bodies trying to pull back into position. A very important lesson you had yet to learn before taking matters into your own hands." Her eyes flash and I shrink back, feeling sick. "Not to mention the psychological trauma of traveling to a war zone."

Heat rises to my face. "Everyone went willingly. I—I *had* to."

"What you did was foolish and dangerous, and utterly irresponsible."

"The city?"

She sighs and looks out the window. "I'm afraid I don't know what happened there. It'll be a while before we feel the full effects of what you four have done."

I drop my head back against the pillow. Was it all in vain? Did we lose Zanum?

Three pairs of eyes are on me. I squint against the light.

"Hello, sweetheart," my mom says.

I look at Dr. B. "Can I have some water, please?"

He almost leaps out of his chair to find me a bottle of water.

Mom plants a kiss on my forehead. "Miss Maggie and her team of doctors say you're recovering nicely. Heatstroke is not a light matter. You could have been badly hurt. You really need to be more careful, Pams." She glances at Miss Maggie with gratitude. "We're lucky you were found when you were. You'll be up and around in no time."

I nod, not trusting myself to speak. I don't know what Miss Maggie has told them.

Dr. B. returns with an ice-cold bottle of water and a warm hug.

Chapter 23

We're hanging out under the oak again, but this time we're under tight supervision. Celia's nearby, close enough to keep an eye on us, but far enough away that we can have a decent conversation in the open.

"Are you still going away, Pam?" Gayla asks. "To Kenya for a year?"

I nod. "I need to get away from my mom's scrutiny for a bit. Get to know—" I stop just short of saying anything about Dyal. "More about my ability."

Etienne tosses the stick into the bushes, causing Celia to jerk her head up. She sighs and shakes her head before returning to her laptop.

"You can do that here," Etienne says. "With Miss Maggie."

I stare off into the branches above us before looking back at her. "I want to find my own answers. Maybe being closer to the actual land, in my own time and my own body, will help... I don't know. I just know that Zanum is also my home. Those people were—*are*—my family, as much as my mom and Dr. B. And you all."

She nods. "I know what you mean," she says. "We'll miss you. It'll be quiet around here without you."

All three of us turn to stare at her. She puts a hand on her hip. "What?"

Sharlene leans across and gives her a quick peck on the lips. "You're such a softie, Tee, deep down inside."

"I'll miss you all, too," I say.

"Did you ever hear from Bobby again?" Gayla asks.

I nod. "We'll keep in touch. He said he makes frequent trips to Nairobi because he has family there. We'll probably try to connect at some point."

Sharlene cocks her head to one side. "It's funny, isn't it? How one summer can change everything? I mean, I've gotten way better at talking about my family." She goes quiet for a moment before giving me a weak smile. "My biofamily, that is. I'm going to let Gayla take a peek into this one memory I've been scared to look at."

I give her hand a squeeze. "Wow. That's a big step, Shar."

Etienne drapes an arm across Sharlene's shoulders.

Sharlene laces her fingers through her girlfriend's and shrugs. "I just want to move on, you know?" She looks up at me and I see deep wells of longing.

I know it'll take years to learn all the layers of her story. I hope I'm around for all of those years.

"It's true," Gayla says. "One summer can change thousands of years."

"Have you found out what happened with Zanum?" Etienne asks.

I take a shaky breath. "I probably wiped more people out than any invading army could."

"Pam," Sharlene says, reaching out to stroke my arm. "Don't do that to yourself."

Gayla shakes her head. "Zanum couldn't have been wiped out. We're still here." She smiles. "If Zanum was destroyed, we wouldn't be here, or at least we'd be here very *differently*."

I nod slowly, hope rising in my chest. "That's true. I don't know what happened, but I plan to find out."

"Let us know if you need any help," Gayla says.

I smile. "I will." I glance at the time on my cell phone. "I should go. Mom and Dr. B. are taking me out for a celebratory dinner."

Gayla raises her eyebrows. "What are you celebrating?"

I give her a half-hearted grin. "The successful completion of my internship at the Margaret Schroff Leadership Academy and Residence for Girls."

Etienne laughs. "Now you're all set on your path to becoming a famous TV psychologist! Dr. P... has a nice ring to it."

Sharlene scrambles up to hug me. "I will definitely see you soon," she says. Her voice is muffled against my shoulder. "Either live or in spirit."

By the time I'm done hugging Gayla and Etienne and Celia, and saying good-bye to Miss Maggie, my lashes are damp. And the sting of leaving behind loved ones again is lodged like a boulder in my chest.

It's time. I throw my window open and sit next to it, listening to the leaves and the wind and the darkness. It's the night before my flight, and I'm ready for whatever this trip and the people I meet have to teach me.

I pull back into my room and slide the window down. The rhythmic breathing of my mom and Dr. B. reaches me from down the hall.

I close my eyes and slip easily into the fold of the Dark. It feels like a long time since I last ventured here, and my heart aches with remembrance. I revel in it for a while, reaching my arms out and twirling.

I sense around for the strands. I see the one I've known from the beginning, there, just to the right. It wafts airily next to me, like an old friend. A golden thread of spider's silk, beaded with dew.

I look around and am surprised to see that there are no others. It becomes a magnetic force, insistent. I move closer, eyeing it carefully, and walk around it to see how it moves.

Are you a friend?

There is an answer. It's from Dyal. "I am you."

"Yet you're not me," I say.

The strand pulls up and forms an outline of sparkling light. "I was Dyal once, full of light and love and laughter. But over the years, I became something unrecognizable—no longer human. Yet my essence was strong. My power, infinite. Everyone wanted me for their own. In the end, it was my brother who ensnared me, using my emotions like barbed wire to surround me. I loved him with all my heart. He was all I had left after the battering we both endured from our family. I allowed him to slip a collar around my neck because by his side was where I wanted to remain." Her sparkle fades in some spots as she trails off.

"But he used you."

The sparkles burst into blinding globes with red halos. "He did far worse. He knew he had more power with me at his side. He let something evil take root and it consumed us both. I was his harnessed fire, and he directed me. Some of the things he made me do are unspeakable. No soul should ever know what I've endured at his hands."

"And now?" I ask.

"Now you have breathed in my essence—the essence of thousands of souls through time. Without me, you fall. And without you, I float forever in a semi-existence, neither dead, nor alive."

"So you're always a captive? How can you be free?"

"If I knew the answer to that, I would already be free. But we two, you and I, are both captives," she says. "Together, we stand a chance. Apart, we do not. Our liberation is entwined, like our serpent fires. My power combined with yours gives you control over the Dark, as well as the Winding Steps of Time."

The significance of her words washes over me, but she reinforces it. "Now you navigate not only time, but the Eternal

Womb from which all of Creation emerges—the Dark. You can control the rate at which time flows, age at your desired pace, and create and shape events, people, all of the manifestations of Life."

"Are there others like me?" I ask.

"Of course. Together, you create many realities."

The shadow form condenses and stretches back into a thin strand. "Come now. Let us continue this strange journey we've begun."

I struggle with the meaning of her words, turning them over in my thoughts, rearranging them, trying to make sense out of it all. There is so much I don't understand. So much about my own ability, and the Dark, that I still need to learn. Maybe Dyal is right. With her, I might be able to navigate it better. There are things she knows that I don't, and vice versa.

But the one thing I know for sure is that she isn't going anywhere any time soon. I take the strand in my hands to test the feel. Then I begin to walk.

The walk is a good pace, my feet stepping like a heartbeat, trusting the strand, trusting the Dark and yes, trusting Dyal.

Soon, the darkness begins to lift. I flow into a soft, hazy mist as a light drizzle falls gently onto my skin. I emerge into the light and hear the sounds of people on the other side.

I step out onto the rich dirt of freshly plowed land.

"Mika'Arini," Pasea says, smiling warmly and dropping her tools.

"Pasea!" I run into her embrace. "Where are we?" I ask when I can finally speak.

She casts a glance around the expansive open fields, a half-erected wall in the distance, and the river's edge way off to one side. "In a valley. We are not far from our beloved homeland, but far enough away to be safe. We shall begin anew, Mika. We are learning to shield ourselves better. And we are creating stronger forces. The Tablets are safe. We will build new temples, continue to pass on the teachings of our ancestors and the wisdom of our Laws. One day, it will be time for your generation to pass the light of knowledge to those who follow you."

She points beyond the perfect lines in the earth, toward a newly-forming city, then bends down to reach for her tools again.

I know Haram still leads an army bent on the destruction of an ancient people and their wisdom. I know his bitterness will turn him into the monster he later becomes. Unless things are changed.

But for now, I begin to walk toward this new city. Dhan is in there somewhere, waiting for me. I can feel his energy reaching toward me like arms outstretched. I know that I can rest in those arms, assured that he, Pasea, Atesu, the city, and people like me and the girls at the center, are safe.

At least for now.

Epilogue

If you look up Zanum, you will find nothing related to the city I knew. You may find, through extensive searching, references to the Indus Valley, where we ended up. But the images they have are not of the city I helped build. Dhan is not in those images with his camels. Pasea is not in those images, fashioning her pottery and tilling her land. Yonaweh is not there creating his seals, and Miraly is not dancing in the temples.

It was not difficult for Atesu and the High Council to recreate Zanum in their new home. The people of Zanum dug tunnels and fashioned tubes to move waste out of the city. They created a great central bath for rituals and ceremonies.

Over time, they built a colossal mound after which they named the city. This holy mound was where the High Council members would reside and shielded ceremonies would take place.

Having learned from their mistakes, Atesu and the High Council fortified the shielding tenfold, weaving dense walls through the Dark, miles deep and impenetrable, so no one would ever again breach the bounds of sacred Zanum space.

There was a river that Atesu called upon periodically, and an ocean nearby. She would stir blades of grass, or certain roots, in jars of water to bring the rains. They would flood the land until enough water was stored in the reservoirs. Food was plentiful and predators were few. It was the perfect spot to begin a new age.

The Zanumites were great manipulators of the Dark. Like the Blesseds, they were handpicked by the Dark itself. Far before The Conquest—before men began their crusades and journeys of discovery, the people of the valley were flushing toilets. They were storing water and grain and building temples, advancing the intention of the Dark, and communicating across vast distances. They were charting territory and mapping the stars, building monoliths and megaliths and great structures that would stand through the millennia—structures containing one layer of accumulated knowledge upon another.

They were, in fact, forging temples of wisdom that would help ascend all of humanity to the stars in the great vast darkness, above, where we belong.

About the Author

Born in a rural Punjabi village, Neesha Meminger grew up in Toronto, Canada, and now lives and works in the mega-urban metropolis of New York City. She has a fascination with ancient history and the stories we're not told.

Neesha's first novel, *SHINE, COCONUT MOON*, made the Smithsonian's list of Notable Books for Children in its debut year and was listed on the New York Public Library's *Stuff for the Teen Age–Top 100 Books for Teens*. The book was also nominated for the American Library Association's *Best Books for Young Adults*. Her second novel, *JAZZ IN LOVE*, was picked by the Pennsylvania School Librarians' Association for their top 40 selections for young adults and was a recommended summer read by Bookslut. Both *SHINE, COCONUT MOON* and *JAZZ IN LOVE* were nominated for the online CYBILS award. *INTO THE WISE DARK* is Neesha's third novel.

www.NeeshaMeminger.com
On Twitter: @NeeshaMem
On Facebook as Neesha Meminger

Into the Wise Dark

by Neesha Meminger
QUESTIONS FOR DISCUSSION

1. There are many different kinds of family in *Into the Wise Dark*. Identify some of the family units in the novel and discuss how these units are similar to, and different from, conventional notions of family.

2. The theme of belonging features strongly in this novel. Why would a sense of belonging be so important to the characters? Pick two characters for whom belonging is especially important, and tell us about their journeys. Why do they want to belong? What do they want to belong to? And what happens if/when they find they don't belong anywhere?

3. Several times in the novel, characters refer to keeping realms separate. Pasea and Atesu constantly remind Pammi that she is from another time and that's where she belongs; during the scene at Geneva Mall, there is great alarm when Dyal is about to merge two different planes of existence. Why would it be so important to keep things in their proper place?

4. Pammi is a different kind of hero because she doesn't save Zanum by herself. She is the guide, or the vessel, but she would not be able to complete the task without the help of everyone else. How are Pammi's relationships shaped or changed by this reality? How might her relationships be different if Pammi was the sole hero in this story?

5. The search for truth is something the Zanumites hold sacred, but many of the characters in the novel are either punished for speaking their truths, or forced to negate them. In what ways is truth subjective? In what ways is it absolute? In what ways is this distinction illustrated in the novel?

6. How do the themes of birth, death, and rebirth play out in the lives of the characters? What are the symbols used to represent these themes?

7. Pammi often sees herself as "in-between" and, at one point, she is referred to as a "living portal." In what ways does Pammi bridge completely different realities? In what ways does she offer a window, or door, to another reality?

8. At the end of the novel, Dyal says to Pammi, "We two, you and I, are both captives. Together, we stand a chance. Apart, we do not. Our liberation is entwined, like our serpent fires." Why would she say they are both captives? And how would their liberation be entwined?

9. Discuss the use of snake and serpent imagery in the novel. What do these symbols represent? How is this similar to, or different from, what snakes and serpents normally symbolize?

10. What is the Dark, exactly? How are themes of light and dark used throughout the story?

*For more information about Kumari Kandam,
the Indus Valley Civilization, and other research
that went into the writing of this novel, please visit
www.NeeshaMeminger.com*

Also by Neesha Meminger

Jazz in Love

"What made Jazz in Love so enjoyable ...was the narration, which reminded me a bit of Meg Cabot both in its humor and how Jazz remained endearing even when you know she's making a mistake."
—Kirkus

Shine, Coconut Moon

"A beautiful and sensitive portrait of a young woman's journey from self-absorbed naiveté to selfless, unified awareness."
—SCHOOL LIBRARY JOURNAL
"An enjoyable, difficult-to-put-down book."
—VOYA